SEASON OF THE WOLF

JEFFREY J. MARIOTTE

WFP
WORDFIRE PRESS

QUOTES

"Make no mistake, Season of the Wolf *is one hell of an entertaining novel.* Season of the Wolf *will go a long way to further Mariotte's reputation as one of today's best writers of horror and dark fiction. It is highly recommended."*

—TT Zuma, *Horror World*

"With outstanding characterization, a complex plot, and the hypnotic voice of a storyteller, Season of the Wolf *is definitely an outstanding thriller. This is one novel where you can't wait to get to the end and then are sorry that the book ends."*

—MysteriesGalore.com

"Season of the Wolf *is a quick read, but it's one that imparts an important message about the delicate balance between our actions and nature. Mariotte turns the tables, and shows us what it's like to be among the hunted, not one of the hunters —having our safe havens invaded and taken away, friends and family killed and shown no mercy. It's a great read, and while it doesn't fit into my usual genre, I believe that any reader, whether they enjoy mystery, thrillers, fantasy or just fiction in general will find something in Season of the Wolf that will draw them in."*

—Becca Lovatt, ArchedDoorway.com

"*I could hear echoes of Stephen King and Dean Koontz while reading* Season of the Wolf *and, for this genre, there's no better praise than that.*"

—Lori Spier, Goodreads

Season of the Wolf

by Jeffrey J. Mariotte

SEASON OF THE WOLF
Copyright © 2013, 2019 Jeffrey J. Mariotte

EBook ISBN: 978-1-68057-003-8
Trade Paperback ISBN: 978-1-68057-001-4
Hardcover ISBN: 978-1-68057-002-1

Cover design by Janet McDonald
Cover artwork images by Adobe Stock
Kevin J. Anderson, Art Director
Published by
WordFire Press, LLC
PO Box 1840
Monument CO 80132

Kevin J. Anderson & Rebecca Moesta, Publishers

WordFire Press eBook Edition 2019
WordFire Press Trade Paperback Edition 2019
WordFire Press Hardcover Edition 2019

Printed in the USA
Join our WordFire Press Readers Group for
sneak previews, updates, new projects, and giveaways.
Sign up at wordfirepress.com

❦ Created with Vellum

DEDICATION

They've all been for Marcy Spring—wife, best friend, and inspiration. This one is, too.

CHAPTER ONE

Bark had been scraped off the ponderosa pine, leaving a light streak against the bare trunk. Mike Hackett moved in closer. Elk rubbed against trees, but so did bears. So, sometimes, did hunters. This spot, though, had a little velvet snagged at the edges, curling down like Spanish moss he'd seen in Georgia.

He was on the track of a good-sized bull, based on its hoofprints. They were cut especially deep in the wet muck around a wallow he'd found about an hour before. Judging from those tracks, the animal might be big enough to keep him and his wife in meat for much of the coming winter.

Mike Hackett hadn't intended to be out alone. Frank Trippi was supposed to hunt with him, but Frank had sprained a wrist the other day. Slipped in his own damn bathtub and caught himself the wrong way. Mike had a license, though, and the first rifle season only lasted a few days, so here he was. In one of the later seasons, he could come back out with Frank, and in the meantime, he'd have meat in the freezer.

Truth was, he didn't mind hunting alone. He occasionally enjoyed Frank's company, though that was an enjoyment better sustained on a limited basis. A few hours here and there were plenty. On an all-day or an overnight trip, Frank's nonstop jabbering got old quick.

Mike felt much the same way about most of the folks in Silver Gap. He was basically happiest when he was by himself, flat on his back looking up into the innards of an automobile. Spending time with his wife was okay, too. Marie didn't talk too much or demand a lot from him, and that was what he liked in a woman.

He was wearing camo pants, a long-sleeved black T-shirt under a camo shirt, and heavy boots. A blaze orange vest was cinched around his gut, and a hat of the same brilliant hue covered his flattop. Orange was supposed to make a person stand out so he wasn't shot by other hunters, but these last few years the pines around here had been turning orange and brown, like spreading rust, and he was starting to think he would be safer in some other color. Green, maybe, which was quickly vanishing from this elevation. People said beetles were to blame, and he guessed maybe that was so. He fixed cars; what he didn't know about bugs would fill an encyclopedia. He didn't like it when they bit him or got into his house, but that was about the sum of his insect wisdom.

What he did know was elk, or *wapiti*, which meant pale butt or something like that. White rump, that was it. A nice six-pointer decorated the wall of his living room, and he had room for another. He was hoping for a 7x7 this time, but he'd take what he could get. The .338 Winchester Magnum rounds loaded into his Remington would stop any bull elk he could draw a bead on.

The summer had been hot and dry. There had been one decent snowfall since, and on this mid-autumn day he encountered only remnants of snow, a few frozen patches on the north side of boulders or ridges where the sun never reached. Mike tromped across earth strewn with discolored needles and up a steep rise. At the top he paused for a moment, catching his breath and taking in the view, searching for the fleeting movement that would indicate his target.

The trouble with tracking elk was that every sense they had was stronger than his. They could see him at a greater distance, smell him. He didn't worry too much about them hearing him, because elk in the wild were not the quietest creatures themselves. But he tried to move slowly and carefully, sticking close to the tree line, and he had put on scent control to neutralize his odor.

As Mike's gaze drifted down he saw antlers, tawny fur, and the familiar pale yellow behind of an elk. But he also saw white and red—jutting bone and spilled blood—staining the dirt and the fallen pine needles. Something had beaten him to his prize. He drifted closer, Remington at the ready with his finger resting lightly on its trigger guard.

The big animal—the seven-pointer he had hoped for, in fact—had been ripped open at the haunch and up the belly. A strip of skin, meat gnawed from it, hung to one side like the canvas flap of a tent opening. Its organs were gone. Tufts of fur were scattered around the carcass, blown about by the breeze or scattered by whatever predator had done this.

If he didn't know better, he would have thought wolves had taken the elk down. But this was Colorado, and Colorado didn't have wolves. He squatted beside the gory mess, breathing through his mouth but still catching the musky, sour-sweet aroma. Fat flies buzzed about the thing. He put a hand on its still side. Not yet cold.

Silver Gap was in Larimer County, close to the Jackson County line. He might even have crossed over that line, on the hunt. Both counties abutted Wyoming, where gray wolves had been reestablished. There, and in Montana and Idaho, the damn enviro-libs had practically put out bowls of Alpo, inviting wolves down from Canada to predate livestock and game animals.

Coyotes wouldn't have brought down such a magnificent beast. And he hadn't heard about any wild dog packs in these mountains. No, it had to be wolves. He rose and walked around the carcass, finding paw prints in the blood. That wedge-shaped rear pad and four clawed toes. Definitely doglike.

Mike swore and spat into the dirt. *Wolves. Shit.*

They had stolen his prize, and they would pay for it. Wolves had been expelled from Colorado decades ago. If he had his way, he would elimi-nate them again.

He started following those tracks. Six or seven different animals, he thought, but they were all on top of one another, so it was hard to be certain. After a while, he wondered why they had left the elk behind with so much uneaten. Crossing a slender axe-edge of a valley and starting up the far slope, he remembered something he had read in *Field & Stream*—along with *TV Guide*, the only magazine to which he gave any credence at all. Wolves, it had said, would eat until they were full, and if they had not finished consuming their prey they would go someplace nearby to rest, then return to the prize later. But they wouldn't go far, and they rarely left a meal altogether until they had exhausted the supply of meat.

Sweat tickled his upper lip and streaked down his sides.

They might be nearby. Watching him right now, even.

Hunting wolves was one thing. But if they were hunting him?

Something else altogether.

A shadow crossed the sun at the top of the ridge. Mike scanned but didn't see anything. It could have been the wind blowing tree branches in front of the sun, except the pines on that ridge, like many around here, had been stripped of needles, their branches bare.

He heard something off to his left, a sharp intake of breath. Like a sniff.

Then he saw the first dark, furry muzzle. Yellow eyes gleaming in the sunlight. Lips peeled back to expose huge, sharp fangs.

He raised the Remington to his shoulder, aimed quickly, and fired. The round went way wide. He tried to rein in growing panic and fired again, but his hands betrayed him. They were shaking, and he couldn't slow down his heartbeat or hear anything but blood rushing in his ears. He snapped off a third round—or was it? One in the chamber, three in the magazine. Had he already fired one or two? He couldn't remember.

There were more of them now, coming toward him from different directions. He couldn't shoot them all.

He hurled the rifle at the nearest one. It spun in the air and missed by more than a foot. He turned and started to run.

That was the worst thing he could have done.

CHAPTER TWO

Charles Durbin took a last look at the lobby of the Mountain High Lodge. "Lodge" was an over-inflated word for a motel, but he had tried to maintain a traditional western lodge atmosphere in the lobby, with mounted animal heads and high ceilings with huge wooden beams from which antler chandeliers were hung. The stone fireplace usually had a fire roaring in it, but it was cold now, its ashes swept up. The knotty pine floors were mostly free of the heavy wood-and-leather furniture that had once occupied them. Most of that was piled in a back corner, along with rolled-up Indian rugs. He'd thrown tarps over it all to keep the dust off. In a couple of weeks, a dealer from Fort Collins would be up, and Charles hoped he would buy the whole lot. He'd had no takers for the lodge, though. He had inherited the place from his parents, had grown up in it, and now he had driven it into the ground.

He had tried everything, but in the end, the place was doomed because Silver Gap was not one of Colorado's major winter or summer recreation hotspots. There had been some good cross-country skiing in the area, a few popular snowmobiling spots, and hunting and hiking were always in style. But when the economy had turned sour, people started vacationing closer to home, or they stuck to the tried and true: Aspen and Vail, Denver and Colorado Springs. And when it finally bounced back, they didn't return. The condition of the forest hadn't helped; nobody wanted to spend time in a wooded wonderland that looked like it had been ravaged by fire.

After the fourth deathly slow summer in a row, swimming in red ink, he gave up. To keep the place open would use up every last bit of savings he and Clara had, driving them deeper into debt. As much as he despised the idea, which felt like a betrayal of both his family legacy and his convictions, he had accepted a job at one of the national motel chains, down in Fort Collins.

Clara was waiting in the car, too upset by the reality of leaving Silver Gap to accompany Charles on this final walk-through. Maybe if she had been bringing in another income, they could have stuck it out another year. Instead, whenever she wasn't needed at the lodge, she had volunteered at Reverend Gil Calderon's Chapel in the Woods. She enjoyed the work, liked the church and its parishioners. But although it might have brought her spiritual comfort, it didn't bring in any money.

They needed to get on the road. It was a couple of hours to Fort Collins, and the sun was already sinking. The winding mountain road below Silver Gap could be treacherous at the best of times, even for locals who drove it often. It was even worse at night, when you never knew if a deer or elk or bear might wander onto the pavement.

He switched off the overhead light, plunging the lobby into darkness. Stepping outside, he noticed that the hinges were squeaking, and thought about the can of WD-40 in his maintenance closet. But he stopped himself with a grim smile—*not my problem anymore*—and pushed his key into the lock. The *Vacancy/No Vacancy* sign that had always kept the parking lot bathed in buzzing pink light was silent, its glow extinguished.

He heard a vehicle rushing up the road. Somebody's pickup truck, probably, heading home after a run into the city or a hunting trip. It would race past, as they always did. Likely never notice that the lodge's lights were off. Charles paused in the gravel lot. He could barely see Clara, sitting in the passenger seat of their Buick, but from the angle of her jaw and the way her hands were raised to her face, he suspected she was still weeping.

Those hours into Fort Collins would be long ones.

Instead of racing past, though, the vehicle turned into the parking lot. Low beams washed across the Buick and Clara looked up, her eyes wide. A Lexus SUV bounced over that bump at the lot's edge that Charles had always meant to grade, and spat gravel as it came to a halt, pinning Charles in its headlights.

The driver's door opened and a man climbed out. A couple of other people waited inside. The man was handsome, early forties, Charles guessed, but with a five-year margin of error in either direction. Deep crags joined the edges of his nose with his lips, and shallower ones edged the corners of his eyes. Longish, light brown hair splayed out from beneath a dark blue ball cap with a leather bill. He was trim, bundled up in a bulky leather coat and gloves, dark jeans, and hiking boots. "Excuse me," he said. "Is this place open? Looks kind of quiet."

"Not anymore," Charles said.

The guy looked at him, confusion showing on his face. He wasn't a big man, maybe five-nine, but he looked sturdy enough. He offered a kind of half-smile. "Not open anymore, you mean? As of when?"

"About ten minutes ago."

"I'm sorry, I'm a little ... are you the manager?"

"Manager, owner, head janitor, you name it."

"And you're closed?"

"That's right. Out of business, I'm sorry."

"Is there any place else in town to get some rooms?"

"In Silver Gap? No, sir. Might be able to find something over in Walden."

The guy peeled off his cap and scratched his head. "Man, I don't want to go that far. You say you own the place?"

"That's right."

"Well, I don't know anything about your business, but since you're standing here and all, what if I offered to rent all your rooms at whatever the going rate is, for say, two weeks? Would that make a difference?"

"*All* the rooms? How many people are coming?"

The guy jerked his thumb toward the SUV. "There's three of us. And some equipment."

"Then why do you need all the rooms?"

"I don't. I just want it to be worth your while to let us stay in a couple of them, and, you know, clean the showers, change the sheets, that kind of thing."

Charles considered this for a moment. Clara watched intently from the Buick. She longed to stay in Silver Gap, a longing so fierce it scared him sometimes, so he knew what her answer would be. Charles, though, had different concerns. He had accepted a job. He was supposed to start in three days. If he didn't show up, he would forfeit that. Renting every room for a couple of weeks would put some money in the bank, though, maybe keep them solvent until winter. A good snowfall might bring out the snowmobile crowd. He had not yet had the utilities shut off, so it wouldn't cost much to reopen. With only three guests, he and Clara could staff the place themselves.

Another thought struck him. "What kind of equipment are we talking about?"

"Some film gear."

"You're making a movie?"

"That's right."

"It's not a porno, is it?"

The man grinned, shook his head. "No, nothing that exciting. It's a documentary."

"About Silver Gap?"

"About global warming. Climate change."

Charles tried to do some quick mental gymnastics. Global warming was bullshit, but money in the bank was not. And there might be publicity value in having a filmmaker stay at the lodge. Maybe he'd even put the lodge in the movie. Publicity could be good for long-term business, put them in the black, so he wouldn't have to go to work for some faceless bureaucracy. His gaze swept between the man and the expensive SUV.

"I guess maybe I could open up again for that," he said. Playing it cool. "There'd be some start-up costs to get everything back up and running, of course."

"Would a grand up front cover it?"

Charles tried not to grin. "That'd probably do."

The guy stepped forward, peeled off his gloves, and offered his right hand. Charles took it. The handshake was firm, but the hand lacked the calluses of most people he knew. "Alex Converse," the man said. "Thanks for doing this."

"I'm Charles Durbin." Charles nodded toward the Buick. "That's Clara. Welcome to Silver Gap, Mr. Converse."

Alex Converse returned to the Lexus. Charles beckoned to Clara and unlocked the front door, flipping the switch up again. Light from the antler chandeliers flooded the lobby. He passed through to the office, where the first thing he did was trip the *No Vacancy* switch, sparking a jittery buzz directly outside the window. Once again, a pink glow filled the parking lot. When he looked out, he saw Clara hurrying toward the door wearing a huge smile.

The next thing Charles did was call the home of Alden Stewart, Silver Gap's mayor. Alden answered on the second ring.

"Alden, it's Charles Durbin."

"Hey, Charles, what's up? I thought you'd be on your way by now."

"Change of plans. We're staying open."

"You are? That's awesome news. What happened?"

"Let's just say there's a new man in town, Alden. A crazy man. A *rich* crazy man."

"That's the best kind."

"Yes, sir, Mr. Mayor, you got that right." Charles unleashed a deep chuckle. "You got that right as hell."

CHAPTER THREE

L et's go," Alex said, ducking his head back into the hybrid RX 450h.
Peter Hasselstrom unfolded his lanky, six-foot-three frame from the front passenger seat and gave his shaggy mane a shake. "Dude ripped you off." Peter was the palest blond person Alex had ever met in Los Angeles, but he was a skilled cinematographer. Even more significantly, he was available and interested in Alex's project. "He would have jumped at any chance to stay open. You could have taken two rooms and he'd have creamed himself."

Alex shrugged. "It's only money."

"You're the only person I've ever heard say that who meant it," Ellen Playfair said. The pixyish brunette sitting in the backseat was Peter's sound tech. Also his girlfriend. Alex had deduced that she was more skilled at the latter than the former.

"I guess it just doesn't mean that much to me." A facile answer, he knew, but honest. He had never *not* had money. He had been born with it, raised with it, and had inherited much, much more. Ellen, like others he had known who had spent their lives without it, was obsessed with money. He had it, but it was blood money and he didn't like to talk about it.

He went to the back and grabbed a couple of equipment cases. Peter was in charge of the actual shooting, while Alex would be doing on-site research and showing Peter what to shoot. Peter was fanatical about his cameras—or Alex's cameras; he had purchased them, but Peter treated them like they were his, and as precious and fragile as Fabergé eggs. So Alex carried in the other gear and left the cameras to Peter. The documentary was Alex's project, conceived by him and self-financed, but he wanted to be seen as part of the crew. Unless there was disagreement, at which time he would not hesitate to pull rank.

When he had deposited the cases on the flagstone walkway linking the rooms, he tried to peer through the darkness at the trees beyond the parking lot. In daylight, on the way up the mountain, he had seen plenty of healthy-looking evergreens. At some elevations, bark beetles were destroying the big pines, but he didn't know the situation right around Silver Gap. He would find out, come morning, whether the surrounding trees were a vibrant green or a dull, rusty red.

"I'll check us in," he told Peter and Ellen. "I guess you two have your pick of the rooms, so let me know if there's one you want."

They were still standing in the parking lot. The rooms were individual cabin units, pine-walled and steep-roofed, spreading out around them and disappearing into the trees. "Far away from yours seems like a good idea," Peter said. "Ellen's one hell of a screamer."

"Thanks for the warning." Alex started toward the office. He didn't mind if Peter and Ellen were way out in the woods. He hadn't brought them along to be his friends, but to do the job he was paying them for.

When he stepped through the doors into the lobby, bare but for a pile of what looked like furniture under a blue tarp, he heard the motel owner saying goodbye to someone on the phone. Alex made his way to the front desk, which, like the rest of the room, had been stripped of everything functional.

He had his mobile phone, if anyone needed to reach him, and he didn't expect any calls through the motel's switchboard. As long as there were still beds in the rooms, they would be fine.

Charles Durbin passed through a doorway behind the counter, smiling, and Alex reached for his wallet. He had a feeling he would be doing a lot of that over the next few weeks.

There *were* beds in his room, two of them. Those and a straight-backed chair and an empty dresser with scratch marks on it where a TV had sat were the only furnishings. Two nights earlier he'd been at home in Santa Monica, in a nice California bungalow eight blocks from the beach, on a street where the neighbors were appropriately progressive and culturally diverse. He owned two homes next to one another; the second served as the offices for the Alex Converse Foundation.

The night after that was spent at a Hilton in St. George, Utah. Nothing special, but the bed was comfortable and the room had a TV and a dresser, towels and sheets, a working sink, inoffensive artwork on the walls—all the amenities one would expect.

This place, not so much.

The room had been stripped. The mattresses were bare. The TV and anything resembling the traditional clock radio were gone. Dark spots on the wood-paneled wall showed where pictures had once hung. There was no toilet paper or tissues, much less little shampoos or paper-wrapped soaps.

The Durbins had promised to bring linens soon. Alex guessed they had canceled their linen service and would have to rummage up somebody's personal sheets and towels. He just hoped they were clean.

Before leaving LA, he had checked out the motel online. He had tried to make reservations, but the phone was never answered, and finally he had decided to take the chance and drive up. If the place had been full, he would have offered somebody cash to check out early, or rented a house or cabin locally.

Renting the whole place might have been extravagant, but such a small indulgence was a drop in the bucket. A minor sin. He was responsible for much greater, and the fortune that weighed on him came from a catalog of horrors he didn't like to acknowledge, although it confronted him every time he looked in the mirror, and haunted his dreams at night.

He had to shake off this mood, try to focus on the positive impact his film could have if he could bring it off right. But it was hard; he was tired and he was starving and at this moment, his greatest desires in life were for clean sheets and towels and maybe some toilet paper.

Just in case.

CHAPTER FOUR

Alden Stewart, the mayor of Silver Gap, descended the four front steps of Town Hall and started across the street. Whenever he passed through the big, weighty double doors of the building, he felt a thrill of pride. Silver Gap was *his* town, and he was the town's devoted servant.

He had sought the job not because it paid well—because it didn't—and not because it conferred on its holder a great deal of power. Because it didn't do that, either. The town council retained most of the power, and not only could they enact legislation without his approval, they set his salary, which—in the interests of the taxpayers, they claimed—they kept on the low side, barely enough to keep him from having to attend to his duties buck-naked and barefoot.

But he had, as a younger man, read the author and public servant John Buchan's autobiography and been struck by his claim that politics was "the greatest and most honourable adventure." He had determined then that he would have a political career. Now, he figured, it was too late to correct his error.

Silver Gap was a small town, with all of any small town's trials and tribulations. But it was a good town, its people mostly fair-minded and willing to do for one another. He had been to other places, towns and cities that felt, to him, as if evil thrummed beneath their streets, turning those who walked them sour and mean. Silver Gap had its share of tragedies: death and betrayal and heartbreak, as any place inhabited by that failed tribe known as human beings would. On the whole, though, her townsfolk cared. They made an effort. He could do no less on their behalf.

He and his wife Belinda lived mostly on proceeds from the Cup & Cow, the restaurant and bakery that Belinda ran. She served beer and wine, but not hard liquor; most of the town's heavier drinkers spent their paychecks at Spud's. But people came to her for food, especially her baked goods.

From the middle of the street, the aroma of steaks on the grill inside the C&C reached his nose, perking him up. Alden had never known a better cook, and he was glad she had opened the restaurant and found an appreciative audience. He'd had an early supper, and the smells made him consider adding a second one to his day.

Instead, after he pushed through the glass front door, ignoring the tinkle of the bell that hung on a leather thong from the handle, he veered straight for the bakery counter. "Any doughnuts left?" he asked.

An attractive woman who clearly enjoyed her own cooking gave him a smile and a nod. Her hair was dark and basically helmet-shaped, her eyes twinkling, her grin impossible to look away from. At least for Alden. "I can probably scrounge one up," Belinda said. "You hungry again?"

He looked down at a stomach that had, sometime during the past two decades, bulged to the point that he had to lean forward to see his feet. He had never thought of himself as a fat man, but he had to accept that he had become one. Thanks, primarily, to his deep and abiding appreciation of his wife's cooking and baking skills. "I wasn't, until I walked in."

"We like to hear that."

"I was really coming over to tell you to raise your prices."

"In the middle of a recession?"

"Charlie Durbin says there's some kind of nutty millionaire in town. Bought out the entire Mountain High for two weeks, just for three people. Says he's making a movie."

"A movie? Here?"

"That's all I know about it. Except it sounds like he's got money to burn."

"If I raise the prices, the locals won't eat here." She slid a glazed doughnut on a plate across the glass case toward him and turned back toward the coffee pot.

"This guy spends enough, we won't need 'em to."

She returned with a brown earthenware mug of black coffee. "He's only here for two weeks. After that, we'll still need the locals."

"I know." Alden sipped from the mug and eyed the plate. Best doughnuts in town.

They were also the only doughnuts in town, but that didn't negate the point. "I'm teasing about the prices. Mostly. But I wanted to let you know they're here, three of them, and apparently they're happy to share the wealth."

"If they come in," Belinda said, "we'll take good care of them, just like anybody else."

"That's what I love about you, Belinda. What do I owe you?"

"For you, Mr. Mayor? A buck fifty."

"That's the other thing I love. You don't cut anybody a break."

"My silent partner would pitch a fit if I did."

He *was* the silent partner, and she was right. He always paid full freight. But it all went to the same place, so he didn't mind.

He carried his doughnut and coffee to an empty table near the window, greeting other diners on the way. He had run for office because he believed in government, in the idea that government really should do what it could to help the people it served. He also knew that politics went hand in hand with government, so he never wasted an opportunity to be seen around town, supporting local businesses and being friendly.

He had just sat down and bit into the doughnut when his cell phone buzzed. He eased it from his pocket and saw the name "Deeds" on the screen. Morris Deeds, the chief of police. Alden always took his calls, day or night, though they rarely brought good news. "Hello, Morris."

"Alden," Morris Deeds said. His voice was dry and tight. "We might have us a situation here."

"What is it?"

"I've just been over to see Marie Hackett. Mike went out after elk yesterday. Was supposed to take Frank Trippi with him, but Frank sprained his wrist and backed out."

"So Mike went by himself?"

"That's right. And he hasn't come back, or called. Marie expected him last night, latest. Now it's almost another full day gone by and she's worried sick."

Alden glanced out the window and drummed his fingers nervously on the table. "What do you want to do? It's dark now."

"I'd like to pull together a search party, go out at first light and see if we can't find him. In the meantime, I'll have some of my guys drive the back roads looking for Mike's truck."

"That's a good idea, Morris. I'm away from my desk now, but I'll head back over there and start making some calls."

"Thanks. That'll help."

"You know Mike better than I do. Is he a good hunter? Good outdoorsman?"

Morris paused a moment before responding. "He's not bad. He's brought home some trophies. But I wouldn't say he's the most careful man who ever picked up a gun."

"That's what I was afraid of. Keep me posted, okay?"

"Will do."

"And let's hope for the best."

CHAPTER FIVE

After getting unloaded and into their bare-bones rooms, Alex, Peter, and Ellen met up again, piling back into the Lexus and tooling into town to look for some dinner. There wasn't much of town, five or six blocks along the main street, lined with brick buildings housing shops and businesses. Side streets appeared residential and quiet. Fully a third of the storefronts were empty, and "For Rent" signs plastered walls and windows. The only place that looked busy was Spud's, a square brick building with blacked-out windows illuminated by neon beer signs.

Peter wanted to go in, but Alex overruled him. He would hear about that for an hour, he was sure. Peter was a skilled cinematographer—more than skilled, he was maybe a genius, and that wasn't a word Alex slung about easily. But he was insufferable. If people considered him merely a genius, Peter thought they underestimated his true worth. He brimmed with opinions, each the true and final word on any given subject. Ellen was happy to feed his ego, which Alex guessed was why he kept her around.

He pointed at a sign that said, "Cup & Cow Bakery/Cafe." The windows were clean, and the interior appeared to be as well. Several of the tables were occupied, but he could see a few empties. "Here we go," Alex declared.

"It'll do, I guess," Peter grumbled.

"Looks yummy," Ellen said. She wore perkiness like a badge of honor.

Alex found it draining and wondered how Peter could stand it. Then again, he wouldn't be able to put up with Peter's glum cynicism for long, either, so maybe they balanced one another out.

"It's charmingly rustic." Peter oozed sarcasm. "Sort of like that motel you found us. I'd think it was the place Janet Leigh stayed at, in *Psycho*, except that one had shower curtains. It's not exactly the Ritz, is it?"

"You wouldn't stay at a Ritz," Alex countered. He eased the SUV to the curb. "It's much too bourgeois."

"Yeah, well, it sure as hell isn't the W, either."

The restaurant smelled great, the scents of grilled meat and fresh coffee and baked goods combining in a sort of aromatic hug. They were greeted at the door, seated in a booth alongside a pine-paneled wall, and had placed their orders within a few minutes.

While they waited for their meals, Peter left the table. A burly guy in a down vest was talking on a pay phone—arguing with someone, Alex thought, from the pained animation of his face—and blocking much of the narrow hallway that led to the restrooms. Peter squeezed past him, but he must have muttered something as he did, because the guy's face turned dark red and he dropped the telephone receiver, which spun and dangled on its cable, and stalked after Peter.

"Shit," Alex said. "Wait here." He bolted from the table and hustled to the hallway. Pine lined both sides of it, and a handful of framed photos that visiting minor celebrities had autographed decorated the walls. Alex caught up with the big man just about the same time he reached Peter, who had pulled the men's room door open.

"Listen," Alex said. He put a hand on the big man's shoulder, startling him. The man looked away from Peter and fixed Alex with an angry glare.

The guy was huge. Bigger than he had looked from the table. He was Peter's height, only without Peter's lankiness. A curly red beard clung to his chin, seeping down his neck and beneath his plaid shirt. "What?"

"I don't know what my friend said, but he's tired. We've had a long trip, and he might have mouthed off or something, but he didn't mean anything by it. He's sorry. Tell him you're sorry, Peter."

"Sure," Peter said with a shrug. He looked anything but sorry. "Like he said, I'm tired."

"Tired is one thing, but rude is something else."

"It's the California in me," Peter said. "Takes a while to slough off when I go someplace civilized."

The big man almost grinned in spite of himself. "I hear that."

"Can I buy you a beer or something?" Alex asked. "Make it up to you?"

"I can buy my own beer."

"I know you can; I just wanted to do something for you."

"Then tell your pal to keep his hole shut."

Alex lowered his voice to a stage whisper. "Brother, I tell him that every day."

The big guy laughed. Peter shrugged again and disappeared into the men's room. "You're okay," the man said. "Your buddy there, he's an asshole."

"You don't know the half of it."

"Maybe I should kick his ass just on general principle."

"Wouldn't help," Alex said. "Did you look at him? People have been kicking his ass since birth. He's used to it."

Alex had only known Peter for about two months, but he was on a roll, and the more he insulted the cinematographer, the more the big man relaxed. The burgundy color faded from his face, and he suddenly remembered his phone call. "Damn it!" he said, brushing past Alex and lunging for the receiver. "Baby, you there?" he asked when he picked it up.

When Alex returned to the table, Ellen greeted him with a smile. "That was ballsy," she said. She sat on the bench with her legs crossed under her, wearing a tight, white, ribbed cotton shirt with long sleeves, snug over small breasts and a flat stomach.

"What?"

"That dude's about as big as you and Peter put together. He could've snapped you in half like a toothpick."

Alex put his hands under the table. They'd started shaking as he realized how right she was. He hadn't even considered that, had simply rushed to make sure Peter didn't get them involved in a scrape on their first evening in town.

Peter returned from the men's room without further incident, and their food arrived soon after. As they ate, chatting casually about their plans for the next few days, a couple came inside and spoke to the woman behind the counter, the one who seemed to be running things. Her face took on a grave appearance, and within a few minutes word spread throughout the restaurant. The people in the next booth told Alex, Peter, and Ellen, as if they were locals. "Mike Hackett's missing," a woman said. "There's gonna be a search party out, first thing in the morning."

"I don't know Mike Hackett," Alex said. "But we'd be glad to help search."

"We're meeting in the parking lot behind Town Hall, at seven."

"We'll be there."

"We will?" Peter muttered.

"You started us out by pissing off one of the locals," Alex said, keeping his voice low. "This'll be a good way to get them on our side, and what we're doing here will be much easier if they like us."

"What if it's dangerous?" Ellen asked.

"How could it be dangerous? We'll be with a bunch of people. They know the area and they'll probably be armed—"

"What's more dangerous than a bunch of Cletuses with guns?" Peter interrupted.

"Look, the guy's probably sleeping off a drunk under a tree someplace, you guys. The whole thing probably won't take more than an hour or two. We walk around in the woods, make some friends, and then when they find out why we're here maybe they'll go easy with the pitchforks and torches."

"Seven is awfully fucking early."

"Peter, we're making a movie about climate change. These are rural people, mountain people, who probably don't believe in it. They're going to think we're a bunch of assholes from the city, and so far you're proving them right. We've got a chance here to make them go easier on us, and we've got to take it."

Peter shrugged. He did that a lot. "You're the head honcho."

"That's right. So get to bed early tonight. And set an alarm—I doubt the motel has a wake-up service."

Peter nodded his assent, and Alex turned back to the people in the next booth. "Excuse me. If I wanted a guide, someone who really knows these mountains well—I mean, after the search party's done, of course—is there someone you'd recommend?"

The man didn't even have to consider the question. "Robbie Driscoll," he said. "Don't you think, Mae?"

"Yes," his date agreed. "Robbie's the best. Just look for Driscoll's Outfitters, here on Main. It's, what, four doors from here."

"Driscoll's," Alex repeated. "Thanks. Thank you very much."

"Enjoy your meal," the man said. "The pork chops here are the best I've ever had."

Alex forked a chunk into his mouth, and he couldn't disagree.

Ellen waited until both men were looking away, then shifted her grip on her steak knife and brought it back above the table. As soon as Peter had bumped into the big man, she had snatched it up and been ready to move. She had known a guy like him in Miami—fuck *known*, she had been *with* him, and shading the truth from herself wouldn't do her any good. He'd been a city guy, not a mountain man like this dude, but physically aggressive men shared enough similarities for her to recognize one: the way his chin ticked up when he spoke, the tightness at the back of his jaw. She had watched the man's hands when Peter got in his face, his fingers poised to clutch a knife or a gun or to curl into fists. Peter wouldn't have had a chance, and even Alex's interference wouldn't have helped.

Hence the knife. She was out of her comfort zone here, and it didn't pay to take chances.

Ellen was a survivor. Her father had died when she was a child, and her mother had dealt with that loss by becoming addicted to a variety of pharmaceuticals. When she went to prison, Ellen went into the system, too, and a series of foster homes had taught hard lessons. She had figured out early in life that she would always be small and not strong, but that if she latched onto someone who was powerful, she would be protected. Once in a while she took a beating—men who liked to punch weren't always particular about whom, where, and when—but never more than one.

Eventually she had figured out that power didn't only come from physical strength; that, in fact, lasting power emanated from less flagrantly obvious sources. Wealth, for instance. Influence. That newfound knowledge had led eventually to Peter, a man she believed to be on the cusp of doing big things. This documentary of Alex's was just the beginning, the project that would take Peter to the next level.

She wanted to be with him on that ride. If that meant being ready to knife someone who might hurt him, then that's what she would do.

Just the same, she was glad it hadn't come to that yet. With luck, it wouldn't.

She would be ready, though, just in case. She always was. Survival demanded no less.

He was underground, in the dark. The walls were close, and the lights had flickered and then gone out, and the air was thick with choking black dust. He had fallen to the ground when the earth shook, carrying with it a noise that seemed to come from everywhere at once, from all around him and deep inside, first a ferocious boom from the mine bump as the support pillars collapsed, then a rumbling that seemed like it would never end, but that stopped abruptly, leaving behind only the patter of rocks falling from walls and ceiling, and the screams of the lost and injured.

Lost? That was him. When he regained his feet—lucky to be alive, he knew that much; doubtless some of the shafts and rooms had collapsed entirely—he didn't know which way was which. One direction might lead him out of the mine, to safety and breathable air. The other would take him deeper in, where his chances of being caught in a secondary cave-in or explosion would increase with every foot he traveled. He fought back against the panic that tore at his throat, trying to think, to reason.

But it was no use. The world was pitch-black; he couldn't see his hand an inch from his face. The dust gagged him, and he stumbled along, coughing and spitting and vomiting, with no clue where he was going. For all he knew, he could have passed into seams long since closed off by the company but opened again by the tremors.

Time had passed—he had no way of knowing how much—when he heard another tunnel burst. He couldn't tell if it was ahead of him, behind, or in a shaft that was parallel or adjoining. His face was slick with dust-caked blood and he was weak, stumbling often, panic ebbing but being replaced by a sense of futility. The shafts could be filling with mud and debris that would drown him before he had a chance to die of hunger. Either way, he would never see sunlight again, never take another breath of clean air.

Then the man was there, as he always was. His name was Jared Flannery, and he could see Flannery, as if the miner had his own perpetual glow. He was blackened from head to toe, but his ruddy brush of a mustache stood out, and green eyes shone like lanterns. *This way, man*, he said, though his mouth didn't move. *Come on, this is the way out.*

And he followed Flannery, willingly, only once in a while fearing that Flannery was some sort of mine sprite, a Tommyknocker or other creature here to lead him into certain destruction. Flannery seemed to know the way; he was confident, at least, and he kept up a running patter as they moved through the shaft. *This is the way, won't be far now, this way to the surface, boss.*

He didn't know why he should trust Flannery, but he did. And they did seem to be going up, mostly, and the air did seem to be clearing a little. He was still scared, *terrified*, but he started to allow himself to believe that there might be a way out, that escape was possible, if not likely.

And then Flannery stopped, and there was a door behind him, and he put his hand on the door handle. *This is the way, boss*, Flannery said, *this is it, right through here.*

But as he drew closer to the door, something behind it made a noise. Another bump, he feared, another collapse, but no, it wasn't that. It was on the other side of that door, and it was a growling, deep and resonant and fierce. Not just growling, but snapping and slavering, and he knew that if Flannery opened that door, they would charge, all teeth and claws and ripping, tearing, and as Flannery pulled down on the handle and the door started to gap open and light, blinding light with shadows moving in it started to leak through, he said "No, Flannery, don't open it don't let them in I won't I'll do—"

Alex woke up thrashing, sheets and blankets wrapped tightly around him, binding him. Sweat covered him like ice water, and he was shivering, his teeth clacking together.

The dream was always the same, and yet it wasn't. It varied in its details; sometimes Flannery took him to a great shaft from which he could see light, at a distance that seemed like a miles-long, impossible climb. Twice, the miner had taken him to a place where light fell on a signpost, and the sign read "Silver Gap." Sometimes Flannery led him around in circles and then abandoned him, though always with a promise to fetch help and come back.

The dreams, though—and no one else knew it, surely not Peter and Ellen—the dreams were why they had come. He had been looking for some sort of redemption. The idea of a documentary had been itching at him, and he had seen that sign: Silver Gap. He looked it up and found out about Silver Gap, Colorado, and learned about the bark beetles, and the fairly direct link between their spread and the blister rust infection that was killing whitebark pines all over the western states, and his plans had crystallized almost at once.

Now, he was here. And instead of going away, the dream was back, worse than ever. Before, at the end of the dream, scary as it was, there had been some hope. But this one, tonight, had offered none. There was only one way out, Flannery seemed to be saying. Through that door. And when he opened that door ...

Alex shivered again, got out of bed, flicked on the overhead light. There were no bedside lights, no bedside tables. He sat on the edge of the bed in the bare room, wrapped the blanket around himself, and waited for the dawn.

CHAPTER SIX

Alex woke up again at six.

He had an internal alarm that worked as well as any store-bought clock he'd ever had. He wasn't sure when he had fallen asleep again—he was still at the edge of the bed, his legs dangling off—but obviously he had. When he'd turned in, there still hadn't been any hot water in the joint, but the owner must have got the water heater going because when Alex tried the shower, he only had to wait a couple of minutes before the bathroom filled with steam. While he was out to dinner with Peter and Ellen, someone had come in, made the bed and left towels and soap.

Although he traveled with his own soap, shampoo, and conditioner, he used the motel's because he wanted whoever had left them to notice that *he* had noticed. Alex Converse might have been the heir to the Converse Coal fortune, but he tried to remember that not everyone had been born rich, and that even hotel housekeepers—which he doubted this place had, at the moment—deserved respect and needed to feel appreciated.

His family business had been responsible for terrible environmental degradation, for clogging rivers with sediment from mountaintop removal, for clear-cutting forests, for pumping tons of carbon into the atmosphere. Alex couldn't make it never have happened. He couldn't even shut down the company, because stockholders controlled it now, and he had only a minority interest.

Instead, he did everything he could to counteract the destruction that had made him rich. The Alex Converse Foundation funded groups fighting climate change and other environmental battles and supported political candidates who shared those goals. Those were baby steps, though. You helped elect someone and then maybe that person voted the way you wanted, and maybe they didn't. You worked for months or years to get a bill inching through a state legislature, or Congress, only to see it fail or be watered down so much that it lost its teeth. Alex tried to be patient, but sometimes he felt like a feather in a tornado, trying to make headway but forever blown in circles by forces far more powerful than he could ever be.

Finally, the idea for the film had come to him. He had never made a movie, but he understood the persuasive powers of moving images. He was no celebrity, no Al Gore or Michael Moore—his name was known mostly to the fundraisers for the groups he supported—but he had done a lot of research on climate change, and he thought he had an approach that would attract some notice. Plus, he could afford to market the hell out of it.

Only a couple of decades ago, in the wake of Gore's movie, people had believed in climate change—what had once been known as "global warming." Since then, though, the deniers had made headway, thanks to phony interest groups backed by oil companies—and, he knew, other big energy industry companies, including Converse Coal—buying off scientists who helped spread the lie that climate change was nothing but a liberal hoax.

The evidence, in fact, was all around. Here in the Rocky Mountains, glaciers were melting, and bark beetle devastation had come about when winters ceased being cold enough to kill off the beetles every year. Elsewhere, there were disappearing wetlands and prolonged drought, powerful storms and warming oceans and calving of the Antarctic ice shelf and enough other symptoms to convince any, he thought, but the willfully blind.

When he got out of the shower, he dressed quickly and walked down to bang on the door of the cabin that Peter and Ellen shared. She answered, already dressed, and told him they were up and getting ready. Surprised, but pleased, Alex left them to it and walked back to his cabin.

A few minutes after seven, he parked the Lexus in the lot behind the big brick Town Hall building, where a crowd of about fifty had gathered.

Many, as he had expected, carried rifles or shotguns, and more than a few had handguns on their hips. Someone had set up a table with two coffee urns, hot water, teabags, and several steel trays of doughnuts. Alex recognized the woman who had been running the restaurant last night, the Cup & Cow, standing behind the food table.

Alex, used to the temperate southern California clime, had outfitted himself in a Mountain Hardwear Sub Zero SL jacket, North Face Outbound pants, and fur-lined leather gloves. His boots were from Asolo, and by themselves had probably cost more than most of these people had spent on everything they wore. He saw plenty of flannel, denim, and down.

The vast majority of the people were white, but there were a handful of Latinos and a couple of black men. The guy Peter had pissed off at the restaurant was there, talking to an enormously fat man who didn't look much older than fifteen but who almost certainly was. A double-barreled shotgun looked like a child's toy in his hands. A couple of feet from them stood a pair of hard-looking, rawboned women with short, steely hair and masculine clothes.

"Guess we found the dyke contingent," Peter said with a snicker.

Alex hadn't slept well enough to put up with Peter's shit. That, or he needed caffeine even more than he wanted to admit. "Try not to offend anyone for at least an hour, Peter. Try really hard."

Alex was overdressed, considering that the autumn had not yet turned really cold, even at this elevation. And he was overdoing it with his pricey new duds, compared to the lived-in clothing of the locals. Peter and Ellen hadn't gone so whole hog on the outdoor gear; both dressed as if they were out for a stroll on the Santa Monica Promenade. Peter was unshaven, with fair whiskers stubbling his cheeks, and grouchy.

They were helping themselves to coffee and doughnuts when a stocky man with short dark hair clapped his hands together a couple of times. His mustache was a stiff, mostly black thatch riding his lip. He wore a dark blue coat with a gold star on the chest, and a tan cowboy hat. The crowd quieted and directed their attention toward him.

"Thanks for coming out today, folks," he said. "Looks like I know most of you, but there are a couple newcomers here, and we appreciate you taking part in this effort, too. For anybody who don't know me, I'm Chief Deeds."

He ticked his head toward two officers standing at his left, a tall black man with a mustache rivaling his own, and a shorter, skinny white guy whose prominent nose and receding chin gave him an unfortunate rodent-like appearance. "These here are officers Jones and Honeycutt, for those that don't know them," the chief continued. "We're here to track down Mike Hackett. I got some pictures here that his wife Marie gave me, for anyone don't remember what Mike looks like. I figure he's fixed most of your trucks, one time or another, and you'll recall the smile on his face when he took your money."

There was general laughter in the crowd. Alex felt like a stranger crashing a family reunion. He was pretty sure that he, Peter, and Ellen were the only outsiders, the ones for whom Chief Deeds had intended his introductions.

"I should also thank John Fredericks of Fredericks Mining for buying the coffee and doughnuts. Where are you, John?"

A burly, bearded man in a plaid hunting coat and cap raised one hand. "Right here, Morris!"

"Well, thanks a lot, John. We appreciate it and I know the mayor's wife appreciates the extra business."

"Maybe she can mention that to him next tax season," John Fredericks said, drawing another laugh from the crowd.

The chief continued with an overview of the basic strategy. His officers had located Hackett's truck, so the search party would convoy over to where it had been parked, and fan out from there. Everybody would stay no more than five or six feet from the people on either side of them, because any farther and somebody lying on the ground, maybe hurt and needing help, could be missed. Where terrain demanded it, they would adjust, but that was the plan.

As people flocked toward their trucks and Jeeps, Alex headed for one of the big urns. A slender blonde woman in a puffy down vest, snug jeans, and calf-high boots was moving in the same direction, so Alex stopped short and gestured her in. "Ladies first," he said. "I guess standard city manners apply here in the mountains, right?"

She shot him a frown. "We're not barbarians." With that, she filled her Styrofoam cup and walked away, not once looking back at him.

Blew that one, he thought.

He hadn't noticed until she'd glared at him how pretty she was, her features cleanly carved, a light spray of freckles gracing the curve of her nose, her green eyes direct and sparkling in the soft morning light. The frown had accentuated the bulge of her plump lower lip. Shoulder-length hair framed her face, bangs cutting a straight line across her forehead.

Alex had been married once; married too young, really. He had always seen himself as a married man, a family man, since his early teens, and Steph had played into that self-image. She had seemed perfect in every way: smart, beautiful, able to tell a joke or take one with equal ease. She hadn't come from money but she wasn't freaked out by his, or particularly interested in it. She was a seeker, as Alex had been at that point in his life. A seeker after truth, after beauty, after the answers to every question that life put before her, and they had decided to search together. They married after a seven-month courtship, and two years after that she got pregnant. Alex was only twenty-three, Steph a year older.

Eleanor was four months old when she died. SIDS, the coroner said, adding that it was an imprecise diagnosis, a name applied to various conditions that were only barely understood.

Steph went three weeks later, jumping off a high cliff onto jagged boulders. Police found her body hours later, after the seagulls and crabs had been at it.

To say that Alex was devastated would have been to vastly underestimate his condition. He barely existed in the world of the living for the next year. The foundation limped along, someone coming to his house with a stack of checks for him to sign every week or two. On the few occasions he tried to go out, he found himself breaking down at unexpected times, like once when he went into a movie men's room and saw the pull-down baby changing platform there. He wandered through the rooms of the big house he had talked Steph into letting him buy, convinced they would raise a whole brood of kids there. He still talked to her, sometimes, hoping she would answer, but she never did.

Only one of the dead—the many, many dead, in Alex's world—ever spoke to him. And Flannery didn't answer questions, simply demanded blind trust and faithful obedience.

Gradually, Alex was drawn back into the world. The foundation needed his attention. The planet wasn't fixing itself, and every year that slipped by was one year closer to the irreversible tipping point. He immersed himself in research, letting facts and figures and hard data substitute for human interaction. But his path led toward humans, after all.

Now he found himself surrounded by ghosts and dreamers. Only the dreamers spoke to him, when the voices he longed to hear were those of the ghosts.

Since resurfacing, he had suffered through a few couplings that almost deserved to be called relationships, all of which had ultimately ended for one reason or another—usually because of him, because of the unfinished business he carried inside himself like a separate organ: one heart too many. Interspersed were a handful of LA-style flings, a woman encountered at a party who would go home with him or simply go down on him in her car, a minor celebrity who let herself be seen at trendy spots around town with him to help establish her liberal *bona fides*. Lately he had been so focused on the documentary project that he had let his personal life slide. He hadn't expected to meet someone here; the possibility had not even occurred to him until he saw that woman, the line of her neck and the natural pink blush of her cheeks and the swell of her breasts, and then it had hit him like a baseball bat to the solar plexus.

And he had, in turn, swung the bat into any chance of them connecting, smashing it to hopeless shards.

Now that he knew it wasn't happening, he could concentrate on the task at hand. He carried his cup back to the Lexus, where Ellen and Peter waited. Ellen raised her cup to him, steam issuing from a slit in the plastic lid. "This shit is probably straight-up poison, huh?" she asked.

For the most part, Alex limited his activism to carbon issues and climate change, but within his sphere of acquaintances there were always people happy to point out the many ways in which human beings were killing one another and the planet. "You mean the coffee? It could be. But if you mean the Styrofoam, then yes, absolutely. Styrofoam is loaded with styrene, which is toxic as hell. And the heat in the coffee is probably breaking it down so it can enter our bloodstreams faster."

"Great," Peter said. "Yet another way to fucking die."

"There's no shortage," Alex pointed out. "Some are just quicker than others." They got into the SUV and joined the line of vehicles heading into the higher country. The ride took about twenty-five minutes, through ponderosa pine forest. The higher they went, the more denuded the trees, their needles brown and orange or their limbs completely bare. Once the trees gave up, high winds could knock them over; stumps jutted into the air and in places, tall trunks were scattered like toothpicks shaken from a box.

Vehicles were filling in the empty spaces around a red and white Ford pickup that Chief Deeds had parked his department Tahoe beside. Alex pulled off the road at the first wide spot he found, and they climbed out again.

"Isn't that your new girlfriend?" Peter pointed to the blonde Alex had spoken to. She was exiting a red Jeep about twenty feet away. She didn't glance in their direction, for which Alex was grateful.

"Let's go," he said. "And let's try not to call undue attention to ourselves." He meant attention from that specific woman, who he hoped would forget he had ever opened his mouth. But it would be a good policy overall, too. If they were seen helping the community, and had a few pleasant, non-humiliating interactions with the locals, that would serve their ends. It would be even better if one of them turned out to be a hero, rescuing Mike Hackett from a bear or something.

That was highly unlikely, Alex knew. But he hoped at least they could get through the day without making any more enemies.

CHAPTER SEVEN

Their third hour in the woods, Alex admitted that his initial estimate had been flawed.

"My feet are killing me," Peter complained. "And I'm fucking starving. You got any more granola bars, babe?"

"You ate the last one a half hour ago."

"Chief Deeds said someone's bringing sandwiches up," Alex reminded them.

"Probably peanut butter and jelly, from that same place in town we ate. I think it's the only restaurant in town. You think one of these yokels would run down to The Palm for me?"

"Just look at these trees," Alex said, desperate to change the subject. He waved an arm at the devastated pines. "Think about the footage we'll get up here."

"Yeah." Peter eyed the forest, raising a hand and making a corner from fingers and thumb. Framing the shot. Alex wished he could see the way Peter did, with an artist's eye. "We'll get some awesome footage, if I don't have to have my feet amputated."

"It's not that bad, Peter," Ellen said. "I'll massage them later."

Peter laughed. "You can start there and work up."

Alex didn't want to hear any more. He drifted away from Ellen and Peter—although trying not to stray too far beyond the police chief's requested six-foot distance—and toward a guy who looked like he had grown up in these woods. The man wore patched, faded camouflaged fatigue pants and jacket with a bright orange vest. He carried a beat-up rifle that might have been his age or a little older, maybe from World War II. Or the War of 1812.

"How long have these trees been in this condition?" Alex asked. "All dead like this?"

The man glanced Alex's way, showing him narrow eye slits in a blunt, ruddy face. "I guess maybe it was seven, eight years ago or thereabouts, it started up," he said. "Don't remember exactly. And there's always some of it, right? Just seemed to have got worse around then. Kinda leveled off for a while, but then this past summer it got really bad again."

"It's the cumulative effect of the carbon in the atmosphere," Alex said.

"No, it's bugs."

"Yeah, that's what I'm saying. The cold winters used to kill the bark beetles. Since the winters have been warmer, the trees' natural defense hasn't been there, so the effect of the insects has become much more pronounced."

"I don't know where you were last winter, but it was pretty fuckin' cold up here."

"What I'm saying is, it's cumulative. The hottest years on record have almost all been in the last ten years or so. Glaciers and ice sheets are declining, sea level's rising—"

"Don't start with that global warming bullpuckey," the man countered. "It all goes in cycles, hot and warm. Anyway, the good Lord won't let nothin' too bad happen."

Alex started to respond, then decided against it. He was lecturing, which he had promised himself he wouldn't do. Anyway, science and faith had been in conflict forever, and he wasn't likely to change this guy's mind. Some churches preached that humanity served as the Earth's steward in God's stead, but many continued to claim that the works of mankind couldn't have a significant, harmful effect on His handiwork.

But walking through a forest that should have been an emerald-green cathedral, Alex couldn't fend off the crushing weight of hopelessness. Even the breeze rustling the trees had a brittle edge, instead of its usual smooth susurrus. The air carried a hint of decay.

"Hey!" someone called from about thirty yards away. "Look!"

Alex couldn't see what he was supposed to be looking at, but then he heard the word repeated over and over. "Ravens!" someone said. "Look!"

Now Alex saw them: what looked like twenty or thirty ravens

wheeling about above the trees, some darting down toward the earth or soaring away.

Carrion birds. They looked like ink stains sliding across a crisp blue background. The searchers streamed toward that point from every direction, converging beneath the raven wheel.

Just before Alex reached the group—Peter and Ellen left behind someplace, not running flat out as he was—somebody let out a scream. Alex threaded through the clot of people gathered there, and a woman bumped into him, bent over double, hand over her mouth. She barely got past Alex, who turned to see that she was okay, then dropped to her knees and made retching noises. Someone on the far side of the group did the same.

Alex wanted to run. Whatever was attracting those ravens and making people sick, he wanted no part of.

But he couldn't. People were pressing in behind him, and curiosity propelled him forward. The stink hit him before he could see it, the sick and sour-sweet smell universal to death. Then somebody else moved away, cupping his face in his hands and sobbing out loud, and there was nothing between Alex and the mess that had been Michael Hackett. Blood painted the ground. Jagged bone protruded through pale, torn flesh. Bits of orange fluff were snagged on stiff, dry grasses.

"Oh, God," a man said. Tears streamed down his reddened face, mucus slicked his nose and mustache. "Oh, God, oh, God, Mikey, no!"

Alex's guts flipped and churned. He leaned forward, hands on someone else's shoulders, for a better look at the remains, then closed his eyes against the gruesome sight. It didn't matter; what he had seen was seared into his memory.

"Back off!" Chief Deeds shouted. He waded through the crowd, which parted before his advance like the Red Sea for Moses. "Give me some space here!"

Alex was trying to move away, but he was close enough to see the chief's face blanch. The lawman swallowed hard, twice, but didn't look away. Alex was impressed by the man's steady gaze.

The crowd swept Alex away from the massacre as the chief went down on one knee beside the body. Trauma erased any distinction between outsiders and locals; everybody spoke at once and Alex was in the middle of it all.

"You think it's him?" someone asked, and the responses flew.

"It's Mike. I seen his rifle."

"His hat's right over there."

"What do you think done it?"

"Mountain lion, maybe."

"Could be."

"No, you see them tracks? They're dog, not cat."

"Dog pack?"

"Or coyotes, maybe."

"That or wolves."

"There's no wolves in Colorado."

"Heard about some sightings at the High Lonesome."

"That's south of here. They come in through Wyoming, they could be here, too."

"Never heard about any."

"You look at him? Coyotes didn't do that. I don't think dogs did either."

More discussion about the likelihood of wolves followed, and then the conversation dwindled, down to one searcher talking to the next. The word "wolves" came up often. Alex rejoined Peter and Ellen. They hadn't come close enough to see, or to take part in the analysis.

"'Sup?" Peter asked. He leaned against the trunk of a stripped-down pine. Ellen sat on the carpet of discolored needles around it.

"Wolves, they're saying. Guy's a mess; I'm amazed they can even identify him."

"Really?" Ellen asked. Suddenly she sounded interested, like she might want to check it out.

"I've never seen anything like it outside of a horror movie. Lot of people getting sick over there, and I had a hard time keeping my doughnuts down."

"Nice," Ellen said.

"Some of these guys, hunters I guess, are probably used to it. Field dressing their kills and what have you. But I don't know, I think it might be a while before I can eat meat again."

Peter laughed. "I thought we'd get off this mountain and pick up some burgers in town. Rare and juicy."

Alex's stomach did another quick churn. He blinked, tried to erase the memory. It wasn't going anywhere. "I'll pass, thanks."

"We done here?"

"I guess so."

"Think we made friends among the populace?"

Alex shrugged. "I couldn't say. I hope so."

Other searchers began to drift back toward the road, so Alex, Ellen, and Peter joined them. "Gotta get what's left of Mike down to Dr. Steinhilber," someone was saying. "He'll know what done it."

"Gonna have to scrape him up with a spatula," someone else answered.

"Be a special service tonight at the church, you think?" This was the man Alex had talked to earlier, the one who didn't believe God would let anything bad happen to the world.

"I expect so."

"I'll be there, for sure."

"Same here."

Alex was not a religious person, or particularly spiritual—he had given up that quest when Steph and Eleanor died—though he understood the impulse to seek answers or solace in what he considered the realm of the supernatural. Seeing Mike Hackett's ruined body didn't cause him to become a believer, but he felt a kind of inner pang at the idea that other people would come together in their grief, while he would be sitting in a lonely, empty motel.

He spat to clear an unpleasant taste from his mouth, and trudged toward the SUV.

Howie Honeycutt looked at the remains with what he considered to be a cool, clinical eye. All around him, people were puking, sobbing, threatening all manner of revenge, or simply silent, holding their terror inside. Even Tim Jones, who grew up in Silver Gap and had been on the force for fifteen years, looked green around the gills. Tim would probably judge Howie's reaction, and he would find it lacking, because that's just how he was. That, in Howie's opinion, was how lesser men viewed others, through a prism of judgment and distrust.

Howie was proud of Chief Deeds, though. Deeds was naturally disturbed to find one of his townsfolk torn apart by wild animals, even though that wasn't in itself a crime and therefore was outside his area of responsibility. Still, he was exhibiting strength to the members of the search party, who at this point needed that more than anything. He didn't let them see how torn apart he was, but showed them that he had his act together. Howie would help in any way he could, of course. He was the newest member of the force, with just over three years in, and he had never worked for anybody he admired more.

He looked at the body—the parts, anyway—and tried to figure out how to get them back to town. No sense crying over Hackett; he was beyond any pain or human judgment or possibility of help. He was no longer a person; he was an assortment of tissue and bone. A logistical problem. Howie figured they would need shovels and bags. Body bags if they could be spared, but heavy-duty trash bags would do. Shovels would be the main thing. And gloves. They wouldn't get all of him with that, but they'd get the big pieces. The rest they could leave. Insects would finish off what larger animals didn't. Come spring there might be a few bones scattered about, but that wasn't a problem out here.

Hackett's ribcage arched up from the bloody mass, reminding Howie of a bent bicycle wheel, its spokes catching sunlight. Looking at the body parts, breathing in the scents of blood and raw meat, Howie realized that his engagement with the scene wasn't entirely clinical after all, unless by clinical you meant that it made your pants suddenly fit tighter around the groin area. It stirred memories, that's what it was. Memories that he thought were long buried. All in the past.

Maybe, though, not so much ...

CHAPTER EIGHT

Christy Deeds knew when her husband was depressed. They had been married for seventeen years. She knew all of his moods, and there were many. Depression showed itself in his slumping shoulders, his eyes—especially the eyes, which seemed to fix on some faraway point—the way he held his neck. It was different than the mood that gripped him when work was particularly wearying, when the things that people did to each other grated against his soul.

Morris walked toward her, up the walkway to their front door, and he was definitely depressed. She opened the door before he reached it. "Was it bad?"

He'd already called her with a brief report, but he had left out the grisly details. "What's *left* of him was."

She opened her arms and scooped him against her. "I'm so sorry."

"It was awful, Christy. Animals got to him." His voice, ordinarily gravelly, was lower than usual. She had to strain to hear him.

"Can you take it easy for a while? Have a cup of coffee, decompress?"

He kissed her cheek and backed away, coming inside and shutting the door. "No, I can only stay a minute. Just want to splash some water on my face. I've got to go talk to Marie Hackett before she hears about it from someone else."

"Oh, no, she doesn't know yet?"

Morris met her gaze briefly. "I hope to God she doesn't."

He moved away from her like a sleepwalker, and she watched him go into the bathroom and close the door.

She had been on her way out when she saw him drive up. She had put her purse back on the entryway table, shucked her jacket and hung it back up in the closet. He didn't need to know where she was going, or why.

She busied herself for a few minutes. When he came out, his face was freshly scrubbed, cheeks red. A few droplets of water clung to his bushy mustache. He wasn't a handsome man, but he was striking, with riveting blue eyes and a commanding nose and that black 'stache. His purely masculine physical presence was impressive out of proportion to his size —he wasn't especially tall or broad, but he projected strength and vitality. People respected him, she believed, as much for how he made them feel when he walked into a room as for what he said or did.

When he emerged, his eyes were minutely less sad. He had steeled himself for the task ahead, and that cut some of the edge off his depression. She knew it would be a bad night for him. "I've gotta go," he said.

She hugged him again, kissed him on the lips, holding it for an extra couple of seconds. "You'll help her," she said. "You're good at that. The dependable shoulder to cry on."

"I guess."

"I know it's hard on you. But you do it anyway. That's why you're the man I love."

"Thanks," he said. He offered a smile, but it was forced, lifeless. He opened the door and went back to his car. Notifying people that a loved one had died was always hard on him. He genuinely liked Marie Hackett, and Mike, too, and that would make this one worse than usual. She liked them, too, enough that she was glad she didn't have to make this visit. She stood in the doorway and watched until he was gone.

Then she put on her jacket again, grabbed her purse, and hurried to her Camry.

Eighteen minutes later, Christy Deeds pulled into a parking space outside the Church in the Woods. The church blended into its surroundings so well that someone could drive right past without knowing it was there, just off the highway. The walls were dark-brown wood with native stone accents, the roof a forest green that matched the pines almost precisely. Behind the chancel was a floor-to-ceiling window, clear, rather than stained glass. She had seen deer walking behind it during services, and on most Sundays birds flitted around, up into the trees and back down to the ground.

On the far side, an addition to the church edged toward the woods. Gilbert Calderon, the church's pastor, lived there, in a four-room rectory added in the late 1980s. His quarters had a separate front door as well as a door leading to the office that connected church and home.

The church's front doors were usually left open. Christy pulled on the right one, heavy and cool under her hands. It swung freely, and she stepped into weighty darkness broken only by the emergency exit lighting over the door. The building was silent. She went to the swinging doors that opened into the nave. "Hello?" she called.

Gil appeared at the far door, the one that led toward his office. "Who's there?" he asked. He was looking right at her, and the nave was better lit than the lobby.

"Gil, it's me. Christy."

He smiled as he approached, up the aisle between the pews. "Christy, hi. I couldn't see you. The light—"

"It's not good in here," she agreed. She didn't point out that the nave's light should have been falling on her, illuminating her against the dark background of the lobby area. Gil's vision had never been good, but could it have deteriorated so much in the weeks—no, that was wrong, it had been two months, at least—since she had seen him?

"I haven't seen you in a while," he said. He had always seemed able to read her mind. He took her hands in his, giving them a gentle squeeze. A ministerial squeeze. As ever, she was aware of the softness of his hands, so different from her husband's.

"I've ... I've been staying away."

"I gathered that. It's probably best."

"That's what I thought. But ... Gil, have you heard about Mike Hackett?"

Up close, his gaze found her face, locked on it. A straight brow shadowed deep brown eyes made only somewhat less profound by thick-lensed glasses with tortoise-shell rims. His lips were thin but expressive, his chin firm with a cleft like someone had sliced it out with a pocketknife. "I heard he was missing. I spoke with Marie, earlier."

"They found him. He's dead, Gil. Morris said it was bad. Really bad."

"I'm sorry."

"He's with Marie now. She'll need you."

"I'm here for her."

"You always are." She twisted her hands together. She wanted him to say more, do more. She wanted her cheek to scrape against his afternoon whiskers, wanted her breasts pressed against his broad chest, wanted to breathe in his clean, male scent. But unless he offered, she didn't dare.

He had made that abundantly clear.

She was here, putting herself in front of him. A word, a gesture, and she would be in his arms.

He just stood there, though, arms at his sides, hands clenched almost into fists. Like it was taking a physical effort not to touch her.

The thing was, he made the effort.

"You and Marie were always friends," he said.

"That's right. That's ... I needed to see you. I needed comfort."

"I can pray with you."

Not that kind of comfort, Christy wanted to say. *That's not it at all.*

"Christy," he said. "I can't ..."

"Yeah." She shouldn't even have come here. She tore her gaze away and hurried from the church.

CHAPTER NINE

The day had been more tiring than Alex expected. He'd experienced a jolt of adrenaline when Mike Hackett's body was found, but on the drive back into Silver Gap it had faded, leaving him drained. They stopped at the Cup & Cow and ordered some takeout, since the place was filling fast. Back at the Mountain High Lodge, they broke it out and dug in, sitting on chairs that the Durbins had set outside the cabin Peter and Ellen shared.

Mountain sun had pinked Peter's face even more than usual. His whiskers looked white against it. He slouched in the chair, elbow on the armrest, chin resting on his fist while he picked at an order of baked ziti. The sun had dropped behind the hills, plunging the valley into premature evening.

"What's up for tomorrow?" Ellen asked.

"Tomorrow I'm going to find the guide that couple in the restaurant recommended. Robbie Driscoll. If he's available, I want to go back up into the high country, do some location scouting and research."

"What kind of research?"

"I want to get some core and bark samples. Something's killing trees up here, and it's been pretty convincingly established that it's bark beetles. Just the same, I want to have an independent lab confirm that. The results will give the film more weight, and we might get some backdoor publicity by promoting the research separately."

"Long as you're not talking about a bunch of talking-head geeks in lab coats," Peter said. "Or charts. Nothing kills a documentary faster than fucking charts."

"I promise we'll keep charts to a minimum."

"Dude, you know I'm down with whatever you got in mind. And I think you're right on about getting location footage from the fronts of the climate war that people aren't talking about. I can get you some brilliant shit up here."

"I'm counting on it."

"But you gotta let me tell the story visually."

Alex had already had this discussion, or some variation on it, with Peter several times. Peter was all about the eye, the lens, and he would make a silent movie if he could get away with it. But Alex needed this film to do more than just thrill the eye; he needed it to reach a wide audience and deliver an important lesson.

Coal money was paying for it, and Alex hoped it would go some distance toward making up for the destruction his family business had caused. But there was a lot to make up for, and he wanted it to be done right. If that meant overruling Peter, then that's what he would do.

Howie Honeycutt drove both ways, up to where Mike Hackett's body had been found, and back again. George Trbovich had been assigned to recover the remains; Howie had volunteered to go along. He'd be working a graveyard shift, but he didn't mind being awake. Not for this.

Coming back, especially, George was kind of gloomy. Howie chattered, because he always did when he was excited. Whenever the conversation waned, when he let the chatter die, his mind drifted back, to Hackett and to something else. Something that Hackett reminded him of.

The first dead body Howie had ever seen was that of an accident victim. But she was also a girl he knew from school, and he had sometimes wondered if that had been the key thing about her.

He had just missed seeing it happen, though he'd heard it.

He had been riding home on the school bus, outside Collinsville. The Little Egypt part of Illinois, people called it, mostly country and small towns, closer to Kentucky and Missouri than Chicago. He had enjoyed growing up there, as much as he would have enjoyed it anywhere with his momma being dog-poor and hooking up with a succession of losers, men with quick tempers and hard fists, sometimes men who didn't like making love to a woman in the same room as her son was sleeping, and sometimes ones who liked it too much.

But when he was outside their tiny house, at school or on the bus or even just walking in the open fields, free from the smells of his momma's bad cooking and cheap smokes and spilled liquor, he figured he was happy as anybody. Every adult he knew struggled to buy groceries and pay rent and keep the kids in clothing and shoes. He had a few friends and he liked being around farms, watching animals being born, growing up, finally being slaughtered. That part was best; the powerful feeling that came from seeing a human being snatch the life from a big animal, a cow or a pig, the brutal finality of the killing blow, the almost godlike roar of the saw.

So on that afternoon, on the bus, he had been sorry he'd missed the impact. Karen Carty, a senior who was just about the sexiest female he had ever seen, with her long, bleached hair and the way she switched her hips when she walked, had gotten off the bus at her usual stop. She was flirting with a couple of the football players and didn't see that a pickup truck was racing past the bus, ignoring the flashing lights and the little stop sign that extended from the side. The pickup's driver, drunk and hurrying to get home from his mistress's house before his wife got off work, didn't see her in time, or didn't think she would step away from the open window that boys' arms were hanging out of. He hit her head on and smeared her across forty feet of roadway.

Howie missed the impact, but he got a good look at the aftermath. The bus had to wait for the sheriff to come out, and although the driver told everybody not to look, some of the football players forced open the door and piled out. Howie joined them. He saw Karen Carty with her eyes open and her clothes mostly shredded and torn off, saw her jubblies and the tuft of hair over her ladybits and the guts that had spilled from where her stomach had opened up wide.

He'd had to walk home from the bus stop with his books held in front of him that day, to hide the stain on the front of his pants. His momma wasn't there when he arrived, so he took jelly from a jar and smeared it all over the pants, and told her he had spilled trying to make a sandwich. She had turned her current boyfriend loose on him that night, for wasting food.

But from that day on, whenever he touched himself in the john or in his bed while his momma grunted and rutted in the next one, he thought about Karen Carty. Not how she had looked in life, with her makeup and her hips shaking and her behind encased in tight-fitting jeans, but the other way, in death, naked and spread out for everybody to see.

Even then, he had known that one day, the memory would no longer be enough.

CHAPTER TEN

W olves, you say?"

Morris Deeds sat in the mayor's office, on the second floor of the century-old Town Hall, with large windows facing Main. Alden Stewart could stand at his window and watch traffic in and out of his wife's restaurant, if he wanted to. Morris was pretty sure he did just that on occasion, maybe even going so far as to tabulate the average check so he would know how much she was taking in.

Alden had a big wooden desk and filing cabinets, and a table covered with folders and blueprints and plans for the various town improvement projects he had going. The hardwood floors squeaked and there were rust stains on the ceiling that looked like a bison had been slaughtered in the attic and bled through. Morris sat on a low-slung couch covered in some kind of hideous gold-and-brown fabric that should have been burned in 1979. He hated sitting there, because he had to look up at Alden. The only other chair in the room was a wooden ladder-back, however, and that was piled high with volumes of municipal code.

"Wolves," Morris replied. "That's the conclusion I reached."

"You realize wolves officially don't exist in Colorado."

"Yes, Alden, I do. But I didn't have a chance to check their visas."

Alden peered at him from behind the big desk. He didn't always appreciate Morris's sense of humor. "If wolves killed Mike, what do you propose we do about it?"

Morris had known this question was coming. "I don't know that we do anything about it. Wolves aren't criminals, even if they're trespassing across state lines. And Mike was well beyond town limits. If wolves killed him, they didn't do it within my jurisdiction, or yours."

"That's true."

"And since Colorado doesn't have wolves, stands to reason they were just passing through, right?"

"That might be true."

"We have no reason to believe it's not."

"We didn't think there were wolves around at all until this afternoon, Morris. We've got to consider the possibility that they're here, and that more people might be at risk. Not to mention livestock, pets, and what have you."

Morris had been afraid the mayor might take this approach. As far as he was concerned, Mike had run up against some bad luck. He was sorry it happened, but he didn't think it had to make his life difficult.

Morris Deeds was not a lazy man, but that didn't mean he wanted life more complicated than it had to be. He had expected Alden to go along with his take, not to twist things around so that wild animals became a law enforcement matter.

"I'm not saying we shouldn't be watchful, Alden. I'm only saying I don't want my officers running patrols up in the hills outside of town when they should be here. We're stretched plenty thin as it is. If there are wolves and they become a problem, then I'll deal with it. But we shouldn't go looking for trouble."

"I understand, Morris. Resources are limited."

"Exactly. Any wolf shows his furry ass around here, we'll blow it off, no matter what their 'protected' status might be. But traipsing around the forest—that's not police work."

"I read you. There's only one additional concern I have."

"What's that?"

"Wolves nowadays are like rock stars to the tree-hugger set. A pack of wolves attacking a man, especially in an event as vicious as you've described—that's going to make the news. Statewide for certain, and likely national news. International, if the cable networks get their hands on it. We could find ourselves deluged with wolf advocates. They could get, I don't know, Sting, out here for some kind of save-the-wolf benefit. Or, or, who's that other one, Bono."

"Kind of money these fruits make, you'd think they could afford two names."

"But you see my point, right? We've got to play this right. We have to protect our own, but we have to be careful about the wolves. The key is to limit contact between us and them. Maybe they'll move on, become someone else's problem."

"We can hope that," Morris said. "But one comes into my town, I'll make a rug out of it."

Alden Stewart rose to his feet, his palms flat on the desktop. His gut lapped over his belt. Morris was disturbed by people who didn't take care of themselves. Between the two of them, Alden and Belinda carried enough extra pounds to make most of a third person. "If it comes to that, just make damn sure you bury that thing outside of town. I don't want Silver Gap becoming the centerpiece of a battle over wolf rights, unless it's going to be good for the economy. A lot of attention in the right way could spark a whole new tourism boom here. But the wrong way ... why, that could be the last nail in our coffin. Are we clear on this?"

"Oh, we're clear, Alden," Morris said. He didn't like having to hold the politician's hand, but the man carried a lot of weight with the council, and Morris wanted to keep his job. "Don't you worry about a thing. No wolf is going to show its face here, and I'll make sure our people don't run afoul of them out in the hills, either."

"That's all I'm asking for, Morris," the mayor said. "That'll do just fine."

CHAPTER ELEVEN

George Trbovich had called his wife Gloria from the station to tell her that he'd be a little late getting home. Chief Deeds had made him accompany Howie Honeycutt into the backcountry to bag up Mike Hackett's remains and haul them to Dr. Steinhilber. He admitted that he didn't think he'd ever had a worse day on the job. It hadn't seemed to bother Howie at all, though. Howie had volunteered to go along, and according to George, he'd been chatting and telling jokes and such, all the way up and back. It was all George could do to keep from upchucking, but Howie actually ate some of a sandwich on the way back to town.

Gloria wasn't happy about it. Kyle, their eight-year-old, had been home from school all day, running a fever of 101 most of the time. She had been hoping George would get home early so she could have some adult conversation, and maybe a little help getting Kyle fed, bathed, and put to bed.

Instead, the dinner hour had come and gone. Night had enveloped the valley and the moon was making a valiant effort to rise above the pines. George's dinner warmed in the oven; if he didn't get home soon it would be a warm but inedible glob. Kyle was out on the screened back porch, huddled under a blanket watching *We Bare Bears* while Gloria did dishes. Toweling off a pot, she stepped to the door and took a peek.

He was curled on a wicker daybed, clutching an Indian-print blanket so tightly to his chin that Gloria worried he would overheat. He had, perhaps unfortunately, inherited his father's looks. Kyle Trbovich would never be a screen idol. But he had also inherited George's huge heart and off-the-wall sense of humor, and those things carried a lot more weight than looks. At least, they did with Gloria.

She went to the cabinet, put the pot away, and returned to the sink, glad he hadn't seen her watching him. He was going through a strange phase, his desire for independence in constant conflict with the urge to cling ever more tightly to his mother. At the same time, his daddy worship was a powerful force. Sometimes Gloria wondered if she could handle having two cops in the family, because Kyle seemed destined to end up in that profession.

They lived in an old farmhouse on the outskirts of Silver Gap. Between the house and the woods were a couple of cultivated fields where they raised whatever vegetables would survive the short growing season. Behind the house they kept chickens for eggs and meat in a fenced chicken yard, in which George had built a wooden coop. The door from the porch opened directly into the chicken yard, and as a result it was rarely used; instead, they typically went outside through a mudroom off the kitchen, and into the chicken yard through a gate. The kitchen window faced the backyard, the coop, and a carriage house they used to garage the tractor.

Gloria was drying the last of the glassware when she saw something dark streak toward the chicken yard. At the same time, the chickens went berserk, squawking and fussing. "Mom!" Kyle screeched from the porch. "There's a dog in the chickens!"

"A dog?" Gloria was already on the move, tearing into the mudroom. "Stay there, Kyle!"

George kept a lever action Winchester in the mudroom, a .22, good for pegging rabbits and not a lot else. But it didn't make much noise and the recoil wasn't bad. She snatched it up and banged out the door, chambering a round.

The dog, if that's what it was, was a huge one. German shepherd, maybe. Bigger than any she had ever seen. It had one chicken by the throat, feathers wafting around it like snow. Other chickens had already fallen victim to it, and more pressed against the fence, shrieking, or were fluttering into the coop.

Gloria was raising the rifle to her shoulder when the porch door squealed open. "Go away, bad dog!" Kyle screamed. Tears shone on his cheeks as he stomped down the wooden steps.

The dog dropped the chicken and turned toward the boy. Its lips drew back in a snarl. Its snout was longer than most dogs', and Gloria recalled with a stab of fear what George had said killed Mike Hackett. *Wolves,* he'd told her. *That's what we think, anyhow.*

"Kyle!" Gloria cried. "Run! Inside!"

Her son froze on the steps. The wolf shifted its weight, poised to leap. Gloria pulled the trigger.

The gun seemed loud in the night, the muzzle's flash bright. Her round went high, tearing chicken wire on the far side of the yard. The wolf spun around to face her, and Kyle took advantage of its distraction. He ran, but not back up the stairs and into the house. Instead, he ran through the chicken yard, fumbling with the chain that held the gate closed, then pounding through it. "Mommy!" he shouted. "It got Clemmie!"

Clemmie, Kyle's favorite egg-layer. That was the one the wolf had its mouth when Kyle came outside.

"Run, Kyle!" Gloria readied another round, raised the weapon again. The wolf took a couple of steps toward the gate and she fired once more. This one kicked up dirt in front of the yellow-eyed beast. It reared away, then charged through the gate.

Kyle ran, but toward the trees beyond the yard, not the house. He was screaming, crying, blind to direction or rational thought.

She took off after him, afraid to turn her back on the wolf but not wanting Kyle to get lost in the shadows. "Kyle! No! Come back!"

The wolf lunged through the open gate. Feathers skittered in its wake. Gloria fired a third shot, which creased the wolf's left haunch, even though she held the rifle out in one hand and barely aimed. She raced toward the trees, calling Kyle.

Just past the first of the big pines, she found him. He had shrunken in on himself, skinny arms wrapped around his lean frame, cheeks glistening with tears and snot. His eyes were wide and unfocused. "Kyle!" She dropped to her knees, throwing the rifle down and putting her arms around him. "Are you all right?"

He noticed her then, blinked and nodded and sniffed.

"Come on," she said. "You've got to get home."

"O-o-okay."

She took his hand and led him toward the house. The last time she had seen the wolf, it had decided against chasing the woman with the rifle. Now she caught another glimpse of it, pausing near the tree line, looking back as if to see if she followed. There was nothing between Gloria and the house except open space, and the wolf was well clear.

"Go to the house and get inside and lock the door," she told the boy. "Don't worry about the chickens. I'll be back in a few minutes."

"Mommy ..."

"I'm just going to make sure that wolf doesn't come back."

"But—"

"Do it, Kyle!"

He sniffled again, then tore across the yard and up to the kitchen door. As soon as he was in, she went after the wolf.

That thing had threatened her son.

She would make sure it never did again. She would aim carefully this time, as George had taught her. One shot in its chest, another in the head, at close range. It was wounded already, maybe bleeding. She'd catch it before long.

She levered a round into the chamber and entered the woods where she had last seen it.

CHAPTER TWELVE

As George Trbovich pulled into the drive, a hen wandered into his headlight beams. His fingers clenched on the steering wheel. The chickens were supposed to stay in their yard, and Gloria and Kyle both knew it. Neither would have left the gate open.

He brought the truck to a shuddering halt and shoved the door open. "Gloria!" he shouted. "Gloria!"

No one answered except the hen, clucking excitedly in the dust.

For the drive home, he had taken off his duty belt and put it on the seat next to him. He grabbed it and dashed toward the house.

The front door was locked. George pounded twice and ran around to the back.

Kyle stood behind the window in the kitchen door. His face was wet, his eyes rimmed with red, but he looked okay. "Open the door!" George cried.

"Mommy said not to!"

George's keys were in his pocket, but getting them out seemed like too much trouble. He scanned the trees for intruders. The chicken yard gate was wide open, birds everywhere. Something had gotten in there; feathers were scattered across the ground, pasted to pools of blood and a couple of dead hens. "Open it, son!"

Kyle complied, but slowly, as if in a partial trance. While George waited, anxiety clawing at him, struggling for breath, he buckled on his belt.

"Kyle," he said when the door was open. "Where's your mother?"

Kyle languidly raised his right arm and formed his fingers into a pointer. "Out there. She went after the dog."

"What dog?"

"The dog that killed Clemmie."

"Who?" Then he remembered. Clemmie the hen. "There was a dog?"

"A big one."

The boy's words were as slow to sink in as he was to speak them. Gloria went into the woods after a dog?

It wasn't a dog, though. He understood that much. Not a dog, but a wolf.

And his wife had gone after it.

"Did she take a rifle?"

"She had a gun. She shot it."

"She did?"

"I heard it cry, and then it ran away."

A surge of relief tempered George's growing anxiety. Maybe it was a dog, then, and not a wolf. Maybe Gloria had wounded it and followed it into the woods to deliver a merciful killing shot. That would be her way.

"Which way did they go? Exactly."

Kyle pointed again, more or less toward the same spot as before.

"Okay, I'm going to find her," George said, trying to keep his voice and manner calm. "Lock the door, and stay inside until we get home. Can you do that for me, champ?"

"'Course, Daddy."

"Good. We'll be back soon."

He stepped away from the door, pulling it closed, and waited until he heard the click of the lock.

If she had shot it with the .22, then it might not be seriously wounded. He drew the 4-cell flashlight from its loop on his belt. Clicking it on, he trained its beam toward the place Kyle had indicated and started into the darkness.

The air always smelled sweet around their place, once you got away from the chicken shit. Pines graced the land with natural air freshener, and George loved the warm, loamy scent cast out by fallen needles blanketing the earth. Instead of enjoying it now, he studied the carpet for tracks, drops of blood. He found Gloria's trail right away, and he tilted his head toward the sky and screamed out her name.

Only the night sounds of the forest answered him.

He stayed on the trail. Once his eyes adapted, he was able to make out the wolf's tracks—he *wanted* to believe it was a dog, but he couldn't—and hers, and the occasional splash of dark liquid that let him know the beast was still bleeding.

After a few minutes, he called her again. He had to be moving faster than her; she was no skilled tracker, and she had only the faint trail of an injured animal to follow, while he had the big streaks and scuffs left by her shoes. Until they married, she had been a city girl, and though eleven years in rural New Mexico and then Silver Gap had put a patina of country on her, it hadn't made her into a hunter. George had been raised in the country, brought up with shooting and tracking. In his professional life he hunted people, and in his free time he hunted game.

He kept going. His flashlight cut a funneled swath through the darkness, around which soared the big trees, whispering their disapproval in the breeze. Every now and then, he caught a glimpse of stars in the night sky. He shouted for Gloria again, and this time he heard a reply.

Again, he cried, "Gloria!"

He heard her call to him once more, and he dashed through the trees. Limbs snagged at his uniform, clawed his face and hands. She kept shouting and he followed her voice, and in another minute, his light picked her out of the gloom.

"Gloria!" He sprinted to her, crashed into her, careful to keep his weapon pointed away. "Are you okay?"

"Yeah, fine. I'm fine, baby." She returned his squeeze, then shifted the rifle out from between them. "I just ... that thing pissed me off so much. It almost went for Kyle. I didn't want to let it live to attack us again."

"Is it really a wolf?"

"It's a big one." She held her left hand out, palm parallel to the ground, about three feet up. "So high. Solid."

"Kyle said you shot it."

"I winged it. It's close by somewhere—I was hearing it whimpering when you called. I think it's dying."

George realized with a start that she had nothing in her hands except the rifle. "You've been tracking it without a light?"

"I know, I should've brought one. Stupid. I wasn't that far behind it, and I could hear it most of the time."

"You're amazing."

Her lips parted and her gaze sought his, then lowered to the ground. "Thank you."

"Here," he said, pressing the flashlight into her hand and drawing a smaller one from his duty belt. He pointed back over his shoulder. "You took kind of a roundabout route but if you go straight that way you'll be home in no time."

"By myself?"

"You got here by yourself," he pointed out. "I'll stay out here and finish the thing off. Call the station and have them send a couple of guys out here with lights and guns, just in case. I've got my radio."

"You sure?"

"Babe, Kyle's home by himself. He locked the door, but you know that kid ... he's as likely to come looking for us as he is to stay put."

"You're right."

"So go. Hurry. I'll be fine."

"You want the rifle?"

He showed her his Glock 9 mil. "It's already wounded. I'll be okay with this."

Gloria kissed him and started for home, flashlight illuminating her way. She was only about ten minutes away, if she took the straight shot instead of winding all over creation.

Once the racket of her passage had faded, he listened for the wolf she'd said was whining. He wanted to wrap this up quick. It had been a hellishly long day, most of it spent in the woods, and all he wanted was a cool one and a meal and maybe some TV.

CHAPTER THIRTEEN

"She's asleep, Doctor."

Dr. Steinhilber stood in the doorway, bidding goodbye to a couple of the visitors. He acknowledged Deborah's whisper with the slightest nod. "Is that all of them, Mrs. Morgenstern?"

"I'll check." Deborah made a pass through the living room and the kitchen. The bathroom door was open, but she glanced inside. Nobody else was downstairs. They had left casserole dishes, two pies, a bowl of macaroni and cheese, and a dish of salad big enough to feed a dozen rabbits. She understood the impulse—she had done it, herself, when a neighbor's family had suffered a loss—but how on God's green earth these people believed that Marie Hackett could eat so much food before it spoiled was beyond her. The poor woman hadn't eaten all day and probably would barely peck at a meal for months to come. She wasn't that big to begin with, just a slip of a thing.

Deborah Morgenstern lived right down the road. She and Henry had never had children of their own, and since Henry was gone, she had more or less adopted the Hacketts, stand-ins for her own nonexistent family. She was their nearest neighbor, since the Fellowes family had moved away early in the year. The For Sale sign still ruled a corner of the yard, but it had a decided lean to it, and no one had been around to straighten it for some time. Deborah had been mostly living at Marie's since Mike took missing, and Dr. Steinhilber had appointed her her neighbor's keeper.

He was closing the door as she returned. Outside, she heard the crunch of tires on gravel as the last car pulled away. "They're all gone," she announced.

"Thank God. They mean well, I know. But one of them's nosier than the next. I thought they were going to start going through her mail. And maybe her underwear drawer."

Deborah's face heated up and she knew she had gone crimson. A doctor had to be matter-of-fact about all sorts of things, she knew, and Dr. Norman Steinhilber seemed to take pride in saying things to shock the people of Silver Gap. She found him entertaining, if sometimes a bit hard to take. But she knew what he meant about the people he had just shooed away.

"They've brought far too much food," she said, leading him into the kitchen. "She'll never eat it all. You should take some."

"I just might," he said. "It's a pity Henry's gone. He did love a good casserole, I seem to recall."

Henry, her husband. Dead nine years now. Dr. Steinhilber had been at his bedside when he went. "He did, at that."

"Then there's the Mitchell family," he said. "Those three kids always look underfed. I could take a dish or two over there. If you don't think Marie would miss them."

The Mitchells lived on the edge of town. If Silver Gap had ever had a railroad, they would have lived on the wrong side of it. They were the worst sort of trash, Deborah thought. For all she knew, Kelly Mitchell fed his family by trapping rats in the woods. His common-law wife Bernice was barely out of her teens, and seemed to be with child more often than not. And Dr. Steinhilber wanted to feed them? "You are full of Christian charity, aren't you?" she asked.

"I don't know that I'd characterize it that way," he said. "But I won't argue with you."

"Take whatever you like," she told him. "I'm sure Marie and I will have more than enough."

"You're going to spend the night?"

"I'll sleep on the sofa down here. It folds out."

"Good. I don't want her to wake up alone. Not that I expect her to wake up for a good long while. What I gave her would knock out a rhino."

"I'll be here, Doctor."

He picked up a few dishes, balancing them precariously. "Call me if you need anything," he said. "Or if she does. You know the phone's always on."

"It shouldn't be. A doctor deserves a day off, same as the rest of us."

"Not when he's the only one in town." He tucked the top dish under his chin and held them that way, between hands and head. He was in his late sixties, same as her, bespectacled and on the portly side, but he had a jaw like FDR, like Dick Tracy, taut and firm. It was a good way to carry things, for him. "Could you get the door please?"

"Of course." She passed him, pulled it wide.

On his way by, he raised an eyebrow in farewell. "I'll be back in the morning."

"Get some rest!" she ordered him. She thought she'd have to go down the steps and open his car door, but he managed, setting the dishes on the floor and the passenger seat. She closed the door and went back into the living room, sat in the big chair that Mike loved so much—he wouldn't be needing it, after all—and clicked on the flat-screen. The picture was so much sharper than her old TV.

She had barely settled in when she heard a knock at the door. Dr. Steinhilber, no doubt. He had decided he wanted a couple more dishes, maybe one of those pies. She rose, dragged herself wearily to the door, and opened it. "What did you forget?"

But it wasn't Dr. Steinhilber.

"Oh!" she said. "I thought you were the doctor."

"Sorry to disappoint," the visitor said. "How you doing, beautiful?"

"I'm well. I'm sorry, you can't see Marie," she said. "She's sleeping."

"That's okay, Deborah honey. Maybe I just came to see you."

She giggled and started to blush again.

Then she saw the knife.

Deborah Morgenstern was a useless old crone, a biddybitch, withered away like a dried-up apple. Doing her was easy, almost fun, and it was also a way of easing back into what had never really been a habit, but could probably have more accurately been described as a goal.

She had started to scream, but he shut her up with a quick shot to the throat. She fell backward, tripping over her own scrawny legs, and he shoved inside, slammed the door and locked it. When he turned back to the old biddybitch, she was gagging but trying to get to her feet. She glared at him through teary eyes, and he could see she was trying to tell him off—she had always been good at that. He took a big step onto his left foot, then brought his right up in a fast, swinging kick that caught her just below the nose. It broke under the toe of his boot, spurting blood everywhere.

He finished her fast, with a quick slice across the throat he had already damaged. She bled like a pig, but he already knew he'd have to burn those clothes.

Anyway, she was incidental, an in-the-way busybody fucking biddy-bitch who he would forget in minutes. What he really wanted was Marie. She was younger, slim and sexy, with a face that would have been pretty if she just had a little money to spend on the right haircut and makeup. Life had worn her ragged, but then being married to Mike Hackett would do that to anyone. At least she was shut of him now.

Biddybitch had said Marie was sleeping. Had to be upstairs, in the master bedroom. He had been in the house once before, remembered thinking that Marie deserved a nice place, a bigger one, with a walk-in closet full of nice clothes instead of the giveaway auto parts T-shirts and discount-store jeans she mostly wore.

A light burned on the staircase, but the upstairs was dark. Dr. Stein-hilber had been the last to leave, and no doubt he had sedated Marie. That would make things easier. He found the bedroom and went in, leaving the door open so light from the stairs would illuminate his path.

She was out. Curled on her right side, covers tucked up around her, she looked like she hadn't budged since someone had arranged her here. He drew back the blankets, admiring her slumbering figure, and she moaned and moved her arms a little. She was wearing sweatpants and a long-sleeved Pennzoil T-shirt. Her hair was short, a dirty blonde, her face unlined in sleep.

Yes, she was a fine-looking piece. Hackett had never treated her right, never done her as she needed to be done. He realized that he had always been aware of it, of her unspoken longing for what he could offer. Funny it had never pushed itself to the forefront of his brain until now, when her hopeless, hapless husk of a husband had left her behind.

Life was like that, he guessed. Brains were unknown territory to those who carried them around. His rarely steered him wrong, and he knew what he was doing now was only proper and correct.

He was doing it for her. It was what she needed.

"Marie," he said softly. "You're coming with me, okay?"

She mumbled something and moved her head to the side. "Don't suppose you can walk." Another mumble. She wasn't walking anywhere.

No matter. He had brought a pair of handcuffs in with him, and he fastened them around her wrists. Not too tight, just enough to restrain her. Her eyes fluttered open, then closed again, and her moan was louder. He used his bloody knife to hack off two sections of sheet. The first he balled up and stuffed in Marie's mouth, and the second he twisted into a narrow strip, tying it around her head and over her mouth to hold the gag in place.

Now her eyes opened and understanding dawned. He could read the terror in them, see her fighting for consciousness. Still, her struggle was hampered by the drugs, more by the cuffs, and yet more by the secret longing that burned in her breast. He hoisted her over his shoulder, ignoring her kicking and squirming, and carried her down the stairs and into the backseat of his car. He closed her in, then got behind the wheel and drove away.

"I'm sorry it took me so long to figure things out," he said into the darkness. He knew she would be able to hear him, to understand his meaning. "Don't worry, though, Marie. I'm finally going to give you what you've been craving."

CHAPTER FOURTEEN

Going the way George said, instead of following her own path back, felt wrong. But he had always been more comfortable in the woods than she was. Sure enough, after only a few minutes of hiking in as straight a line as the trees would allow, she saw the lights of their home, and then she was there. The chicken yard gate was still open and the chickens were scattered. She scooped up a couple that she passed along the way and shoved them back in, but suspected that most of them were lost.

Hurrying inside, she gave Kyle a crushing hug, congratulating him on his bravery and thanking him for staying put. Then she snatched up the phone and hit Morris Deeds's personal mobile phone on the speed dial. He answered on the second ring, and Gloria took a deep breath, then told him in as briskly efficient a manner as she could what had happened and where George was.

"He has his radio on," she said. "So your men should be able to find him okay."

"I'm on the way," Morris said. "I'll bring Ortega with me. Don't worry, Gloria, George knows his way around. He'll be fine."

"I know. But thanks. I trust him, but that doesn't mean I don't worry."

"Of course. You stay put, and we'll be there directly."

She hung up the phone and looked at their son, watching her with interest and concern. His eyes were still red, but he had stopped crying and had been entertaining himself with action figures when she got home. "Are you all right, Kyle?"

He nodded gravely. "When will Daddy be here?"

"Soon. He'll be back soon."

"Okay."

"I promise."

Kyle raised a Batman toy toward her. "If you want, Batman can keep you company till he gets back."

She almost declined, then thought better of it and accepted the toy. "Thank you, Kyle. And Batman. That's a big help."

Carrying the toy to a chair close to the window, she sat down to wait.

The wolf was on the move again.

Wherever Gloria had hit it hadn't been a vital spot. The beast had lost some blood, but not enough. George heard it crashing through low branches, less graceful than it would ordinarily have been. At least she had done some damage.

It cut around to the north, following the floor of a canyon. On a couple of occasions, George thought he might have a shot at it, if only there were better light. Once he did squeeze off two rounds, but they went high. If the wolf continued in this direction, it would lead past the Church in the Woods and eventually toward town.

George froze, listening. In the darkness of the trees, his best hope of tracking the thing was by sound. He heard the whisper of paws scraping across pine needles, not far ahead, and a steady chuffing sound that he thought was the wolf panting with exertion.

Then from behind, he heard something else.

He whirled around. His flashlight's beam cut the darkness, but didn't penetrate far. His eyes were as accustomed to the dark as they were going to get, and he couldn't see anything beyond the screen of pines silvered by moonlight. The sound came again.

It was unmistakably the sound of something breathing.

He strained to hear it, to determine how far off it was.

Then his radio squawked, static drowning out any other sound. George recognized the voice of Chief Deeds, although he couldn't make out more than a couple words. One of them was "forty."

"I'm not too far from the church," he replied. "To the south and east a little. Over."

More static. He couldn't tell what Deeds was trying to say, so he repeated his location and cranked down the volume. Listened.

The breathing was closer. More than one of whatever it was. Coming up behind him.

Wolves?

Had he been following one without realizing that the rest of the pack was tracking him? Wolves hunted in packs—it wouldn't make sense that there would be one out by itself, unless it was one of those proverbial lone wolves.

He hadn't thought this through.

Letting Gloria take the rifle and go back to the house by herself. Stupid. He should have gone with her, let this animal go. Two were better than one.

The church wasn't far away, though. He could hole up there, call Gloria, make sure she was okay. He'd have better radio reception, maybe, and could call Deeds on his cell. Anyway, the radio had a GPS chip, so the chief could find him if it came to that.

Forget the wounded wolf. It could live or die, he didn't care.

He struck out toward where he believed the church was.

The first wolf came about two minutes later. George heard heavier footfalls, then a snarl. He looked behind him just in time to see it soaring through the air, mouth open, fangs gleaming. He tried to dodge, and his ankle twisted beneath him. He fell.

George threw out his left arm to steady himself. A fang caught sleeve and flesh, rending both, and the thing landed hard, spinning around the way canines can do. George bit back the pain and raised his Glock, squeezed off a shot.

The round punched a hole in the wolf's skull. Still it managed two steps toward him before dropping.

Close behind, another wolf yipped.

George broke into a sprint. Around the animal's body, tree limbs slapping against him. His left arm bleeding, numb.

The world receded into two things, the narrow cone of light ahead of him and the sounds of his pursuers. They'd given up the quiet approach, and were charging through the trees, yipping and growling.

George held the Glock over his shoulder as he ran, pulled the trigger. The report, so close to his right ear, was deafening. Another mistake.

Chances that he had hit anything were almost nonexistent, but half his hearing was gone. The wolves sounded more distant, an illusion.

Another wolf lunged from his right. Black fur, pink tongue, white teeth. George halted his progress, backed up. The wolf corrected, seemingly in midair, and his maw caught George's right thigh.

George let out an agonized scream, clubbed the beast's head with the Glock, then shoved the muzzle into its fur and yanked the trigger. The blast echoed in the night and the wolf fell away.

George tried to run. His thigh was shredded, gushing blood. The leg wouldn't support his weight. He tried anyway. He could see the church now, light streaming through the big window behind the altar. Someone—Pastor Calderon, he thought—stood in the parking lot, looking his way.

"Calderon!" George cried.

"Who's there?" he heard. "Is someone ...?"

"Gil!" George called. The man was staring right at him. "It's me—"

But his shout was cut off by more wolves, one hitting from behind and one from the left. Their fangs tore through clothing, flesh, and muscle. Another snagged onto his right hip.

George, already slipping into shock, hardly felt them.

CHAPTER FIFTEEN

Morris Deeds had been hoping to sleep in. The day before had been a long one, and difficult, what with the early-morning search party, the discovery of Hackett's body, sending men back into the woods to recover it, then visits to Marie and Dr. Steinhilber and a meeting with Alden Stewart, and generally trying to calm everybody down, himself included. Finally, an emergency summons from Gloria Trbovich had sent him and officer Tommy Ortega into the woods looking for George. A second call, from Reverend Calderon, had ended that search in the worst possible fashion.

He had closed out his night with a couple of drinks and a sleeping pill, a combination he both frowned upon and relied on from time to time, when a day became overly draining.

But Christy shook him awake shortly after six, telling him he had an urgent phone call from Althea, the department's overnight dispatcher. He took it and told Althea to send Howie Honeycutt over with a cruiser. He didn't know if he would have time for coffee, and though he could do police work without it, he was damned if he wanted to drive uncaffeinated.

He dressed quickly, and when Howie pulled into the drive ten minutes later, he was standing on the porch waiting. Christy already had coffee going, as it turned out, so he drained the rest of his cup and left it on the little metal table that stood between two porch chairs, descended the three steps, and slid into the passenger seat. Howie backed out as Deeds fastened his safety belt.

"You know where we're going?"

"Hackett's house," Howie said. He was short, at five eight just above the departmental minimum height. Skinny, but he worked out, so his arms and shoulders and neck were big, his chest deep. He had bright red hair and a freckled face and couldn't grow a beard on a bet, and it all conspired to make him look barely post-pubescent.

"Everything quiet last night?" Deeds asked.

"Mostly." Howie described a couple of DUI stops, and four teens picked up for trespassing and vandalism when they broke into a vacant house to party. Silver Gap was a quiet town, but it and the state of Colorado and the United States all had laws, and wherever there were laws there were people who broke them.

When he finished, Deeds said, "Althea tell you what's going on?"

"Sounds bad," Howie said. "Wolves, again. First Mike, then George, and now this."

"I don't know what's brought them here, but I don't like it." He knew he was understating it, but he was still trying to wrap his mind around the whole thing. Colorado didn't have wolves. But in one day he'd had to look at the bodies of two men he knew, both killed by what appeared to be wolves. Now he was on his way to Marie Hackett's house, where a neighbor had reported that wolves had slaughtered Deborah Morgenstern.

According to Althea, Bill Tyler had been walking his collie Grizelda around 5:30. Tyler lived on the other side of Deborah Morgenstern, and he usually walked his dog past her place and the old Fellowes place and the Hacketts' and down to where the woods met the town. On this morning, Grizelda started going berserk as they neared the Hackett home, barking and straining at the leash and sniffing at the ground. As they got closer, Tyler noticed tracks, not unlike Grizelda's but much larger. A little nearer the house, he saw what looked like blood in some of the tracks. Then the dog almost tore loose from his grip, and he saw a mutilated body part on the Hackett lawn. He wrapped the leash several times around his hand and investigated further, stopping when he saw a woman's upper body and one arm, separated from the rest of her, and recognized her as Mrs. Morgenstern.

That was when he rushed home and called the police. Deeds knew that the scene would be bad, and he knew that the dog tracks would turn out to be wolf tracks, because that's just how his week was going.

A little more than half the six hundred and some residents of Silver Gap lived in the blocks around its small downtown. The rest lived on more isolated country roads winding in and out of the forest and sometimes snaking between hills. Freamon Road, where the Hackett place was, had no sidewalks but enjoyed municipal power, phone, sewer, and water service; much farther out, though, and homes relied on wells and septic systems, and satellites for TV and internet.

Howie turned onto the curving country road, and when he rounded the bend right before the Hackett place, ravens took to the air in a black cloud. "Shit," Morris said. The presence of the carrion birds meant that Tyler hadn't been dreaming or hallucinating. Morris was sure the man had used LSD back in his youth. He still wore his hair on the long side, had never married, and occasionally had men from out of town as overnight guests. It all added up to an untrustworthy source, as far as he was concerned.

But by the time Howie brought the cruiser to a stop, Deeds could see some of the parts the man had mentioned. What looked like a foot sat by itself in the middle of the yard, and another mass of tissue was closer to the open front door. The Hacketts had a porch, and at the top of the steps was what he feared would turn out to be Deborah Morgenstern's head.

"This isn't necessarily a crime scene," he said. "But it still wouldn't hurt to be careful where you step, and try to preserve as much evidence as you can. You bring a camera?"

"It's in the trunk."

"Get some pictures. We'll never take wolves to court, but if we end up needing to bring in state wildlife officials or anything, it'd be good to be able to show them what we're up against."

"Yessir, Chief." Honeycutt idolized him in a way that Deeds had always found a little disconcerting. Although the kid looked like a rat drowned in toilet water, he had the raw makings of a decent cop. But he was a brown-noser of the highest order and sometimes he seemed just a bit off-kilter. When he had described the night's activities, he had spoken at a rapid-fire clip, and his fingers were drumming on the steering wheel the whole time. Drug testing was part of the department's regular procedure, and Deeds wondered if perhaps he oughtn't to move up Howie's next specimen collection.

Then again, Howie had worked most of the day yesterday, volunteering on the search party and the retrieval of Mike's body. Then he'd had a few hours to sleep before starting his night shift. Chances were, he was simply exhausted, and like Morris himself, anxious about coming out to a house where they knew they would find a horrible scene.

Howie almost tripped getting out of the cruiser, but he caught himself and went back to the trunk. Deeds didn't wait for him. Watching where he stepped, so he didn't trample any of Mrs. Morgenstern's parts or get blood on his shoes unnecessarily, he walked past the foot and the other bloody, meaty bit lying in the grass. Pawprints were everywhere in the dirt around the yard, and bloody ones tracked down the stairs from the porch.

The worst was what waited on the porch. Deborah's face was barely recognizable. The wolves had ripped off her left ear and part of that cheek and jaw. The whole piece was torn off just above her breasts, and as Bill Tyler had described, one shoulder and arm were attached to the ragged neck, with a little bit of spine protruding from it.

Morris's stomach turned against itself. He couldn't decide if he was sorrier that he'd only had coffee for breakfast, or that he'd only had time for one cup. He knew he had to go inside the house, to check on Marie, but his feet were glued to the top step and they didn't want to budge.

Just inside the door he saw a wide swath of blood. He forced himself onto the porch, giving Marie's upper portion as wide a berth as he could. As he approached the door the stink reached him, and bile rose into his throat with a burning sensation. He looked back and saw Howie keeping his distance, photographing the carnage on the lawn. "Get in closer!" he called.

Howie gave him a look he couldn't quite read, but he stepped onto the grass. Morris figured if the kid could overcome his distaste, he had to do the same. He stepped into the house, avoiding the smeared blood on the hardwood floor. Inside, the smell was worse, slaughterhouse thick. Big flies walked in the smear. He took another few steps inside and found the rest of Deborah, or most of her, hidden at first by a couch. Her legs were spread and the other arm was there, still attached to her torso. She had been opened up in the middle, though. Organs were missing and her intestines trailed from the gap like sausage dangling from a butcher's display.

He looked away, toward the staircase. "Marie!" he called. His voice snagged in his throat. He cleared it and shouted louder. "Marie, it's Chief Deeds! Morris Deeds! You up there?"

Nobody answered.

He swore again and raced up the stairs. Although daylight streamed in through the downstairs windows, he noticed that the staircase light was on. He checked the master bedroom first, found bedcovers that were pulled back, but no evidence of a struggle or any wolf tracks. He checked the other rooms upstairs. Nothing.

He hurried back down. The wolf tracks were all over the place down here—they had walked in blood, then investigated the kitchen, dining nook, and bathroom. He looked behind everything, called out Marie's name again and again.

Finally, Honeycutt came to the door. "What's up, Chief?"

"She's not here," Deeds said. "Damn it, Marie's not here!"

CHAPTER SIXTEEN

Alex woke in the morning feeling sore from his long hike the day before, but otherwise surprisingly well rested. The Durbins had brought some more furnishings, including clocks and TVs, so the room felt a little more like a motel and less like an abandoned warehouse. When he awoke, glowing red numbers on his bedside clock showed 08:23, and he was astonished to learn he had slept so late. His night had been without dreams, or if he'd had any they weren't the kind that wrecked his sleep and remained with him into the day.

The Durbins had also restored continental breakfast service in the lobby. The meal consisted of a dozen doughnuts and a few Danishes brought in from the Cup & Cow, along with two pots of coffee, one French roast and one hazelnut, a third pot of hot water, and an assortment of Twinings teas. Alex had the French roast while Ellen squealed in delight at the Irish breakfast tea. Peter sat quietly in one of the big leather chairs that had been taken out of wraps, fingers wrapped around a china mug. He was slow to engage in the mornings, Alex had found. Earlier in his life, Alex had been a big fan of sleeping, too, but when the dreams started to come, that had changed.

This morning, he had a particular agenda in mind, so after a shower, breakfast, and brief conversation in the lobby—with everyone but Peter —he drove into downtown.

Driscoll's Outfitters was not the kind of shop where he would feel at home. The front window was half-covered with fliers detailing the complex schedule of Colorado's various hunting seasons and license requirements, advertising groups looking for participants on wilderness trips, and people looking to buy or sell hunting, fishing, and camping gear. Arranged behind those, in haphazard fashion, were a hunting bow and a quiver of arrows, a pair of snowshoes, and a stuffed and mounted bobcat, all of it dust-caked and looking to be about a hundred years old.

He pushed open the glass-and-steel door and caused a sensor inside to bong twice when he passed through. Inside, the place smelled musty, as if a roof leak or plumbing disaster had not been adequately dealt with. Above shelving and wall-rack units holding maps and backpacks, tents and guns and fishing rods and other equipment Alex couldn't name, the walls were lined with mounted animal heads. Driscoll, or perhaps, Alex reasoned, friends, family, and customers, had brought down black bear, elk, moose, bighorn sheep, and mountain lion, along with smaller game like rabbits and some sort of wild pig. Taxidermy birds perched on shelves and display cases.

There was nobody in sight, but an open door at the back of the long, narrow space revealed a lighted back room. From here, it appeared even more cluttered than the store. Alex heard somebody moving about. He was about to call out when he heard a feminine voice say, "Be right there!"

"Okay," he said. He waited another minute, and then a woman emerged from the back carrying several boxes of boots. His attention fixated on the logo on the boxes, it took him a few seconds to realize that she was the pretty blonde he had encountered at the search party's gathering point. The one, he recalled, in front of whom he had embarrassed himself so utterly that he hoped he would never run into her again.

"Decided you wanted a closer look at the habits of the great unwashed?" she said. She was smiling when she said it, so that was something.

"Look, I'm sorry for what I said yesterday. I didn't mean it the way it sounded. I was trying to be funny, and it didn't come out that way."

"Not really."

"I'm looking for Robbie Driscoll," he said. "He was recommended as a guide."

"Best there is." She put the boxes down on a table next to a display of hiking and hunting boots and extended a hand. "I'm Robbie."

Alex went from moderately embarrassed to deeply chagrined and, he guessed, red-faced. He took her hand, shook it, and held on while he said, "You must think I'm a total idiot."

"I don't know you well enough for that," Robbie Driscoll said. "So just a partial idiot, for now. Anyway, I know it throws folks sometimes. But Roberta is just so girly, don't you think? Obviously my parents didn't know me when they named me."

He released her, shaking his head sadly. "I'm not normally so socially awkward," he assured her. "Honestly, some people actively seek out my company."

"I'm sure that's true. Some people seek out all sorts of punishment. It's a thing."

"I guess I deserved that." He realized that he had committed yet another *faux pas*. "By the way, my name is Alex Converse. And, while I'm at least partially an idiot, I really did come looking for you because I was told you were the guide I needed."

"Let's talk, then. What are you after?"

"Oh ... I'm not hunting, if that's what you mean."

"That's usually what people need guides for, around here."

"I'm making a movie," he explained. "A documentary."

"Heard about that."

"We'll be shooting in various locales around the world, but we're starting here. I need to get out into the woods and look for some locations. Places where the bark beetle infestation is really bad, where it's decimated the pines."

"So it's a feel-good movie," she said. The smile hadn't left her eyes since she had first started tormenting him, but her delivery was dry, deadpan.

"Maybe not so much. But I think it's worth doing, or I wouldn't be sinking my own money into it."

"Heard you have a lot of it."

"I guess word travels fast in a small town."

"You know us barbarians. Nothing to do but gossip."

"Are you ever going to let me live that down? And I never called anybody barbarians. That was you."

"Probably not. And yes, I admit that. And I don't know."

"Don't know about what?"

She raised her hands, palms up. "About being your guide. There's a lot going on in town. I'm not currently engaged, but depending on what happens over the next few hours, that could change. I don't know how much you've heard about it."

"Since Mike Hackett? Nothing, really."

"Apparently there have been other wolf attacks. Closer to town."

"Which means it would be an exceptionally bad idea for me to try to find my way around without a guide."

"A guide, a posse. Maybe a tank."

"I've got none of the above," he admitted. Despite his initial failure to connect with this woman, and what seemed like nothing whatsoever in common with her, he couldn't help finding her fascinating. A faint scar he hadn't noticed before ran down the left side of her face, from the corner of that eye to midway down her cheek. She was dressed in a slate-gray, ribbed turtleneck sweater and faded jeans, both tight enough to outline her impressive physique: strong, broad-shouldered, but curvy. She was not the least bit unfeminine. In fact, there could have been no disguising that femininity, even at a hundred yards on a dark night. He found that fascinating, too. "But I do have money, and I'd love to hire you to take me out into the woods, find me some places I can use in the film. And I need to do a little scientific research while I'm out there, so I'll need somebody watching my back."

She moved behind the sales counter and took a loose-leaf notebook from a shelf. Paging through it, she said, "Business is looking thin on the ground for the next little while, and I do have bills. The roof is leaking and my Jeep hasn't been serviced since I don't know when. I'm thinking there's going to be a wolf-hunting party put together, and they'll want me on it. But that could take a while. How much time would you need?"

"I guess that depends on how far we have to go to find what I'm looking for. Based on what I saw yesterday, I'd guess not very far."

"If you're looking for where the trees are the color of rust stains on a bathtub, then no. You need to get a little elevation from here, but it won't take long to get up there."

"So how about it?"

She gave a sigh that he couldn't read. He hoped it was resignation. "I guess it'll take some time for anybody in an official capacity to make a decision. We can head up for the morning, if you want. But if I get an emergency call we'll have to come back."

"Deal," Alex said.

"Don't you want to know my rates?"

"I guess, if you think it's important."

"I don't do this for free."

"I'm not asking you to. I'm just saying I'll pay whatever's fair."

Robbie chuckled. "Yeah, I know. Crazy rich guy, right?"

"If that's what the gossip says."

"Should I write a number down on a slip of paper and hand it to you discreetly? Or just say it out loud?"

"Out loud," Alex said, "is fine."

Alden Stewart sat with Chief Deeds in the town hall's conference room. He had been in conference rooms in real cities that could hold twenty or thirty people, but this one started to feel crowded with five or six. There was a speakerphone on the table, a device that looked more like a kid's toy spaceship than a telephone, though, and when the door was closed the occupants had privacy and an absolute lack of outside distractions.

On the other end of the call was Doug Wolters, of the Colorado Division of Wildlife. "And you're sure it's wolves?" he was saying. "I mean, I saw those pictures you emailed. The damage to the victims is certainly extreme, and the tracks are canine for sure. But there aren't any wolves in your part of the state."

"There weren't," Deeds said. "But there are now. Gloria Trbovich saw one."

"And what's her expertise?" Wolters asked.

"She doesn't have any," Alden said. "But she saw it. So did her boy. And then her husband, who's a good cop and was armed and ready, was torn to shreds. It wasn't dogs that did that."

"Chances are it wasn't," Wolters said.

"Well, we say it was wolves, Doug," Deeds said. "This is an emergency, and we're going to throw ourselves a wolf-hunting party. I don't care what Colorado law is, when we find those bastards we're going to kill 'em."

"Don't let's get carried away, guys," Wolters said quickly. "I've been in touch with US Fish and Wildlife, and we're sending a joint team up to see what you have going on. In the meantime, if you guys start shooting wolves, then sportsmen in Montana and Wyoming and Idaho are going to get all worked up about their wolf limits."

"Sorry, but I don't see that as my problem," Deeds said. "The wolves around here right now are my problem, and I'm not going to sit on my ass while the government plays with itself."

Alden knew that people who settled in rural communities, including mountain ones, often did so because they didn't want to be in more high-density areas. Bigger, more crowded places required cooperation and contact and, often, more direct intervention by government. He was well aware of the antigovernment sentiment of many of Silver Gap's residents, including, perhaps ironically, quite a few of those employed by the local government. Including the police chief, who sat across the table from him. Chief Deeds didn't believe the state government did much that was helpful or useful, and he tended to think of the federal government as vaguely sinister at best and a potential enemy at worst. Morris's response to almost any crisis was to determine whether there was any action he could take, action that as often as not would involve physical violence toward somebody. The town kept him around largely because the payouts they'd had to make to settle various civil suits were minimal compared to the lean, efficient way he ran the department. Anyway, Morris Deeds knew everybody's secrets, and he had proven to be tight-lipped.

Alden didn't much like the man, but he had to work with him, and he tried to keep the relationship civil. He also didn't agree with Morris's sociopolitical views. Government, he believed, comprised a lot of people who did their jobs to the best of their abilities. When it worked, they made people's lives more secure and sometimes better. Government couldn't do everything, and there were some problems about which it could do nothing and shouldn't try. But it was not, by its nature, a malevolent force.

At this moment, however, he leaned more toward Morris's immediate-action plan than the government's wait-for-us approach.

"We're doing our best," Wolters said. "If you can hold off a little while, that'd be great. If not, then I guess we'll deal with it as it comes up."

"That works," Morris said.

"Thanks for your help, Mr. Wolters," Alden said. "Keep us posted."

"Will do," Wolters said. He ended the connection and the phone buzzed until Alden pushed the off button.

Morris fixed him with a steady gaze. "We can't wait for them, Alden. Those things are killing our people."

"Trust me, Chief. I'm aware. I just wanted him to understand the urgency."

The police chief sat there for another few seconds, seemingly gathering his thoughts. When he pushed his chair back and rose, something hanging off his nylon belt banged into the table. "Sorry," he said. "It's a little tight in here."

"I know." What Morris meant was, government can't even build a functional conference room. To which Alden Stewart's unspoken response was, not without a sufficient tax base.

Which meant they couldn't let the taxpayers be eaten by wild animals.

Before Morris reached the door, there was a double knock, and then it swung inward. Frank Trippi stood there. He was a tall, stocky guy with small hands and feet and a gentle manner surprising in what appeared to be a big grizzly bear of a man. His curly hair and the short beard clinging to all of his chins had gone mostly gray over the years he had been Silver Gap's postmaster. And the sole post office employee, for that matter. Sometimes Morris joked that if Frank ever went postal, he would just quietly commit suicide. He was at least partly right—everything Frank Trippi did was done quietly. His voice was deep, resonating from some-place inside his large bulk, but he rarely raised it above a level that would have met the approval of any librarian in the land. In addition to his post office duties, he was Silver Gap's snowplow driver, a task for which he earned time-and-a-half but which saved the town having to hire an inde-pendent operator. This year, he had not yet had occasion to pull the plow from its barn, though November was only a couple of weeks away.

"What is it, Frank?" Alden asked.

"I got the TV on in the PO," Trippi said. He gestured toward the southeast corner of the room, which was where he kept the set at the post office, and Alden noticed that his wrist was wrapped in an Ace bandage. "It's been quiet today. Anyhow, I was watching Fox News and they mentioned Silver Gap."

"They did?" Morris said, excitement evident in his voice. He was a big Fox News fan.

"Uh-huh," Trippi said. "And I checked CNN and we was on there too."

"What about Silver Gap?" Alden asked, afraid he already knew the answer.

"Wolves," Trippi said. "They're sayin' we got wolves. People from all over says they's comin' to Silver Gap to hunt 'em."

"That didn't take long," Morris said. "Figure Doug Wolters wants his face on TV?"

"Could've been someone at DOW," Alden admitted. "But it could just as easily have been someone calling her sister or his grandma in some other state, and that sister or grandma calling someone else. Doubt there's any way to find the source. We just have to deal with it."

"How, Alden?" Trippi asked.

"Shouldn't be a problem for you, Frank." He turned to the police chief. "But you might want to think about hiring someone to replace George Trbovich, Morris. I expect things are going to get ugly in Silver Gap, and I expect it's going to happen fast."

CHAPTER SEVENTEEN

Alex would have been happy walking through these woods even if he hadn't been accompanied by what he believed, given his limited experience, was the most attractive woman Silver Gap had to offer. The pines didn't offer their usual cool, verdant comfort because bark beetles had killed them from the inside out, and what should have been lush and green was instead reddish and brown and skeletal. But the earth and rocks were unscarred and the quiet—especially compared to Los Angeles and environs—was unworldly.

They hadn't gone far from town. Robbie had said she couldn't, explaining without excessive pride that she was the best tracker, hunter, and rifle shot in town, and might be needed in a hurry. She had pulled on a down vest, loaded Alex and a couple of rifles into an ancient red Jeep Wrangler with no roof, a winch on the front, and gas cans strapped to the roll bar, and driven out of town, taking a right on a narrow country road a couple of miles out. That road passed a few houses, some of them the sorts of comfortably worn places he had dreamed of living in, back when he was too young to know how much wealth he would inherit. Then the pavement ended but the road kept going. It was graded dirt for a while, passing another house or two, and then it started climbing. Before long it was a pair of rock-studded dirt ruts that only a high-clearance vehicle could navigate. Robbie drove it fast, as though she had taken it a hundred times.

The farther from town they got, the more her spirits improved. Soon she was smiling and talking casually, telling Alex about what they were passing, pointing out hills and meadows that had special meaning to her. Then they crested a little rise, and all the pines on the other side were shades of umber and orange, like survivors of a fire. "This what you were looking for?" she asked.

"It'll do for starters, yeah."

She pulled the Jeep off the little trail and killed the engine. "You want to look around?"

"Yes."

"Knock yourself out." She unbuckled her seatbelt and climbed out without using the door. Alex didn't think he could do it as impressively, so he got out the regular way. When he had his feet on firm ground, she was slinging a rifle over her shoulder. "You want one?"

"I'd be more likely to shoot myself than anything else," he said. "You think we'll need them?"

"Ordinarily, I'd say no," she said. "Although I wouldn't come out here without one. But there have been at least three wolf attacks in the last twenty-four hours or so. You don't want to carry one, it's okay. Just stay close to me."

Alex had no problem with that instruction. He had liked watching her drive, the way she smiled in fierce concentration when the road required careful navigation, climbing up a rocky step in low gear with the four-wheel drive activated. She had lines at the corners of her eyes and around the sides of her mouth, and when she smiled broadly or laughed, dimples split her cheeks.

Her features were broader than most of the professional beauties he'd known in LA, but they worked well together and made her feel somehow more real, more present. He had known women who were regularly on magazine covers or splashed across movie screens sixty feet wide, but in person they were like vapor. Robbie Driscoll was solid; flesh and bones and muscle and blood and hair. That hair was mostly a kind of summer-straw yellow, but shot through with darker strands, light browns and coppers, and that flesh was tanned but not leathery or artificially bronzed, and that solidity was something that, in spite of himself, he couldn't stop thinking about holding.

"You said you wanted to do some research?" she said.

"That's right." He'd been lost in reflection, he knew, and he hoped she didn't ask him what he'd been thinking about. He'd have to say it was the trees, and since he'd had his back to them and been facing her, that might have been a hard sell. He got his backpack from the Jeep, and she didn't ask.

He took a few core samples and scraped some bark into plastic bags, marking each specimen with the date and approximate location. With a digital still camera, he shot photos of the trees, mostly longer shots encompassing as much of any individual tree as he could, but also close-ups of the needles and the telltale holes that bark beetles had left in the wood. He wished there were a way to capture the absence of the typical fresh pine aroma.

After a while, he noticed that Robbie was holding the rifle in her hands, and her forehead was furrowed. "Something wrong?"

She held a finger to her lips and walked closer. Her footsteps were silent. "You haven't heard it?" she whispered.

"Heard what?"

"Something's coming."

Two days earlier he wouldn't have been alarmed at the sound of those two simple words. Now he was. Robbie was too, from the alert tension in her jaw, the shifting of her green eyes. "What?"

"I'm not sure." They were quiet for several seconds, and then he saw her flinch. This time he heard it, too: the crackle of fallen twigs and needles.

"Wolves?" he asked.

"I don't think so. But I don't want to take a chance."

They had wandered a good distance off from the Jeep. "What do we do?"

She pointed out a cabin he had been entirely unaware of, half-hidden by trees on a nearby hillside. A rutted dirt track led up to it. "Maybe we can hole up there until we see what it is."

"You probably wish I was carrying that gun."

"Damn skippy. Come on. Quiet but quick."

She led the way and he tried to follow in her path. He made more noise than she did, but not a lot, and he was relatively proud of his amateur woodsmanship. They reached the cabin after a hurried three-minute hike. It was rustic, not a place somebody lived, but a pinewood hunting cabin, probably used only a few times a year. The only door was padlocked shut, and shutters over the windows were bolted on the outside.

"We could shoot the lock off," Alex suggested.

"If we have to, yes. But that'll let everything in the whole forest know where we are. So far it just sounds like one animal, and I'm not sure what."

His heart was thudding in his chest and ribbons of sweat pasted his cotton Henley shirt to his ribs. If wolves did come, would she be able to hold them off? Would shooting one or two convince the rest to seek easier prey? Or could a whole pack take them down, even though he was here with the apparent offspring of Calamity Jane and Annie Oakley?

Whatever it was, it did not seem to be taking special pains to stay silent. They huddled near the corner of the cabin, using the building for cover. Tension grew in Alex as he thought about what might be out there —what might, in fact, be circling quietly behind them while the one in front made all the noise.

Then Robbie relaxed visibly, lowering the rifle's barrel toward the ground. "What?" Alex asked.

"It's just an old elk," she said.

"That's good, then. Right?"

"It's good. Mostly," Robbie said.

"Mostly?"

He could see it now, passing between the trees, twenty yards away. It knew they were there, but it didn't panic, just kept going on the path it had probably followed for years, if not decades. It was a big animal, powerfully muscled. Scars from battles fought branded its haunches and sides and left a deep, graying smudge on its muzzle. Battles won, or at least survived. Alex didn't know much about elk, but he could tell this one was old. It had a rack of antlers that would have looked impressive on any wall, but he was glad it was here, in the wild—where it belonged—and not dead, stuffed, and mounted.

"Go on, granddaddy elk," Robbie whispered. "Get back to your herd."

"Wait," Alex said. "What was that you said about 'mostly' good?"

"It's not with the herd," she said. "It's alone."

"So?"

"So wolves eat elk. Especially injured elk."

"You think they're watching it?"

"It's possible. One or more could be nearby."

"And we wouldn't see them?"

"Eventually, we'd see them. By then, it could be too late."

Alex considered the implications of that statement. The memory of Mike Hackett's remains made those implications breathtakingly clear. "Maybe we should head back to town."

"Do you have everything you need?"

"I've got a start, but no. Not everything."

"Then we'll stay. I don't know how much time we'll have, but once I hear from town officials, we might not get another chance to get out here."

"As long as you think it's safe."

Robbie touched his arm. The contact was fleeting, but he felt it long after she had moved her hand away, and he liked the sensation. "Alex," she said, "You can be eaten by a wolf in town. You can catch a deadly virus. You can be hit by a truck. Out here, you can still be eaten by a wolf, but the other two are less likely."

"I guess that's true."

"So we're staying," she said with firm finality. "Get to work, professor. I've got your back. It's what you're paying me for, right?"

He got to work, reflecting, as he did, on the warm comfort he took, knowing that Robbie Driscoll—Silver Gap's best hunter, tracker, and rifle shot, after all—had his back.

CHAPTER EIGHTEEN

They followed the general path the big elk took, keeping it in sight as they headed toward another stand of beetle-damaged trees. Alex was fascinated by the huge animal. He would have had a hard time negotiating the forest with a two-foot spread of antlers on his head, but to the elk, with his thick, muscular neck, that was just part of life. The elk moved easily between the pines, occasionally flicking its ears this way or that to pinpoint a sound, or glancing back toward the humans, but not spooked by anything.

"I guess I'm getting soft," Robbie said.

"What do you mean?"

"There was a time I would have taken him without thinking twice. Now, I'm happy just to watch him."

"Is it still elk season? That's what Hackett was after, right?"

"Yes," she said. "Season's still on, but I don't have an elk tag this year. That's okay, there's plenty of meat in my freezer."

"You're not a sport hunter?"

"Not for years. I either hunt because I need meat, or because somebody's paying me. It's my profession, not my hobby. And I'll tell you, I'm losing my patience for clients who are just out for trophies. These creatures deserve better than that."

They walked on a little farther, skirting the rim of a deep ravine, approaching another patch of rust-colored trees, when Robbie put a hand on Alex's shoulder. "That's weird," she said.

"What?"

She pointed toward the elk, who was heading back in their direction, but on the far edge of the ravine. "Granddaddy elk went around," she said. She indicated the slope into the ravine. "This isn't even remotely too steep for him. If he's going over there, why didn't he just go down this side and up the other? He's traveled well out of his way, for no reason. Doesn't make sense."

"Just following a known path, maybe?"

"But if that's the case, if this is a regular route for him, why wouldn't the path go through the ravine? One thing about animals, they don't do nearly as many things for totally arbitrary reasons as humans do. If they make a conscious choice, there's a purpose for it."

She veered off course, stepping down the slope. Alex didn't mind diverting from their agenda for a little while. It was obvious that they would be able to find plenty of damaged trees to shoot, and he appreciated the insights she offered into the forest and its inhabitants. She was coming at it from a much different perspective than he—a perspective gained through on-the-ground experience.

After about ten steps, she threw a hand up in warning, and froze. Alex was off-balance, in mid-stride, but he brought his foot down and followed her example. Slowly, she moved her hand, extending it down and to their right, pointing. "Wolf," she whispered. "Do you see her?"

He didn't, at first. The ravine was choked with brush and trees, and the only thing moving was a dark brown bird flitting from branch to branch. But he kept looking, trying to divide the ravine floor into quadrants and scanning each quadrant separately, and then there it was, stepping between a couple of low-lying bushes.

Even from this angle, the wolf looked bigger than he had expected. Its fur was dark gray, almost black except on its long legs where it bleached to near-white, and shaggy, with a thick tail. It was taller in front, at its powerful shoulders, than in the rear, though not by much. Its ears pointed up. From here, its eyes looked red, but he thought that must be an illusion, a trick of the light. It was aware of them, looking up at them, though not letting their presence interfere with its plans. To Alex, the animal seemed alert, even intelligent.

"That's why the elk skirted the ravine," Robbie said in a low voice. "He knew the wolf was down there."

"Should you shoot it?" Alex asked. The thing was more than a hundred feet away, and downhill, but looking at it—knowing it was watching them —made the fine hairs on the back of his neck stand up.

"She's old, and hurt," Robbie said. "Look, she's limping."

Alex saw it, then. Not a pronounced limp, but enough to give it a slightly clumsy appearance as it passed through the brush. "Yeah, I guess."

"If she had tried to take the elk, she probably wouldn't have survived the fight," she said. "That elk was a tough old bastard. I think this wolf left the pack to die, not to hunt."

The thing shot them a final glance, then disappeared into the trees. "Anyway, wolves don't attack people," Robbie said. "I mean, not without good reason. There are no documented attacks in North America by wolves that weren't somehow prompted by the human victim. They know what they like to eat, and we're not it. That one's done, though. She's not going to hurt anything bigger than a field mouse, and not even that for long."

"Have you seen a lot of wolves?" Alex asked.

"Not in Colorado, but out of state, sure. I've seen my share. There was something strange about that one. I can't put my finger on it, but it didn't look quite right to me."

The elk was gone, having disappeared behind a ridge on the other side of the ravine. The wolf was out of sight, too, and though the thrill of seeing the two wild animals had not waned, Alex was beginning to feel the weight of responsibility bearing on him. He wanted to finish up and get back to town, see what Peter and Ellen were up to, and move forward with the project.

Robbie didn't argue when he suggested stopping at the next stand of red pines. "This is so sad," she said. "All these dead trees."

Alex took a knife and peeled back some bark from one of the nearby pines that had not yet died and changed color. He showed her beetle larvae, smaller than grains of rice. "Here's the culprit," he said. "Bark beetles infest the trees and lay eggs. The larvae grow up feeding on the trees, interfering with the flow of nutrients. That kills the tree. By then, the adults have moved on to another one, and when these larvae reach adulthood they do the same. It's still spotty here, but these forests will likely be fully infested soon, and within another year or two it'll be hard to find a living tree."

"Where did they come from? The beetles, I mean?"

"They're indigenous," Alex said. "They've always been here, but in the past, cold winters have killed them off every year, preventing widespread infestation. They can't survive temperatures below about minus twelve or thirteen. These last several years—last decade or more, really—winter temperatures have been staying milder, allowing the beetles to get a better foothold."

"So, global warming?"

"I prefer the terminology climate change, but yes. That's ultimately what we're talking about. And it's even worse than what I'm saying, because it becomes a self-fulfilling cycle."

"Meaning what?"

"Meaning, healthy trees—forests—are a great carbon sink. They suck in carbon from the atmosphere and hold it, keeping it from contributing to warming. But only when they're alive. Dead trees release the carbon they've held in, making the whole situation that much worse. Nature's just full of tricks like that."

"Such as?" she asked.

Alex would have continued even without the prompt. He was on a roll, now, with an indulgent audience. "Such as, permafrost holds in methane, which is a greenhouse gas probably more destructive than carbon dioxide. When it melts, it releases the methane, warming the planet more, melting yet more permafrost. At higher elevations, permafrost helps contribute to healthy forests. When the permafrost goes and the temperatures warm, trees are dry and stressed. Drying trees essentially call out to the beetles, saying 'eat me!' Around the world, tundra fires are increasing, releasing ever more greenhouse gases. In the Arctic, ice sheets are thinning and shrinking. That has a double-pronged effect. The Arctic icepack works as a natural cooler for the northern hemisphere, so melting ice contributes to warming that way. And white ice reflects heat back into the atmosphere, while dark water draws it in, just like a white car stays cooler than a black one in summer. A shrinking icepack means less white ice and more dark water, exacerbating the effects. And subsea permafrost is starting to melt, releasing yet more methane. The whole thing is a natural feedback loop that has the potential to make things a lot hotter, a lot faster, than earlier models predicted."

"Thank you for the lecture, Al Gore," Robbie said with a mischievous grin.

"Whatever you might think about Al Gore, on this one he's got like ninety-seven percent of the world's climate scientists on his side. Really, the only ones who aren't on board are the ones employed by extractive industries, and their whole goal is to muddy the water, to make it appear that the science isn't in. But it is." He indicated the dead, red pines. "It's right in front of you."

She studied the trees, nodding her head slightly. "You said you're not a scientist."

"I'm not. I've read a lot about it, and I understand some of what I've read. I've also talked to people in the field. You'd be surprised at the access money buys you. Or maybe you wouldn't."

"So you're just a rich guy who's interested in it? What's that word? A dill ..."

"Dilettante," he confirmed. He had stopped by one of the trees and started working on a core sample, glad it gave him something else to focus on. "And thanks. But yeah, I guess that basically sums it up. I'm an interested amateur, and I'm trying to affect the conversation by making a movie."

"Where'd your money come from?"

He acted like he didn't hear the question. He liked Robbie, liked her a lot. She didn't seem antagonistic toward the idea of climate change, though she wasn't ready to embrace it. She was not highly educated, but she was smart and well-spoken, and very capable in her chosen field.

Which was, he reflected, more than he could say for himself.

Bored, tired of waiting for Alex to get back, Peter and Ellen had gone into town—what there was of it—to explore the shops. It turned out there were not many, and the ones they found were far from exciting. They were strolling through a place called Earl's Emporium, about which they had shared a good laugh before going in. The storefront of the grand-sounding store was maybe thirty-six feet across, and it had a depth of a couple of hundred feet at the most. "I'd expect an emporium to have five floors, at least," Peter said as they entered. "Plus an annex or two. This looks more like the Feed N' Seed."

Ellen laughed. "What's that?"

"Something I just made up. But don't be surprised if we find it on the next block."

"If there is another block."

Part of what he liked about Ellen was her willingness to go along wherever his own inherent wackiness might lead. He was prone to flights of imagination, to free-associating his way through life, except when he was working. Cinema, he took seriously. Sex, too. And good weed, when he could get it.

Everything else? Better when viewed through skewed lenses, he thought. One of these days he would shoot the world's most perfect porn film while high, and then he could retire, having achieved the pinnacle of all his interests at once. Retire, or die. Until then, having someone like Ellen along for the ride helped keep life endurable.

They passed through a display of kitchenware, plates and glasses and cheap pots and pans, and suddenly found themselves surrounded by maternity clothes. Beyond that there appeared to be a toy section. On the next aisle to the left, Peter saw sporting goods: basketballs and hoops, ice skates, golf clubs, and more. "This place really does have everything," he said. "If by *everything*, you mean anything made in China and sold over here at cheap enough prices to drive American manufacturers out of business."

"I guess it serves the needs of the town pretty well, though," Ellen countered. "I mean, where else are you going to get baby formula *and* lumberjack shirts *and* Bic pens? There's probably no Walmart for a hundred miles."

"Thank God for small favors. This is just the sort of place they love to target and destroy."

Peter was actually trying on one of the aforementioned lumberjack shirts—red and blue and yellow plaid flannel—when he overheard another customer mention wolves. The word spurred a thought he'd had earlier, but hadn't brought up to Ellen yet. "That's really what our movie should be about," he said.

She was looking through an assortment of T-shirts with bad cartoon art on them. "What?"

"The wolves," he said. "Or rather, the reaction of the townspeople to them."

"What's that got to do with dead trees?" Ellen asked.

"I don't know. Nothing, I guess. But how boring are a bunch of beetles? Wolves are elemental, primal. Nature's perfect hunting machines versus human beings with the technology to destroy them, once and for all. But will the wolves stand for it? And will the humans marshal the resources necessary to pull it off? Will they cower in fear as the wolves take them apart, one by one? Or will they reach some sort of mutual accommodation, each species allowing the other a place on Earth?"

He tore off the flannel shirt and tossed it onto the floor beneath the rack it had been hanging on. Job security for someone, he figured: cleaning up after he visited a store. Ellen was still pawing through the T-shirts, so he reached around with his right hand and grabbed her right breast, using his left to cup her ass. She giggled and squirmed a little, pressing her behind more firmly into his grasp.

They had made it another aisle over, a wonderland of tacky colored baskets and displays of plastic flowers, when he overheard more of the conversation that had sent him off on the wolf tangent.

"... ask me, they ought to slaughter every one of 'em," a man was saying. He was white, middle-aged, with a pasty face, short brown hair, and a bulging gut overhanging the waistband of his khaki pants. The same description also applied to his companion, a woman who could only have been his wife, except that her hair was a little longer and artificially blonde, and her pants were sea green. Peter thought she had probably been a real beauty, thirty years or so earlier. "Liberals keep stoppin' people from driving them into extinction," the man continued, "they'll just keep comin' back. Some things don't deserve to live, and wolves is one of 'em."

Peter exploded. "See?" he said loudly. "This is what I'm talking about! The minute there's a potential conflict, the response is not, 'what can we do to ameliorate or mitigate this?' It's, 'what can we fucking kill?'"

"I wasn't talking to you, pal," the man said. "I never seen you before in my life."

"Which means what, that I'm not allowed to express an opinion?"

"Means I sure as hell don't care what your opinion is."

"Peter," Ellen said, tugging at his sleeve. "Let's go."

He ignored her and raised his voice even more. "Maybe if you were exposed to a few more opinions, you'd make more sense! You want to drive a major mammalian predator into extinction? Do you have any idea, the remotest clue, what that would do to the ecological balance?"

"Come on, Titus," the man's wife pleaded. "He isn't worth it."

But Titus paid his wife no more attention that Peter had Ellen. "Right now the only thing I want to see extinct is you!" he blustered. "My Winchester's out in the truck, too."

"That's perfect! Got a problem? Shoot something! Difference of opinion? There's a bullet for that! Jesus Christ, your kind makes me sick!" He was pushing too far, but the governor that most people had in their heads that kept them from going over the line had never been entirely functional in his case. He turned to the man's wife, who regarded him as one might a mentally defective pet that had just pissed all over an expensive rug, and held his thumb and index finger about two inches apart. "I bet Titus has a tiny little dick, doesn't he? That's the only thing that could explain him. He's got to be a blowhard to compensate for not being able to pleasure you."

By now, store employees were rushing toward them. The wife's face had gone crimson, while Titus's was eggplant-colored. His mouth had disappeared, his hands balled into fists. With one of the store employees screaming his name, Titus punched Peter in the solar plexus. The blow was surprisingly solid, considering that Titus looked like he might last have been in good physical condition around the time of the Reagan presidency.

Still, all it did was send Peter further over the edge. He gave Titus an open-handed shove, which sent the man reeling into a display of baskets. Titus fell to the ground, baskets raining down around him.

His wife let out a piercing screech. A trio of employees—one elderly man, one middle-aged woman in a red apron, and one young man, a stock boy, Peter guessed—surrounded Titus. The two men started trying to help him up while the woman stormed toward Peter, rage darkening her face. "How dare you?" she cried. "How dare you? Shame on you!"

"Lady, he started it," Peter said. But he wasn't sure if that was the case. Titus had thrown the first punch, but Peter could have let him express his opinion, instead of getting in his face. Maybe he hadn't been asking for a fight, but surely his actions had led inexorably in that direction.

"Mr. Johnston must be twice your age!"

"Then he should be old enough to know better," Peter said.

"Peter, apologize to the nice man," Ellen said. "And then let's get out of here."

"Don't think that either of you are going anywhere, young lady," the woman said. "I've already called the police."

"Oh, fuck me," Ellen said.

"Don't make it worse," the woman said. "You stay right here and keep your filthy mouth closed."

"Fine," Peter said. "Whatever. Just—he *did* start it. That's all I'm saying. He started it."

CHAPTER NINETEEN

D r. Norman Steinhilber's office had always fascinated Reverend Gil Calderon. It was not a big room, but it was jammed with more stuff than any three antique stores. And it wasn't always the same. Gil had seen old books—ancient ones, practically, seemingly turning to dust right there on the shelves—on one visit, then the next time those books were gone, but there were others, massive volumes of the paintings in the Louvre, maybe, or castles of the Rhine valley. Once he had seen a plastic toy of Magilla Gorilla, a character from an old cartoon show. But the next time he had been there, in the spot where the toy had been was a set of surgical implements from the Civil War. On yet another occasion, Norman had shown him a tiny oil painting, maybe three or four inches square, that he swore had been painted by Rembrandt.

This time, he sat in his usual chair across from Norman's big desk, but it seemed that all the lights in the office had been dimmed. There was a cone of light in which he could see; around the edges, though, everything was dark, blurred. Indistinct, that was the word. His world had become indistinct.

"I won't lie to you, Gil, I'm concerned," the doctor said. "The glaucoma has worsened since the last time. You really need to see a vision specialist, down in the city."

"I'll drive right down there," Gil said with a bitter laugh.

"Okay, not the best idea. But surely, you've got somebody who would drive you. You'd want to plan to spend the night there, but I'm sure Silver Gap can get by without you for thirty-six hours or so."

"I know that," Gil said. "It's not just that. It's ... I'm just so tired of it. Of everything."

Norman heaved a great sigh. "Living with illness isn't easy. Ever. And living with a significant loss of something so basic as sight, such a huge way of how we perceive the world, is especially traumatic. On the bright side, if you get it properly treated, your vision can stabilize. It doesn't have to keep getting worse. But that will require treatment that I can't give you here."

"I know, Norman."

"And there are tools you can use, as well. Magnifiers, adaptive appliances with extra-large readouts. Hell, you can use simple paint to create contrast, around things like light switches and doorways, to help you cope."

"My congregation will love that."

"Gil, they love *you*. You're the reason they attend the church. They'll be fine with anything you have to do to function. Don't worry about that."

"Thanks, Norman," Gil said. He appreciated the reassurance, though he already knew it was true.

He came to the doctor for sound advice and friendship, as much as for medical reasons. He already knew there was nothing Steinhilber could do about his vision, which was getting worse all the time. He had really come hoping that the opportunity would arise to discuss another concern—less medical than psychological—but one that was just as grave. If not more so.

He was convinced—had been for some time—that he was a sex addict. The problem wasn't that his flock didn't love him, but that some of them loved him too much, and enabled his addiction.

He had grown up in the Catholic Church, but had left it because he couldn't stand the enforced celibacy. Nobody expected him to be celibate now, not at the nondenominational Church in the Woods. But they expected him to leave the married women alone, and the young ones, the teens. They expected him not to spend hours every night surfing porn websites when he should have been ministering to the sick and writing sermons.

He had hoped that moving to a small town would limit his opportunities, help him keep his urges under control. But it hadn't. The women and girls he was with all seemed more than happy to keep his secret, even when they learned that they were not the only ones. He'd had sex with at least a dozen of his congregants. And he wanted more.

He believed that as his vision worsened, his other appetites grew stronger.

Stronger, and more extreme. Harder to resist.

He couldn't bring himself to say it, though. Norman would understand, would offer sage counsel.

But that counsel would be to knock it off, to get a grip on his sick self-indulgence.

He'd already heard that advice. He'd been giving it to himself for years. He had never heeded it, and he wasn't about to start now.

Twenty-eight years, he had made his living by arguing that God made man in His image and gave humanity free will, so people could choose to turn to Him. Now he was a slave to his own lizard brain, shackled by his lusts. A walking, breathing lie.

"There something else, Gil?" Norman asked.

"No. No, I think that does it. Thanks for your help."

"I mean it, Reverend. There are some great eye guys in Denver. I can refer you."

"I'll keep it in mind, Norman. Thanks again."

Gil got to his feet, unsteady at first—surprising how much vision impacted balance—then lasered in on the door. He didn't run into anything on the way there, which he counted as a small blessing. He sent a silent prayer toward the heavens, and negotiated the hallway to the front door, and then out to his car.

On the way back to town, Alex and Robbie had come within cellphone range, and he'd had three messages from Ellen telling him that Peter had been arrested. They had gone directly to the jail, and Robbie waited while he handled the logistics. They were on their way to the Jeep when someone called his name.

At the second "Mr. Converse!" he turned around. The jail was actually three cells in the basement of the Town Hall building, with a separate entrance at the back of the building. There was also a back door up six wide steps, and the police chief was standing at the top of those stairs, the door slowly swinging closed behind him. Alex remembered that his name was Deeds. The chief was burning a stare into him, his hands on his hips, star on his deep chest. His mustache twitched a little. Alex got the sense of a man who commanded others not through ability and experience so much as force of will, as if Chief Deeds, having decided he should be the police chief, or having been appointed to that job, had figured out that he needed to project power. It didn't seem to rest all that naturally in him, though, and Alex got the sense that he was eternally struggling with it, quashing weakness and mining himself for strength.

"Yes?" Alex said.

Having been acknowledged, Deeds started down the stairs. Softly, Alex said, "Get in the Jeep," and he started toward the staircase. He would meet the chief halfway and see what the man wanted.

"Heard you bailed your friend out."

"He's my employee," Alex corrected. "I don't know that I'd call him my friend."

"That's even better," Deeds said. "We can't always control our friends, right?"

"Or our employees, apparently."

"I guess so."

"Look, I'm sorry for any trouble he caused. I'll cover any damages. But I don't own the guy, okay? He works for me, but he's his own man."

Deeds ran a finger across his mustache, smoothing it down. "I understand that. And I understand that you're a wealthy man. Lots of money buys lots of influence in some places. Back in Los Angeles, I expect you can pay your way out of all kinds of trouble."

"That's really not what I'm about," Alex tried to say, but Deeds talked over him.

"That's not how things work here, though. Here people mind their manners. Do the right thing. We don't attack our elders, then call for a rich man to get them out from under."

"That's really not what happened," Alex said.

"This town's got some real trouble right now," Deeds went on, ignoring him. "We don't need outsiders coming in here and stirring things up, making things worse. I keep a safe, orderly town, and—"

"Morris!" Robbie was stalking across the parking lot toward them with her arms crossed over her chest and her brow furrowed into a frown. "You're not even listening to the man."

"Robbie, this isn't your affair," Deeds said.

"I've spent all day with Alex," she said. She closed in and came to a halt. Alex would not have wanted to see that fire directed at him. "He's not some rich asshole who's here to make trouble. He's a serious man, and a good one, and you're jumping to conclusions. Again."

"Now listen, Robbie—"

"No, *you* listen for a change. You run a lot around here, but you don't run me. Alex and his people are here for a reason. I might not agree with every one of their beliefs, but I accept that they have a right to express them. And while they're here, they're pumping money into the local economy, which we badly need. When they're finished, their movie might bring more people here. Scientists, tourists, whatever. They're not here to cause trouble, and they'll behave themselves from now on. But you've got to back off. Okay?"

"I'm just saying," Deeds countered. "We don't need any extra problems right now. There's enough going on without that. People who make trouble are going to spend time in jail. Believe that." He still spoke firmly, but his volume was down, his ire reduced. Alex was impressed by the influence Robbie had over him—just one more of the many ways he had been surprised by someone he was coming to see as a remarkable woman.

"Understood, Chief Deeds," he said. "I'll talk to Peter. You don't have to worry about us."

"I am keeping my eye on you, Mr. Converse, and your friends. The trouble didn't start till you showed up. I don't hold you responsible for wild animals, obviously, but if I find out you're connected ..."

"You won't."

"Let's hope not." The chief turned around and clomped back up the stairs.

"Thanks, Robbie," Alex said on the way to her Jeep.

"Morris Deeds is the most self-absorbed person I've ever known," Robbie said. "Everything that happens is all about him. Other than that, he's not really a bad guy. But he has to be nice to me—he knows if he's really got a wolf problem, he needs me."

"It's good to be needed."

"Yes." She reached the driver's door. Peter and Ellen were huddled in the backseat. "Yes, it definitely is."

Titus was down at Spud's, probably scoring his drinks for free on the strength of his story. Barb Johnston had no doubt that the tale had raced around town—too many people knew about it, what with everybody in Earl's at the time, then everybody at the Town Hall who would have seen that California hippie taken there in handcuffs. Titus liked the limelight to begin with, and this event would make him a celebrity. By Silver Gap standards, anyway. She was sure he would come home drunk, which in his case could mean happy and horny—though often unable to live up to the demands his own libido made on him—or it could mean ... well, mean.

She expected the former, tonight. His drinks would be free, after all. Everybody would be gathered around him, sympathetic to his pains and begging to hear the story. He would be jovial, sucking up the attention. When he came home drunk, he would still be riding that high. And yes, in heat, most likely, and really there was nothing wrong with that. She enjoyed a good hump as well as the next woman. And if Titus wasn't always good—hell, he was rarely good, these days, drunk or not—he was at least enthusiastic, and that counted for something.

While she waited, she read a book, a Jodi Picoult novel that her book club would discuss next week. She was enjoying it, mostly, and would have plenty to say about it. She had a classical CD playing in the background, and a glass of red wine on the table next to her chair. Even if Titus never came home, she was having a good night. She was happy.

So when the doorbell rang, she put the book down gently on the table, picked up the glass of wine, took a sip, and swept toward the front door, graceful as a skater on fresh ice. She had a smile on her face and a song, as they said, in her heart.

She checked through the little peephole, aware that the person on the other side could always tell, when the hole went dark, that someone was on the other side—so as a security measure, it left something to be desired. Then she pulled the door wide. "Titus isn't here," she said. "Check down at Spud's, though. Look for the guy everybody's buying drinks for."

"I actually didn't come to see Titus," the visitor said. "I came to see you, Barb."

"Well, I don't know how I can help you."

Her visitor smiled. She had seen that smile before, plenty of times. It was authentic, but a little disturbing, too. "I guess you'll have to find out, then," he said, and then he struck.

CHAPTER TWENTY

C hristy Deeds knew she shouldn't go to Gil again. If he didn't want her anymore—at least in the way that she wished he did—there was nothing she could do about it. Anyway, she was married, and if Morris wasn't the most attentive husband ever, that didn't alter the fact that she had taken vows. Those vows were the traditional ones, and she remembered the words to this day, including the ones that went, "In the presence of God, our family and friends, I offer you my solemn vow to be your faithful partner in sickness and in health, in good times and in bad, and in joy as well as in sorrow."

That "faithful partner" bit she had violated many times over. Worse, she had done it with a man of the cloth, most often at his church. And she was on her way back. She had told herself it was to check in on him, because his eyesight seemed to be deteriorating more quickly than ever. She couldn't fool herself, though. She hoped for much more than a friendly visit. And anything he offered she would gratefully accept, vows or not.

When she arrived, she drove past the congregation parking area to the back. Clara Durbin was parked in front; she would be mopping the floor or polishing brass, something like that. She was the domestic type, Clara was. Christy parked by the rectory, next to the old Sebring that Gil, with his vision problems, should probably give up driving.

The light in his office was on. The office had its own entrance, as it was where he counseled people and worked on church business. It was, he liked to say, positioned between the rectory and the church because it bridged the gap between his life on Earth and his life in service to the Lord. His desk was within sight of the window, and he was seated in front of his computer monitor. She tapped on the window set into the door, and saw him look up, blink a couple of times, then smile. He came to the door and opened it. "Christy," he said. "What brings you here?"

"I just wanted to look in on you," she told him. "I've been worried. About your vision."

"It is what it is," Gil said. "It'll never be good, I'm afraid. But Dr. Steinhilber says it won't necessarily get worse, either."

"That's something, at least."

"Would you like to come in?"

"Yes. Please." *Don't throw yourself at him,* she reminded herself.

But when she stepped through the door, he didn't move out of the way. Instead, he put his arms around her, buried his head in her hair, and breathed her in. "You smell divine," he said. "I've missed holding you so much."

"I've always been here," she said. "You only need to ask."

"I shouldn't."

"I know, Gil. I didn't come here for—"

He put a finger under her chin, tipping her head back, lips toward him, and then he kissed her and kicked the door closed at the same time.

She didn't try to speak again.

After they left the police station, Alex, Robbie, Peter, and Ellen swung by Mountain Grocers, where they ordered sandwiches from the deli counter and bought cut carrots and celery with dip, two kinds of chips, and various nonalcoholic beverages. They took it all with them back to the motel, and Robbie joined them in Alex's room for an early dinner. When they were done, Robbie headed home. Peter said he was fried from the day's activities, but Alex thought it was more a matter of wanting to be alone with Ellen so she could comfort him in her own way. They excused themselves, and Alex let them go with a warning to stay in the room and out of trouble, at least for one night.

As soon as he was alone, he went out to the Lexus. He wanted to talk to the pastor at that church, Reverend Calderon. Alex was no scientist, and he didn't try to pretend otherwise. But different things people had said to him during the day had collided in his head, and he wanted to try to make some sense of it.

Peter had told him that he thought they were making the wrong movie—that they should really focus on the reactions of the Silver Gap townsfolk to the apparent wolf attacks. Alex couldn't argue with his contention that wolves were more dramatic than pine beetles, but he didn't know how wolves fit into his concerns about climate change. Robbie had told him that wolves never attacked humans without cause, and even hinted at the possibility that they might be dealing with a pack of feral dogs rather than wolves.

From the stories he'd heard, it sounded as if Calderon was the only one in town who had witnessed an attack. If he could confirm that the animals were wolves and not dogs, then Alex would put some effort into looking for a way to tie wolves to global warming. If not, he'd stick to his original outline, and Peter would just have to shut up and film some dead trees.

Between the faint light of dusk and his own distraction, Alex almost missed the church driveway. At the last second, he saw the sign in the trees and braked to a sudden halt. As he backed toward the drive, a pair of deer—a mother and her fawn, he thought—emerged from the woods just ahead, as if they'd been patiently waiting for the road to be clear. They crossed the street, illuminated by his headlights, and then vanished into the forest on the other side. He watched them until they were out of sight, then continued backing into the driveway, turned around, and found a space near the church in the almost empty parking lot.

He was barely through the church's front door when an interior door into the seating area swung open. It took him a second to place the woman who emerged. "Mr. Converse," Clara Durbin said. She was a pleasant looking woman, plain-faced but friendly, with round cheeks and small dark eyes and a sharp chin, and she wore a sweatshirt and jeans. Her hair was tied back under a bandanna. There was a rag in her hands, parts of it black with dust or tarnish. The distinct aroma of lemon-scented cleanser cocooned her. "How nice to see you here."

"Do you work here, Mrs. Durbin?"

"I don't call it work. Work is what I do at the lodge. I volunteer here, helping Reverend Calderon with some of the housekeeping and adminis-trative tasks. It's my pleasure, really. Truly, a joy and a blessing."

"Is the reverend here?" Alex asked. "I really came to see him."

"I think he's in the rectory," she said. "He was last I saw him, anyway. I can call him, if you'd like."

"That would be great."

She pulled a smart phone from her jeans and touched the screen. When Calderon answered, she spoke briefly. Then she put the phone away. "He'll be right out." She gestured toward the doors to the church's interior. "If you'd like to take a seat—or a pew, rather."

"I'm fine, Mrs. Durbin," Alex said. "Thanks for your help."

"Well, I've got about a mile of woodwork to polish, and it's getting late. Holler if you need anything."

"Will do. Thanks again."

She passed back through the doors, leaving Alex alone in the entryway. The interior was dimly lit, but lovely, expressing a sense of peace while keeping in tune with the natural surroundings. Lush potted plants and native stone and rich, glowing wood combined to create the impression that instead of a building, Alex had wandered into a grotto someplace deep in the forest, where the trees were all green and there were no destructive beetles or wolves.

A couple of minutes passed before Calderon appeared, coming from a side hallway instead of through the church proper. His cheeks were red and flushed, and when he extended his hand, he sounded out of breath. "I'm Reverend Gil Calderon," he managed. "Clara says you're a guest at the lodge."

"That's right." He gripped the clergyman's hand. "Alex Converse."

"It's a pleasure, Mr. Converse. Welcome to the Lord's house."

"Thank you. I'll warn you up front, I'm not a believer."

A look of disappointment flashed across Calderon's handsome face, but it didn't linger. Almost before it registered, the smile was pasted in place again. "What can I help you with?"

"I wanted to talk about wolves."

"They seem the topic *du jour*, that's for sure. What about them?"

Alex didn't see any reason to beat around the bush. "I'm here to make a documentary film," he said.

"I've heard."

"I know I've arrived at a difficult time for the community, and I'm sorry for the things that have happened over the last few days."

"Thank you."

"But I have a scientific interest in the intersection between human populations and the natural world. Obviously, that plays into what's been going on. And you're the only one I've heard about who actually witnessed one of the attacks attributed to wolves. I was wondering—"

"Yes?"

"Could you tell me what you saw? Were the animals definitely wolves?" Remembering what Robbie had said about the one in the ravine, he added, "And were they standard wolves, or did you notice anything odd about them?"

Calderon's normal coloring had returned, and he was breathing easier now. Maybe he had caught the man working out, Alex thought. Or he had just rushed to greet his visitor. "You're not from here," Calderon said. "And although I'm sure word is spreading, not even everybody in Silver Gap knows. Mr. Converse, I'm losing my eyesight. It's not entirely gone yet, but in some conditions, it might as well be."

"I'm sorry to hear that."

"One of those conditions is twilight. Dusk. When the sun goes down, I'm nearly blind. After dark, if I have plenty of light or use a flashlight to focus, it's not too bad. But for that hour or two right after sunset, outdoors, there's just not enough contrast and I'm useless."

"I know what you mean," Alex said. "I just almost missed your driveway."

"I'm glad you didn't. Anyway, what I'm saying is that when those things caught up to poor George, I could hear him calling for help. I could hear the snarling and yapping, and then I could hear George screaming. Those sounds—what I'm told were the wolves, and George's cries—I still hear every time I close my eyes."

"I'm sure it was horrible."

"You have no idea. At any rate, I prayed and prayed, and then I ran inside to a telephone and called 911. But in that instance, my prayers went unanswered. I asked for the power to help, the power to see, to at least bear witness to poor, brave George Trbovich's final act. All for naught, though. I could tell when George died because the growling changed, and I could hear tearing, ripping noises. Awful, awful sounds. But I couldn't see any of it. Even when Chief Deeds arrived, all I could do was point him in the general direction. The bad light, the thick trees ... it was all beyond my ability to observe. So I'm afraid I can't answer your questions."

Alex thanked Calderon for his time, shook his hand again, and let himself out. A wasted trip. The only eyewitness was no witness at all. He heard animals, but for all he knew they could have been dogs or bears or wolverines. Having made the man's acquaintance couldn't hurt, especially if Peter was determined to make an enemy of everyone he met. But other than that, he had thrown away time he could have better spent in any number of ways.

In the deepest reaches of his imagination, some of those ways involved Robbie Driscoll. But those, he was certain, would always remain imaginary.

Still, it didn't hurt to daydream ...

Morris Deeds was almost home when the radio in his car crackled and squawked and he heard Althea's voice calling his name. He swore and keyed the mic. "What is it?"

"Chief Deeds, we've just had an emergency call from Titus Johnston."

"He's drunk."

"Well, yes. Just the same, he said he got home and Barb's not there. The front door's open. There's something that looks like blood on the carpet."

Morris was quiet for a moment, and Althea filled the space. "You said if anybody else went missing, you wanted to know."

Morris pulled to the side of the road, hit his lights, and made a U-turn. "Get Honeycutt," he said. "Have him meet me there."

"Ten-four," Althea said. "Over and out."

He hung the mic back up and raced toward the Johnston home, a few blocks out of downtown. Over the radio, he heard Althea calling Howie Honeycutt. What he didn't hear was Honeycutt responding. He let that go on for about a minute, then broke in again. "Althea, how about Ortega? You know where he is?"

"Yes, Chief."

"Send him. Make it quick, I'm almost there."

"Yes, Chief."

He replaced the mic, and he wondered what the hell was happening to his town, and how he could put a stop to it.

He stood in a thicket of trees. The cool evening air tasted his flesh where it was exposed, hands and neck and face. There were broken branches and stripped shreds of bark and fallen pine needles under his boots, like uneven layers of carpeting. He breathed in the pine and the scent of urine (his own, he had pissed here in the trees, watching while that rich fuck came in, backing into the lot like the rich fuck he was and parking and going inside, then coming out again, driving that fancy Jap SUV).

Clara Durbin was inside, too, doing whatever it was she did there.

And there was one other person inside, besides the Right Reverend Fuckbuggy.

The chief's wife. She was parked in back, where nobody could see her car if they drove past or parked in the church's front lot. She had gone in the back door. He had watched her drive in, had parked down the road and raced through the woods and had made it to the rear of the church just in time to see the door close behind her. A couple of minutes later, the lights in that part of the building went out. A light came on in the part where the reverend lived, but the curtains were drawn.

He didn't need to see, though. He knew what Reverend Fuckbuggy did with the ladies. Silver Gap was a small town; word traveled.

One day, the chief would find out. He would learn what his whorewife had been up to, and it would break his noble heart. His warrior's heart.

Still, maybe he could help. He had started the harvesting, after all. So far, he had only been harvesting the abandoned, the unwanted. But he supposed expanding his parameters to include the unworthy wasn't too much of a stretch.

Anyway, he would be doing the chief a favor. Who knew what diseases she had picked up from Reverend Fuckbuggy's filthy fuckstick? He couldn't take her tonight; he had his hands full already.

But soon.

Soon.

CHAPTER TWENTY-ONE

Flannery led him through the tunnels.

Blackness surrounded them, broken only by the glow from Flannery's eyes. Alex was sobbing, barely able to talk, but Flannery never stopped grinning. Every now and then he offered encouragement. *Not too far now, boss. Don't worry, boss, we'll be there soon. In the light. In the air that don't clog your lungs with soot. Out where the roof don't fall in and break through that useless helmet—that's for show, right, not for safety, because it don't mean a tinker's damn when the world is crashin' down on your head. We'll be there soon, yeah. There's just this one door, we gotta get through one door, and then we're home free.*

But Alex knew they would never find that door. It was too dark, and the cave-in had filled the tunnels with tons of debris. The earth had turned on them and you couldn't fight the earth. It would let you think you had a chance, but then it would laugh, that loud, loopy, whooping guffaw that shook the world's guts from the inside, turning night into darker night, extinguishing lamps and lives.

No, they would maybe be lucky enough to find the right tunnel, but it would be choked with rock and coal and earth and dust, impassable, impossible. He was hysterical, barely holding it together and that only because of Flannery's calming presence. He fought for control, but then Flannery reached a bend and disappeared around it. Alex had no helmet, no flashlight, no source of illumination at all. Flannery wore a helmet with a carbide lamp, but it didn't burn; all the light came from behind his eyes. Now even that was gone.

Panic overtook him. He ran toward where he'd last seen Flannery, but hurtled headlong into a wall. He saw light then, flashes of it blinding him as he tumbled backward. His head snapped back and crashed into the hard tunnel floor.

Now he was alone, the tunnel silent. Flannery was far ahead someplace. The blackness was existential, definitional, the absolute absence of all light. Alex gained his footing awkwardly, hands out for balance. He left them extended and took slow, shuffling steps, using his hands to feel his way forward. He smelled his own sweat, rank and sour; it filmed his body, soaked into his clothes, trickled down his socks and into his boots.

Then Flannery was there again, beside him, his eyes burning through the dark. He accepted it; dream-reality was different from the waking kind. The panic bubbling up within Alex receded to something more like dread. *Come on, boss,* Flannery said. *You don't want to fall behind in here. Keep up.*

They were moving again, Flannery's eyes cutting a path like headlights on a nighttime road. Flannery kept up a monologue as he marched ahead, but the words slurred into an uneven buzz.

When he finally heard another recognizable word, it was "door." Sure enough, Flannery had stopped before it. Light leaked in around its edges, and Flannery's eye beams showed a big brass padlock hanging in a rusty hasp.

At the sight of that door, Alex's knees went rubbery and his hands started to tremble. He heard snarling and the gnashing of teeth behind it. "Don't open it!" he tried to say. His mouth opened but the only sound that came out was a pathetic whimper.

Flannery touched the lock and it was gone. The door opened with a loud, labored creak that drowned out Alex's further attempts to complain.

Light filled the room on the other side, though it was filtered, as if seeping through drapes. Whatever creatures were growling and snapping were not in the room, which was hardly wider than the tunnel. Flannery led him through it, and although with every step Alex expected to be attacked, the only things he saw in the room were women. There were three of them, with blank stares and silver smiles.

They frightened him more than the beasts he had expected.

He reared back from one who raised her hands toward him. She looked familiar, though he couldn't place her. He couldn't tell if she was imploring or beseeching or trying to grab or caress him, he just saw that empty gaze and that silver smile and those hands reaching for him and he lurched away.

And then he woke, his arms and shoulders and head on the floor, legs still on the bed, tangled in the covers. His T-shirt and shorts were soaked and the sheet immobilizing his legs was soaked. He shivered as a frigid blast from the motel's air conditioner dried the sweat on his skin.

He went into the bathroom and stripped, draping his wet nightclothes over the shower curtain rod. He ran the water in the sink as hot as it would go and washed his face, then his chest and armpits. He studied himself in the mirror, his eyes bloodshot, his chin and cheeks stubbled. Nobody looked his best at this hour, in the harsh light of a fixture over the sink.

He found a dry shirt and a pair of sweatpants, dressed in those, and sat in the room's one chair, his feet up on the ottoman. He turned on the TV and ran through channels with the remote until he found something he could stand to have on, a melodrama from the 1940s, in black-and-white. He didn't know what it was. He had seen the female lead before but couldn't remember her name. He let their words wash over him, not taking in their meaning, and soon he drifted off again.

Engines and honking and shouts outside brought him around. The movie was over, and on the screen before him a woman who had co-starred in a TV sitcom two decades earlier explained how she had lost weight and firmed every part of her physique. Alex punched the power button on the remote and peered out the window, bleary-eyed.

On the road past the motel, a steady stream of cars and trucks headed for town. Pickups were most numerous, some with cabs at capacity and more people riding in the beds. Trailers bore hunting vehicles of various descriptions. He saw gun racks and men in blaze orange vests and camo pants and ball caps, and he knew what it was about.

Wolves.

Somehow word had spread that Silver Gap had wolves, and this was the result. Animals that weren't supposed to be in Colorado at all, according to Robbie, and therefore, animals for which there were no hunting licenses to be had. But now they were here, and people were responding in droves to the opportunity to shoot them. Or, Alex thought, to the possibility of such an opportunity. He didn't know if an open call had been issued for wolf hunters, or it these newcomers had simply decided for themselves that their services were required.

Either way, he expected the woods would be a good place to stay away from until the hysteria had run its course.

And then another thought occurred to him. The costs of renting out the entire motel weren't bankrupting him, but those hunters would need rooms, and he had them all tied up.

He splashed some water in his face and pulled on a pair of jeans and a sweater, socks and boots and walked down to the motel office.

When he passed through the door, the bell rang, but there was nobody behind the counter. "Mr. Durbin?" Alex called. "Charles?"

No answer came from the open doorway behind the counter area. Alex waited another minute, feeling awkward. Durbin had told him that he and Clara lived on the premises, and he could tell from outside that there was a reasonable-sized apartment connected to the lobby. But he didn't know if the doorway led directly into the residence. He didn't want to walk in on the Durbins if they were fighting, or making love, or engaged in any other private couple-type activity.

On the other hand, there had been a series of wolf attacks. They could in there, injured, maybe dying.

He called out once more, then decided to risk it. "Clara?" he called as he went around the counter and through the open door. "Charles? Anybody here?"

Behind the doorway was an office area containing a floor safe and a couple of desks. A computer hummed softly on one, with fractal images shooting across the screen. "Hello?" Alex tried.

On the far side of the office was another open door. One glance told him it led into their apartment. Inside, they were still largely living out of boxes, as if they hadn't quite decided that their reprieve was permanent. Alex knocked on the door. "Anybody home?"

Charles emerged from what was obviously a bathroom, drying his hands on a small towel. "Sorry, Mr. Converse," he said. "The fan in there's as loud as the dickens. I thought maybe somebody was calling me but couldn't tell for sure."

"No problem," Alex said. "I just wanted to make sure everybody was okay."

"Far as I know," Charles said. He ducked back into the room, then emerged again without the towel. "Clara went out a little while ago. It's a little difficult, not having any staff. But not having many guests makes it easier."

"That's what I wanted to talk to you about. I suppose you've seen the traffic out there?"

"Yeah, been a pretty busy morning out on the road."

"Well, what I wanted to suggest was that you could rent them the rooms we're not using. If you don't fill up, I'll still pay for any empty ones. But in the long run, it seems like having more guests—people who could come back again, and tell other people about where they stayed—would be better for your business."

"That's a good idea," Charles said, nodding. "I left my coffee in the kitchen, come on in."

Alex did as the man said and followed him through the small apartment. In the kitchen there was a table with two chairs, the usual large appliances, and an array of smaller ones on a tile counter. On the table was an open cardboard box, which someone had clearly been rummaging in for something or other. A few items had been left out beside it, including some framed photographs. While Charles poured some cream into a cup of coffee—he offered Alex one, which Alex gratefully accepted —Alex picked up one of the frames, which contained three shots from what had to be the Durbins' wedding.

When he focused in on the middle one, showing Charles and Clara Durbin and a third man, clad in their wedding finery, Alex froze. "You okay, Mr. Converse?" Charles asked.

The voice in the quiet room, full of light from a window over the sink, startled Alex. His legs had begun to buckle, and sweat had popped out on his upper lip and his forehead, and for a moment there the world seemed to have gone as dark as the inside of a coal mine.

The woman in the photograph, young Clara Durbin in her wedding gown, a flowered wreath pressed down over long brown hair parted in the middle, was unmistakably the silver-mouthed woman who had reached out to him in his dream. And beside her, the grinning man who was not her husband, his hair longer than Alex had ever seen it and a short, tight beard clinging to his chin, was just as certainly Jared Flannery.

"Alex?"

Alex realized that Charles Durbin was staring. "Sorry," he said. He put the framed pictures back on the table. "I didn't sleep very well, and I guess I'm not quite awake yet. Your wedding?"

"Yeah. Long time ago. Bunch of hippies. Who knew it would last so long?"

"You can never tell." Charles's hair was longer than today, too, and he was about forty pounds lighter, slim and fit and seemingly happy. Alex asked the question, even though he dreaded the answer. "Who's the other guy?"

"Oh, that's her brother, Jared. Our best man. Her father had passed away a couple of years earlier, so Jared really stepped up and filled that role as well."

"Sounds like a great guy."

"Oh, he was. He's been gone for ten years or more, now."

Fourteen, Alex corrected mentally. He kept his mouth closed. That was dangerous territory, and he didn't mean to tread there. Certainly not until he had figured it out for himself.

If he ever could.

He followed Charles back to the lobby, only half-present. He answered in monosyllables, and by the time he got back to his room, he might have agreed to buy the motel, for all he could recall.

Had he seen the pictures earlier, and somehow incorporated them into his dreams? He didn't see how. He had never been to Flannery's home, never met the Durbins before this week, and he hadn't been beyond the lobby earlier. There had been no artwork or photographs in the lobby; it had all been packed up for their imminent move.

And Jared Flannery had been his guide—in his nightmares—for more than a decade.

CHAPTER TWENTY-TWO

Getting into town proved difficult. There was enough traffic to jam the little town's single main road and overwhelm its police force. Once in town, there were no available parking spaces, so Alex turned up one of the side roads. He, Peter, and Ellen wound up walking back to downtown, a distance almost as far as if they had just hiked in from the motel. Peter carried his camera and tripod, while Ellen lugged the sound equipment. When they arrived at Robbie's shop, she was hauling gear to her red Jeep and arranging it in back.

She tossed Alex a harried smile. "Morning."

"I was hoping you could take us out so Peter could do some shooting," he said. "Someplace where the hunters aren't. But you look busy."

"Chief Deeds has me booked up. I'm taking out a few of the town's best hunters—"

"Second best," Alex said. "After you."

"Right. Anyway, he wants us to get those wolves before all these rookies and Sunday hunters get out into the backcountry and start shooting at each other."

"Got room for three passengers?" Alex asked. "I'll pay whatever the Chief is, and then some. We don't want to hunt, but we'd love to observe, maybe film the process."

"I thought your movie was about bugs."

"It's about the effects of climate change," Alex countered. "That can include bark beetles, but it can include other things, too. If there's any link between climate change and the reappearance of wolves into this ecosystem, then that's a worthwhile part of the story."

"And visually a hell of a lot more exciting than fuckin' bug-eaten trees," Peter added.

"And that," Alex said.

He could see that she didn't want to drag them along. She took her job seriously, and she had been hired for a specific purpose. But she kept glancing at him, catching his eye, and every time she did that ready grin slipped over her face. She was weakening, he thought. "We won't be in the way," he said. "You won't even know we're there."

She heaved a sigh and crossed her arms over her chest, giving him her sternest glare. "I have a few rules," she said.

"Name them."

"You only get out of the Jeep if I say you can. If I say to get back in, you do it, fast. If I say hold still, you hold still. If I say move, you move."

"No problem," Alex said. "Peter?"

The tall man nodded his head. "I can live with it."

"Can you get all your equipment in the Jeep with my stuff there? And still find room to sit?"

"We'll make it work," Peter said. He and Ellen helped Robbie load the rest of her gear and worked theirs in around it. When they were done, the front passenger seat was available, and there was room in back for two if they didn't mind sitting close. Alex knew Peter and Ellen wouldn't object to that—he just hoped they didn't decide to have backseat sex.

They eased into traffic, made it to the edge of town, and were stopped there by a police roadblock. A cop that Robbie identified as Tommy Ortega waved them toward a staging area, which was really the parking lot of Mountain Grocers and the couple of streets surrounding it.

On the far side of the roadblock sat some state Division of Wildlife trucks and a helicopter. There were uniformed men with guns around the trucks, which were bristling with what appeared to be state-of-the-art communications gear and antennas. They looked like a military force.

The hunters who had been shunted to the side were massing before the roadblock. Alex heard grumbling and muttered threats and some louder comments about "federals" and "states' rights" and the right to bear arms. He didn't bother pointing out to anyone that the uniformed officials blocking their way were in fact, state employees and not federal.

Mayor Stewart worked his way clear of a knot of official-looking types —lots of suits, and even a few clipboards and walkie-talkies—on the far side of the roadblock. He threaded between two yellow sawhorses, accompanied by another man in a suit who Alex had never seen before. Stewart carried a megaphone.

He stopped just inside the roadblock and raised the megaphone. "Everybody, my name is Alden Stewart," he began. "I'm the mayor here in Silver Gap. A lot of you don't know me, but if you ask around I think you'll be told that I'm a straight shooter. I mean what I say and say what I mean. So I'm not going to tell you that we don't want you here, or that we don't want these wolves dealt with. We do. We had another woman go missing just last night, and while there's no evidence that wolves were involved in her disappearance, they're behind enough others around here that we're not discounting the possibility."

"Someone else is missing?" Alex asked.

"Thought you would have heard," Robbie said. "Barb Johnston. The wife of the man your friend tangled with yesterday."

Alex spun around and looked at Peter. The cameraman was oblivious to the conversation. He was watching Stewart, but paying more attention to the DOW people preparing their trucks. If he had reacted when the mayor mentioned the missing woman, it didn't show. Ellen was looking at Stewart and seemed to be listening intently to his words.

He didn't always like Peter, but he couldn't see him as a killer. He didn't know where the Johnstons lived, but he didn't think even if Peter was more vicious and vengeful than he believed, he would have been able to get there and take Mrs. Johnston away. Alex had gone out in the Lexus, and when he got up in the morning it was parked right where he had left it.

"Are you serious?" he asked Robbie, keeping his voice low. "Is the husband okay?"

"He was out drinking, is what I heard. When he got home, she was gone. No sign of forced entry, and definitely no sign of wolves. Most folks think she just got tired of being married to an asshole and moved out."

"How likely is that?"

"You've never met Titus Johnston. He's nobody's idea of husband of the year. And after being knocked around by Peter, he probably would have been in a worse mood than usual."

"... further ado," Mayor Stewart was saying, "I'd like to introduce Doug Wolters of the Colorado Division of Wildlife, who's going to take charge of the wolf effort going forward."

He handed the megaphone to the other man, who was tall, lean, and tanned, with sandy hair and a reddish beard. He looked uncomfortable in his suit. "Good morning," Wolters said. "As Mayor Stewart said, we're going to be running this operation, and there are gonna be some ground rules."

"What gives you the right?" somebody shouted from the crowd.

"The right to make the rules? We're the DOW, we *are* the ones who make rules about hunting and wildlife management in this state. I think everybody here wants the same thing, which is to see these wolves stopped. Same time, I think you all can understand that we can't just throw out the rulebook and let everybody go wild out there. We'd have a much bigger public safety problem then than we do right now. So here's what we're gonna do. Today, we're going out and track those wolves. By *we*, I mean DOW. You all can stay here in Silver Gap or not, but I want you to keep the forest clear. Last thing we need is for their tracks to be obscured by traffic, or somebody getting into a shot that we need to take. So I'm asking you—I'm asking you, *please*—stay back and let us do our thing. If we fail, then tomorrow we'll run things different."

"I took time off work to be here!" one of the men in the audience called out.

"I appreciate that," Wolters said. "Same time, nobody asked you to, and I can't take personal responsibility for every decision that brought you all out here today. My number one priority has to be those animals. I'm sure you can all appreciate that."

From the sound of the crowd, they didn't. The mayor took the megaphone back. "Look, folks, let's just do it their way, okay? Today's their turn. If they aren't successful, tomorrow's your turn. In the meantime, Silver Gap's wide open to you. Enjoy a meal, a cold drink, relax and breathe in some fresh mountain air."

More grumbling, but the shouting and catcalls stopped. Wolters and Stewart nodded to each other, and then Wolters went back between the sawhorses. He made a corkscrewing motion in the air with his hand, and the propeller on the 'copter started to spin; lazily at first, then faster. At the same time, the truck engines started up, and the uniformed men took their places. Wolters climbed into one and shut the door.

The chopper lifted away from the ground like an ungainly bird taking flight, kicking up a screen of dust, pine needles, and fallen leaves. Through that cloud, the trucks disappeared. In a couple of minutes there was no sign of them but the sound of their engines receding in the distance, and a slight haze in the air.

The mayor was walking amongst the hunters, shaking hands and introducing himself, as if they could potentially vote for him. He had an election-eve smile on his face, and though Alex couldn't hear what anybody said to him, he could hear Stewart's loud laughter in response. "Guy doesn't quit, does he?" he said.

"He's a politician through and through," Robbie replied. "Fortunately, he's also a decent man, so I don't mind voting for him."

"Ellen!" Peter was standing with a clutch of hunters, camera and tripod in one big hand, beckoning Ellen. "Come on!" he shouted. "We're going with!"

"Wait, Ellen," Alex said.

She glanced back at him, but kept hurrying toward Peter, who motioned her on with exaggerated urgency. "Don't worry!" he called to Alex. "We'll get you some great footage!"

"Peter, don't!" Alex cried. But now he saw that Peter's newfound friends weren't alone. Most of the hunters were doing as they'd been asked, standing down for the day. But others were hurrying to their vehicles and ignoring the protestations of the cops posted, driving around the roadblock and after the DOW vehicles.

Peter shot him a thumbs-up and followed the hunters to their truck. Ellen caught up with him. She smiled back at Alex and Robbie, then was lost in the crowd.

"Now what?" Robbie asked.

"I thought you were spoken for today."

"I'll check with Morris, but considering what we just heard, I doubt he'll want me taking anybody hunting today."

"I guess we could do some more location scouting," Alex suggested. "If we can do it someplace where we're not in the way."

"I was thinking about it last night," Robbie said. "I remembered a couple of other places, not far from where we were yesterday, with lots of color. Not the kind of fall color you like to see, but color, anyway."

Alex was strangely pleased that Robbie had been thinking about him overnight. He had hardly stopped thinking about her.

She used her cell to call the police chief. After less than a minute, during which she said very little, she tucked it back into its belt holster. "He's got a lot on his plate today," she said. "Not surprisingly, what with Barb missing now."

"That's two, right?"

"Barb and Marie," Robbie confirmed. "I wish we could blame wolves, but I'm not sure we can."

"You don't think so?"

"Like I said, the word is at the Johnston place, there's no sign of wolves at all. At Marie's, there was, but only downstairs and around Mrs. Morgenstern's body. Dr. Steinhilber says he left Marie upstairs, with enough sedatives in her to keep her out all night. It's highly unlikely that wolves would have dragged her down a flight of stairs and out of the house. And if they had, there would have been blood in her room, blood on the stairs. There wasn't."

"What do you think it was, then?"

She gave him a patient grin. "What's left?"

"People, I suppose."

"Be my guess."

They reached the Jeep and climbed in. Heading out of town in the other direction, there was almost no traffic, just a few vehicles full of hunters who had decided to give up for the day.

Out in the woods, walking quietly, they heard the distant *pop pop* of hunters' guns. "You think they got something?" Alex asked.

"Doubt it. If the wolves were that easy to find, they would never have lasted this long in the first place. And given the damage they've caused, I figure any time a wolf is spotted you'll hear a dozen shots or more. Maybe a hundred."

"I guess so."

"No, that sounds like frustrated guys shooting at whatever they see. There'll be a lot of road signs and mailboxes with bullet holes in them by tomorrow."

They passed through a pristine stretch of forest that seemed, to Alex, to possess the dignity and the reverent hush of a cathedral. He understood how somebody, encountering such a beautiful landscape, could only see the hand of an all-knowing creator at work. The beauty of the scene only made it worse to know that the actions of humans threatened this forest and every other, and that others of his own kind fought back against every attempt to raise awareness and understanding of the problem. Corporate interests battled for every penny of profit, no matter the ultimate cost to the planet.

"You know," Robbie said as they explored, "wolf populations are actually beneficial to the forest."

"How so?"

"Without natural predators like wolves, populations of elk and deer and other grazing animals can boom. They can overgraze an area in no time, resulting in a die-off for their own species and overstressing the landscape that other species rely on. Big predators help maintain a natural balance. Here in Colorado, without wolves, we manage hunting as an alternate method of population control."

"I guess I never looked at it that way," he said.

"Stick with me, baby," Robbie said mischievously. "I can teach you all kinds of things."

"Is that a promise?"

She laughed. "I suppose we could make a trade," she said. "I teach you, and you tell me what deep, dark secrets you're keeping."

"You think I'm a lot more interesting than I am."

"I'm not just good outdoors," Robbie said. "I can read people as well as spoor."

He knew what she was pressing for, but even if he had wanted to talk about it with anybody, after this morning's revelation—that Clara Durbin was related to Jared Flannery, and that she had shown up in his dream, with that strange silver smile—he needed time to process. Something about being in Silver Gap had intensified his nightmares and brought a new element to them. He couldn't understand any of it.

But it scared him to death.

After a couple of hours spent walking through gorgeous forests, speaking only sometimes and then in low tones, Robbie led him back to the Jeep. She had packed a big lunch for the hunters she had been planning to take out, so they raided it. Sandwiches, fruit, salad, crackers and cheese. She offered a selection of beers and wines, juices and soft drinks. Alex wanted a beer but settled for a cola, concerned that if he had one he'd want more, and he was wary about losing the slightest bit of control. He could say the wrong thing, could confess to Robbie how he thought he was coming to feel about her, or could reveal his frankly insane dreams. If they did encounter a wolf, he wanted to be able to react appropriately.

They ate sitting on a tarp in a clearing blanketed with tall grass. When Robbie brought up his "secrets" again, Alex tried to deflect by turning the conversation toward her. "I've never known anybody like you," he said. "How is it you're not married?"

She laughed, and her laugh was as natural as the breeze through the pine needles and the sunshine gilding her blonde hair. "You might have noticed I'm not exactly the most feminine chick," she said. "I know this might be a surprise, but some guys—especially the ones I tend to meet—are a little intimidated by a woman who can handle a gun better than they can. Maybe I should wear more frills and ribbons, you know, and work in a place that doesn't have so many heads on the walls."

"I'm pretty sure that's not the answer," Alex said. "You're beautiful, you're smart, you're successful, and you're fun to be around. I don't see a downside."

"To be fair, you're not really much like the people who usually hire me," she said. "I get the feeling that your ideas about how men and women should behave are a little different from the guys around here."

"That might be part of it," he admitted. "All I know is, if you're happy, then great. But if you want to be with somebody, then someone is missing a hell of a good thing."

She turned her head away, but he saw the spreading rose wash over her neck and cheeks. He wondered how much of what he had said was projection. He was the one who had wanted to take another shot at marriage, a family. With every year that passed, that possibility grew ever more remote.

While they ate and talked, the sun disappeared and the sky overhead turned leaden. Robbie looked up at it for a long minute. "Snow," she said.

"You think?"

"I've lived here for a long time," she reminded him. "I know when it's going to snow."

"I'm not doubting you," Alex said. "It's just, since I got here I've been hearing people saying how surprising it is that there's no snow yet. Guess they'll have to change that tune."

"We'll want to head back to town pretty soon," she said. "But you know, before we do, I'd like to try to find that wolf we saw yesterday."

"Why?"

"Like I said then, there was something strange about her. It bugged me all night, and I wanted another look at her."

"You said she was hurt, or sick."

"Right. But it wasn't just that. We don't have to spend a lot of time at it, especially with snow coming on. But if we can find her trail, I doubt she'll have gone far."

Alex was uncomfortable with the idea of actually seeking out a wolf, even one who was injured or dying. That, he had heard, sometimes made animals more dangerous. But Robbie was the expert.

She took the lead, as usual. She had a rifle in her hands and a pistol

holstered at her hip. They descended into the ravine they had seen yesterday, and Robbie went straight to where the wolf had disappeared from
view. The animal's tracks were visible in the damp earth at the bottom of
the ravine, and her path was almost so easy to find that Alex could have
followed it.

The first flakes fell while they sought the wolf. They were fat and lazy,
drifting down from the solid gray sky as if they hadn't actually committed
to the idea of reaching the ground. Robbie walked faster, concerned that a
serious snowfall would hide the wolf's trail. Alex looked up and saw that
the sun had faded away, not much more now than a pale wafer behind the
flat, gray sky.

The temperature had been dropping steadily, and Alex was close to
giving up on his male pride and suggesting they head for town when
Robbie found the animal.

It had wedged itself into a crevice at the base of a rocky slope. She
summoned Alex over, pointing into the tight space. "She's dead," Robbie
said. "A few hours, I guess. Maybe sometime last night, but no longer than
that."

"Can you tell what she died of?"

"Not here. Maybe Dr. Steinhilber could."

"I thought he treated humans."

"He does, but we lost our only vet last year. We'd have to haul her
down into Bellvue or Laporte to find a vet."

"I guess it doesn't really matter," Alex said.

"Probably not. Help me get her out of here."

"Why?"

She gave him a look that he had already become familiar with,
suggesting that she was becoming more exasperated with him than whatever fee he was paying and friendship might be developing were worth.
He shut up and helped her, glad he was wearing gloves. Together they
lifted the wolf from between the big rocks and laid her out on open
ground. Snowflakes drifted down and melted on her fur.

Robbie stood back and studied the animal. To Alex, it was just a wolf,
large and probably menacing when it had been healthy, but not so
much now.

"I was right," Robbie said.

"About what?"

"She's no normal gray wolf. Look at her."

"I am, but I guess I don't know what I'm looking at."

Robbie squatted down beside the wolf. "Look how short her legs are," said. "At least a couple of inches shorter than an average wolf of this size would have. They're more muscular, too. She might be a little slower over a distance, but she could jump, and in a sprint she could cover some ground."

Alex didn't see it, but he had no basis for comparison. "Anything else?"

She lifted the animal's head, drew back its lips. "This head is massive. And heavy. Look at the size of these teeth. This creature's jaws are power- ful, and her teeth could tear holes through steel, I think. Big shoulders, too." She ran a hand across the wolf's neck. "And neck. She needed those to hold that head up."

"So what are you saying?" Alex asked. "This wolf is some kind of mutant?"

"I don't know," Robbie said. "I've seen wolves. Knowing about big animals is kind of what I do. But mostly I know how to track and shoot them. Wolf physiognomy is not really my field."

"Which leaves us where?"

Instead of answering, Robbie bent over, hoisted the wolf up and over her head, settling the thing across her shoulders and around her neck, like a badly made fur stole. "Let's go home," she said. "We'll figure it out there."

CHAPTER TWENTY-THREE

Ellen thought sport hunting was a barbaric practice. Even this excursion struck her as beyond the pale. The government had marshaled its resources, like an army going to war, and had sent out dozens of armed men to destroy a few wild creatures doing what instinct demanded. A helicopter buzzed overhead like a giant wasp, as if it wasn't bad enough to outgun the wolves on the ground—they needed the option of slaughter from the skies, as well. And then, to top it all off, other theoretically human beings had piled into trucks and SUVs to follow, each member of the party armed, each one hoping he (or she, but Ellen had only spotted two or three women, besides herself, out in the forest that day) would be the one to fire a bullet into an animal's brain.

She knew what it felt like to be prey. She didn't like it.

Peter was as bad as the rest. He was enraptured by the scene. When he remembered to shoot video, he did so with the camera pressed to his eye and his mouth hanging open, as if trying to swallow the testosterone floating through the air. His cheeks were flushed, and when he pulled the camera away the expression on his face—eyes slitted, nostrils flared, lips parted—was so similar to the one he wore when he came that she wondered if he was staining his shorts.

What made the whole scene that much more awful was the grisly way the government hunters went about their task. They were occasionally throwing split-open rabbits, calves, and goats out of one of their trucks.

The truck Peter and Ellen rode in, along with five other men in the bed, three in the cab, was sometimes close enough to the government trucks to hear the carcasses land with a wet thump. When Ellen first noticed it, she complained.

"They're probably poisoned, too," Peter said.

"You think?"

"That's what I'd do."

"What about other animals who eat them? There are other animals that eat meat out here, right? And birds, insects—aren't they putting the whole ecosystem at risk?"

"Like man-killing wolves aren't? If they don't stop these wolves, then this area will be crawling with hunters. They'll do more damage to the environment than a few poisoned carrion-eaters."

"I guess," she said, not entirely sold.

"Anyway," Peter went on, "I guess they think it'll draw the wolves out. I hope they're right—it'd be awesome to get the takedown on camera."

"You really have no compassion for the wolves, do you?" Ellen asked. She was beginning to think that Peter was more like other men than she had first believed. She thought of the cartoon of a fish eating a smaller fish, while being eaten by a larger fish, which was in turn being eaten by a still bigger one, and so on, *ad infinitum*. Peter, she had told herself early on, was an artist, a filmmaker, a creative soul who could see the inherently decent qualities in everyone. Since she had been with him, though—and especially here in Silver Gap—she had come to see him in a different light.

Like the rest of them, he was enthralled by power. Who had it, how to get it. The powerful preyed on the less powerful, and down the food chain it went. He was intrigued by the wolves only because they had proven themselves capable of killing humans. Now he was caught up in the hunt, in the overwhelming force of humans who would, she had no doubt, destroy every last wolf.

She had lived her life as an underdog, often taken advantage of, used, abused. But she had decided to claim her own power, to defend herself against Peter's kind with any means necessary. So far he had not acted inappropriately—he wanted plenty of sex, but that was okay, so did she. He had never struck her or laid a hand on her in anger. If he ever did, she would remove it.

From his arm.

Seeing his fascination with these hunters, his lust for the kill, she decided that their parting would come sooner than that, before he had a chance to devolve far enough to seek to cause her physical pain. Tonight, perhaps, back in their motel room, she would tell him she was leaving. If she could get a ride off the mountain, she would. Maybe Alex would help her out. He was—

"Jesus!" Peter's big hand clamped down on her shoulder, hard. In this case, she let it slide; he hadn't meant to hurt her, and he pulled it away in the same instant, using it to steady the camera he had raised to his eye.

She didn't have to ask what he was looking at. Everybody riding in the back of the truck was staring the same way.

Up on a ridgeline, thirty feet higher than them and about twice that far away, stood a huge, black wolf. It looked like a shadow of a wolf, a silhouette, dark against light. It watched the trucks below, and she could have sworn it understood what it was seeing. It didn't flinch away, didn't try to hide. Just stood and watched, as if observing the approach of visiting emissaries from another kingdom.

"My goodness," one of the hunters said. "Look at the size of it."

"Look at that chunk out of its ear," another said. Her eyes drawn to it by the remark, Ellen saw what he meant. The animal's right ear was almost bisected by it, giving the impression of a single ear on the left and two smaller ones on the right.

"It's a notch," she said.

"Notch," the hunter repeated. The truck was still rolling, but he raised a rifle to his shoulder, sighting along its length. "This bullet's for you, Notch," he said. "It's got your name on it."

He fired. The noise was not as loud as she had expected, flatter, somehow.

Then, as if that had been the signal, everyone was firing. The government hunters blasted away at the wolf, as did the civilians who had followed them into the wilderness. Peter was trying to capture it all on tape, but he was so caught up in the moment that he was swinging the camera wildly, and she knew the resulting footage would be unwatchable, vertigo-inducing. His tongue showed at the corner of his mouth, like that of an excited boy running a relay race in gym class. The racket of all those guns at once was deafening, and when it faded she wasn't sure because it kept echoing in her ears, and the smoke that filled the air was acrid and burned her lungs when she inhaled it.

As the volley began, the wolf turned and ran down the far side of the ridge, out of sight. Bullets chewed vegetation, cut small limbs from trees, flew off into empty air.

No one seemed to care that thirty or forty shooters had failed to find their target. Instead, the hunters whooped and shouted and every vehicle's driver pressed on its accelerator. Unprepared, Ellen fell back against the guy behind her. "Better hold on, little lady," he said with a grin. He pushed her off, getting one hand firmly on her ass cheek as he did. "Ride's about to get bumpy."

She swallowed her response, because he was right. The truck hit an uneven patch and she nearly flew from the truck bed. She grabbed onto the side as the vehicle left the road altogether, charging up the ridge, cross-country, along with the rest of them. The government trucks were in the lead, but not by much. All the wheels kicked up a dust cloud that swamped and overwhelmed the gun smoke.

Ellen couldn't see the wolf anymore, but she assumed that those in the government vehicles could. All the private trucks followed the DOW ones over the hill and down the other side. Brake lights flashed as vehicles fell into single file, or something approaching it, as they raced into a narrowing canyon with high, rocky sides. She heard the crunch of a collision, but nobody stopped.

The truck she and Peter rode in wound up three from the end, because their driver risked a close encounter with a huge pine in order to cut off someone who might have edged him out. Peter was laughing out loud. Ellen was clinging to the side, hoping desperately that the thing could keep its wheels on the ground. The hunters gripped their guns and the truck with about equal ferocity.

Then the front DOW vehicle stopped suddenly. Brake lights flashed again, and trucks skidded on dirt, unable to grip the surface, and slid into each other. She heard lots of banging and shouting and watched one hunter thrown clear out of the truck bed. He landed belly-down in some bushes, and it took him a full minute to gain his feet again. In that time, the truck Ellen rode in smashed into the one in front of it, popping the hood and knocking someone else out onto the ground. The truck behind rammed into them.

"Why are we ...?" she began.

"Oh, good Christ!" one of the men said.

"What?"

The man tried to speak again, but couldn't. Instead, he pointed.

Five or six wolves had appeared on the rock-strewn slopes around them. Then more, showing themselves as if they had simply manifested there, out of thin air. And still more came. Ten, fifteen, twenty-five. They kept coming. Thirty. Thirty-five. She lost count.

A man in the front of the truck bed pounded on the cab's roof. "Get us out of here!" he cried.

The driver tried to accommodate. The engine revved, but they were trapped, squeezed in front and behind by other vehicles. The wheels spun, throwing out dirt clods and dust. Another hunter hammered on the roof, swearing. Peter was aiming the camera at the wolves.

Ellen gripped the steak knife she had stolen from the restaurant. Her only weapon.

She saw the wolf they had called Notch, standing on a boulder, as if daring anyone to shoot.

Somebody did, but the shot missed the big animal.

As if that were the cue they'd been waiting for, the wolves charged.

More gunfire rang out, an unbroken, roaring fusillade.

Wolves fell, but there were more, always more, to take their place.

The two men who had fallen from their rides tried to scramble back onto them. Ellen saw wolves catch one by the legs and yank him down. His scream was long and plaintive and filled her with a nameless dread. The second man was almost into his truck when a wolf leapt onto his back. Huge jaws snapped and the wolf tore off part of the back of his neck and head. Blood flew in a fine, pink spray as man and wolf fell to the ground.

Every driver tried to get his vehicle moving, but most were hopelessly trapped. Wolves swarmed into truck beds and open Jeeps like fierce waves swamping lifeboats. Gunfire and truck engines and shrieks and guttural roars filled the air. Ellen smelled blood and the thick, heavy scent of furred mammals. Panic welled in her, panic and hopelessness and a will to survive, somehow. The men around her were not even aiming anymore, just thrusting gun barrels out of the truck bed and squeezing triggers, and the smoke was gray and bitter and the sound tore at her ears.

And then the first wolf jumped into the bed. The driver tried to free the truck from its prison of steel and rock but couldn't, and a wolf pushed through the open passenger window and in the cab. Peter fell, his throat torn from him, blood arcing into the air and splattering Ellen like paint from a spray can. His camera spiraled up and then down, out of the truck and onto the ground, and a wolf caught Ellen's left arm in its teeth, and she stabbed it and stabbed it and stabbed it with the little knife. It let go once and she thought she had won, she would survive this after all, until she realized it was only getting a better grip. Then there was another wolf in the bed and it had her by the ribs and then another one and there were no hunters left, only her, and she thought: at least I was the last girl standing, and then she—

CHAPTER TWENTY-FOUR

Clara Durbin knew that Reverend Calderon didn't like to talk about his worsening vision, but she also knew that it *was* worsening, significantly, so when he asked her to do chores that he had once done for himself, she didn't mind. She was happy to help, because anything she could do left him more time to interpret the Lord's wishes and words and to minister to those in need.

Today he had asked her to run into town for groceries. He gave her a list and some cash, and she kept cloth bags in the trunk of the Buick because she didn't like those plastic ones they had at the store. She cruised down the road between the church and town, trees flashing past her window, listening to Christian music on the radio.

Until she heard a siren. She glanced in the rearview and saw a police car, the light on top flashing red and blue. She looked at her speedometer. Five miles below the limit, which was how she always drove.

She sighed. At least she had not yet bought the groceries—she would hate to be sitting there while a police officer dressed her down and the reverend's ice cream melted in the trunk. She found a spot where there was room between the road and the woods and pulled over. The police car drew in behind her, and that nice young Officer Honeycutt got out.

She remembered his first name. Howard. He had stayed at the Lodge when he first came to town. Three weeks, he had been their guest, until he found a house to rent. He was an orphan, he'd told them, both his parents killed when he was just a young teenager. She didn't recall now if he had told them how they'd died.

Clara put her hands on the steering wheel. She'd heard somewhere that you should do that, so the police know you don't have a gun. Howard knew she would never carry one, but she wanted to do things right. She waited, hands on the wheel, until he got out of his car and hiked up to hers and tapped on the window. "Mrs. Durbin," he said. "You can come on out."

"Shouldn't I open the window?" She wondered, briefly, how she was to do that with her hands on the wheel. With an elbow?

"Better if you just get out." He tugged at the outside door handle, but of course she kept her doors locked. "Get out of that fuckerfuck car right now!"

At that, she took her hands off the wheel and pressed them against her lap. "I don't like that kind of language," she said. She was no prude— she and Charles ran a motel, after all, and people did all sorts of things in motel rooms. Left behind all sorts of souvenirs, too: condoms and pornography and enough bodily fluids to float an ocean liner. But she was a churchgoer and a God-fearing woman, and she didn't have to approve of such goings-on, or the sort of language often used to describe it.

"Come out of that fuckerfuck or I will shoot you in the head." His voice had gone high, agitated, and when she looked again she saw that his gun was pointed at her.

She lost control of her bladder, just a little bit, a little tinkle on the seat and on her skirt. And she thought, *the skirt I can wash, but Charles is going to notice the seat*. The gun didn't move, so she unlocked the door. As soon as she had, Howard wrenched it open from outside and grabbed her by the arm, hauling her from the seat.

"I don't understand why you're doing this," she said. "I don't think I was speeding."

He holstered the gun and pulled something from the waistband of his pants. Tape, she realized. Duct tape in a big roll. He started to unroll a section of it. "Me to know," he said. "Me to know." He flattened her against the Buick with his body and pressed the tape over her mouth, then wound it around her head, catching hair. "You to find out. Me to know, you to find out."

Then he hauled her by the arms, half dragging her, back to his car. He popped the trunk and pushed her down into it, and when she tried to protest (though the tape made verbal complaint impossible) he back-handed her across the face so hard that she tasted blood. "You'll find out," he said as he held her down in the trunk. He closed the trunk lid over her, repeating the same three words over and over. "You'll find out. You'll find out. You'll find out."

Then it was dark and his voice was muffled. Clara kicked against the inside of the trunk. She kicked and she kicked. But she heard the police car's big engine catch and turn over and then she knew they were in motion.

Still, she kicked as long as she could.

CHAPTER TWENTY-FIVE

The lab was cold, and in spite of state-of-the-art air circulation systems, Alex thought the smell might put him off eating meat for years to come.

Dr. Steinhilber was the only medical professional in a hundred square miles, Robbie explained on the way to town, so he functioned as a medical examiner in some cases. He had a lab set aside with the appropriate equipment, including the stainless-steel examination table on which the wolf carcass they had brought in was now lying. Alex and Robbie had been invited to stay for the necropsy, and another man, a scientist named Cale Conklin, had joined them.

"Dr. Conklin is an expert on wolf behavior," Steinhilber said. "He literally wrote the book."

"It's such an honor to meet you, doctor," Robbie said, pumping the man's hand. She turned to Alex. "His book *The Wild, Wild Wolf* is one of my bestsellers. I didn't know you were in town."

"Just got in this morning," Conklin explained. He was taller than Peter, six-four or six-five, with an underfed mountain-man vibe. His brown hair was curly and unkempt, his beard thick and shot through with silver. He had on a plaid shirt in browns, reds, and yellows, faded blue jeans, hiking boots. He wore little round glasses, wire-framed and thick-lensed, and he looked to Alex like someone who would be more at home in a tent than a building. "Given what's been going down here, I could hardly stay away."

"I'm glad you're here," Steinhilber said. "Since I'm no veterinarian, much less experienced with wolf necropsies."

"Let's just get started," Conklin suggested. "I'm not a vet either, but I'll help as much as I can."

That had been almost an hour earlier. Since then, the doctor had turned the wolf this way and that, poking and prodding, and they had weighed and measured the animal. She was just under six feet long and weighed 186 pounds. "That's big for a wolf," Conklin said. "Huge, in fact. Especially for a bitch."

Robbie rubbed her shoulders. "You're telling me."

Conklin handed Robbie a digital camera and asked her to photograph the entire process. Once the measurements had been taken, the doctor started slicing into the wolf. He removed a bullet from near her ribs, though he said the mass of scar tissue built up around it indicated that it had been there for a long time, and was probably not the cause of death.

With a bone saw, he cut off the top of the wolf's skull and dug a couple of specimens from her brain. "We'll test these for rabies and distemper," Steinhilber said. "In addition to running some bloodwork. Most of the brain will have to be sent over to the state, since they'll want to do their own tests."

"We don't know if this is one of your killers," Conklin said. "And a wolf empties its stomach every six hours, so we probably won't find anything. If we have DNA from any of the scenes—"

Steinhilber cut him off. "I doubt that Morris Deeds and his men are quite that sophisticated."

"Well, if we can locate some, then we can compare it to this wolf's DNA. But when and if we do find the killers, I'm certain we'll find rabies and/or distemper."

"Why's that?" Alex asked.

"Because healthy wolves don't attack human beings. They just don't."

"Are rabies and distemper common in wolves?"

"Not as much as in some other species, but they're not unheard of. Wolves do carry various diseases and parasites. Most commonly, *Echinococcus granulosus*, a tapeworm that can spread Hydatid disease. But that wouldn't result in attacks against humans. Like I said, you can count the number of wolf attacks on people that don't involve rabies and/or distemper on two hands. And you'd have fingers left over."

Steinhilber was about to respond when there was a knock at the door and Morris Deeds entered. "Sorry to interrupt, Doc," Deeds said. "I need you, Robbie. Can you step out here for a minute?"

She agreed, and passed through the door with him. A couple of minutes later she came back and beckoned to Alex. "You might want to be in on this," she said. "I'm sorry, Norman, we've got to go. Dr. Conklin, it really has been an honor. If you'll be in town for a little while, I hope we run into each other again."

Conklin smiled like she had offered him treasure. Alex understood how he felt. "I do, too," Conklin said.

Outside, they passed a couple of other cops heading toward the doctor's office. Robbie led Alex quickly to her Jeep, explaining as they went. Snow was falling at a steady pace, building up on the ground, on roofs and trees, and he zipped his coat against the chill. "They're going to tell Norman and Dr. Conklin what's up," she said.

"Which is?"

"Which is, those people who went out earlier? The DOW trucks, and the hunters that followed them out? They've been attacked."

"Attacked?" he echoed. Then the meaning of her words sank in. "Oh, my God. Wolves?"

"Yes."

"Peter and Ellen were out there."

"Yes. And people I've known for most of my life, and a lot of visitors. I guess one of the people in the party managed to get in touch with Frank Trippi, and said the wolves were overrunning them. The call was dropped —or the phone was—and Frank couldn't get back in touch. He went to see Morris, who told Alden Stewart. Word's been spreading, somehow, and some of the other folks who came to town to hunt wolves are itching to get out there. But of course, the DOW, the mayor, and Deeds want a more organized party, since the last one wasn't exactly a resounding success."

"They're all dead?" Alex asked. His mind was refusing to process what she said. He heard the words, and understood them, but still he couldn't bring himself to accept them.

"They don't know. They just know they can't reach anybody. The DOW chopper was in touch by radio, but then the radio cut out and there was an SOS beacon, and then nothing. They have another one, but the snow and wind are keeping it grounded for now. So they want to send out some vehicles."

"Including you."

"That's right. I'm the best they've got."

"So I've heard."

"I have to go, Alex. It's what I do. And I owe it to my friends, my neighbors."

"I get it," Alex said. Really, he wanted her to tell him she was retiring, that she'd had enough of killing and was going to stay indoors for the next thirty years.

He knew how unlikely that was, though.

They reached the Jeep and he took his usual position in the passenger seat. "I can take you back to your hotel, or—" She let the sentence hang there.

"Do I get a choice?"

"Of course."

"Peter and Ellen are out there. I'm responsible for them."

"You didn't make them get in that truck today."

"I didn't stop them."

"I'm not sure you could have."

"Maybe not. But I could have tried."

"So, you want to go along?"

"I have to."

"Morris won't like it. He doesn't like you."

"I'm not that fond of him, either."

"I can tell. I'm sure he can, as well."

"I guess I'm an open book."

She eyed him for a moment, then returned her attention to the road. "I don't know about that. You've got layers of mystery about you."

"That's just ... just because I haven't told you everything."

"Hence the mystery." They were approaching the lodge. "Hotel, or what?"

"I'm going with you."

"That's what I hoped you'd say." She drove past the motel and into town.

Alex could sense the tension in the air as they reached the small downtown area. There were no people walking casually on the sidewalks, no one carrying bags. Instead, people were gathered in anxious knots. Cars hurried down the street, their drivers grim-faced. Outside Town Hall, police cars and SUVs were parked willy-nilly. Robbie parked in the mix and climbed out of the Jeep, telling Alex to stay put.

Chief Deeds and Mayor Stewart were locked in intense conversation with a man and a woman in DOW uniforms. Robbie joined them. Deeds called another cop over, and he spread a map on the hood of one of the cop cars. There was more discussion, and pointing fingers, and after a few minutes Robbie stalked back to the Jeep. "We're riding with Morris," she said.

"Me, too?"

"Unless you want to change your mind."

"No, I'm in." He didn't like the idea of spending time with the police chief, but he figured it was a trade-off, because he got to spend more time with Robbie.

He helped load Robbie's gear into a department Tahoe, then took a seat in back beside her. An officer named Honeycutt swaggered to the SUV and got in behind the wheel, moving with a sort of official crispness that felt practiced to Alex. It looked like he had an idea about how cops should move, and although it was artificial and forced, he was determined to live up to it.

Deeds took shotgun. He turned around and fixed Alex with a stern glare as Honeycutt started the engine. His eyes were almost slate grey, echoing the sky outside. "You keep out of the way," he said. "Stay in the vehicle unless you're told to get out. You're along because Robbie asked, and that's the only reason. Clear?"

"Clear, Chief," Alex said.

Deeds faced front again, and Honeycutt pulled in near the front of a procession of official vehicles. Alex counted nine, each containing at least three or four people. He saw Silver Gap PD, Larimer County Sheriffs, state troopers, and DOW. Most were male and white, but not all of them. A DOW truck took the lead, and Deeds explained that they had GPS coordinates from one of the missing DOW vehicles.

They were about ten miles from town when Alex heard Deeds's name over the radio's constant crackle. Deeds thumbed his mic and responded. "What is it, Althea?"

"Charles Durbin just called in, from the Mountain High Lodge?" Alex stiffened at the familiar name.

"Right, what about?"

"He says Clara has gone missing. He hadn't seen her in hours. She ain't answering her phone."

"He try the church?"

"Yeah. Reverend Calderon says he sent her into town with a shopping list and some money, but she never came back with the groceries."

"Hell's bells, Althea. A few hours isn't enough time to file a missing person report."

"I know that, Morris. But what with the wolves and all, he's plenty worried. He sounded just about panicked on the phone. Wants a search party put together right now."

"He'll just have to wait a while, won't he? We're stretched a little thin at the moment. I'm concerned about Clara and everybody else who's missing, but right now we got a couple dozen people who need help."

"The phone's ringin', Morris, I betcha it's him again."

"See who's around. Maybe some of those guys that came to hunt wolves will go with Durbin to see if they can find her. Other than that, there's not much I can do."

Finished with the call, Deeds turned to Robbie. "You've been with him all day?" A tick of his head toward Alex indicated who the "him" was.

"Yes, Morris. Since first thing this morning."

"So if Clara went missing over the last few hours, I guess you're in the clear," the chief said. "And your friends went out with the hunting party, so they are, too."

"Small favors," Alex mumbled.

"What's that?"

"Nothing."

After a few minutes of quiet except for occasional bursts of staticky conversation over the radio, Honeycutt met Alex's glance in the rearview and took it for an invitation. "Hear you make movies," he said. "You from Hollywood?"

"I live in Santa Monica," Alex said.

"That's Hollywood, isn't it? Same thing."

"It's Los Angeles. Not precisely Hollywood, but not too far away."

"Do you know Vin Diesel? Or Chuck Norris, anybody like that?"

"Sorry, no. I really don't work in the movie business. I'm making a documentary, so—"

"About the ecology or something, right?"

"More or less."

"You must know George Clooney then, right? Brad Pitt and Angelina Jolie? All those Hollywood liberals?"

"Howie," Deeds broke in. "He said he doesn't know those folks."

"I've actually met Clooney," Alex admitted. Robbie nudged his thigh, and he realized he should have kept his mouth shut.

"Is he a queer? I heard he's queer."

"As far as I'm aware, he's an excessively successful and attractive heterosexual," Alex said.

"I don't like that," Honeycutt said. "I mean, I don't like people being queer either. But I think a man ought to find himself one wife and settle on that. Like Chief Deeds, and Christy. You and Christy have a great marriage, Chief. Don't you?"

Deeds snarled something at Honeycutt, who lapsed back into silence. Staticky voices came from the radio and Honeycutt followed the DOW truck along narrow dirt roads, and the other vehicles followed them. The snow was building up and the sky had gone from gray to almost white, as if the color was being leached from the world.

Then the DOW truck left the road and traveled overland, up a hill and down the other side. Honeycutt downshifted and took the ascent slowly. The mood in the vehicle was tense, but he thought that mostly emanated from Chief Deeds. Honeycutt was a little too anxious, a little too desperate to be liked, Alex believed, but he was young and in uniform and maybe that came with the territory.

On the other side of the hill, the ground leveled out again and the path, clearly marked by dozens of tires, led into a canyon that Alex couldn't even see until they were right on it. The trail wound through the canyon, where it was hemmed in by steep, rocky slopes and boulders that had rolled from them in earlier times, perhaps before the dawn of man but likely a blink of an eye in geologic terms, and then the brake lights on the DOW truck were burning and Honeycutt brought the Tahoe to a sudden, sliding stop behind it.

The vehicle halted at such an angle that Alex could see around the DOW truck. What he saw brought bile to his throat. He swallowed, with difficulty.

Earlier, during the necropsy of the wolf, he had whispered to Robbie, "Remind me never to do that again."

"I guess you've never shot an animal and field-dressed it," Robbie said.

"Remind me never to do that, too."

"I'll keep it in mind."

There, the smells of death and blood and the hot stench of the bone saw cutting skull, the sight of the mangled fur and pink flesh and dark organs, had almost sent him running from the room. He had taken some comfort in the ease with which the others dealt with it, and he told himself that life and death were natural processes, each a part of the other, unable to be disconnected. Looking at it that way, clinically and philosophically, had enabled him to stay in the lab and get through the process.

This was so much worse.

Falling snow blanketed everything, but red had seeped through it like fruit juice through crushed ice. The first recognizable thing Alex saw was a foot, still booted, but severed at the ankle and lying on its side. Then the shapes under the snow took on form and meaning. Most of a body, torso and head and limbs, but the torso was split open in the middle, gaping toward the sky. Something that at first he thought was the bloody back of somebody's head, until he realized it was the front, only all the things that made a face—eyes, nose, lips, ears—had been torn away, leaving pulpy flesh and white bone. The upper part of a man, clawing at the snow as if trying to free himself from its grip, except there was nothing below mid-chest except tatters of clothing and shredded flesh. Here a hand, there an arm, over there snagged on a tree limb, a single flap of skin that could have come from a back or a stomach. Bodies dangled out of open trucks, leaned against doors. Blood coated windows and shards of glass jutting up through the fresh powder. The stink of it filled the air; blood and death and shit, urine from the dead and the wolves that had marked their territory, claimed their kills. It was inescapable. Alex tried to breathe through his mouth but then he could taste it on his tongue.

"Oh, God," Chief Deeds said.

"You okay, Chief?" Honeycutt asked him.

"Had better days, son."

The other vehicles were stopped behind them now, doors opening and closing, people getting out. There was swearing and puking and somebody let loose a bloodcurdling cry of fury and frustration. Robbie got out of the SUV and checked her weapon. Alex started to slide out, too.

"You sure?" she asked. "They might still be around. The wolves."

"I'll stick close," he said. "There a gun I can use?"

"You know how to shoot?"

"I have shot. Not a lot, and not well. But it's not an entirely new concept."

"Layers of mystery," she said. "Howie, is the back open?"

"Should be," Honeycutt said. "Fuckeroonie, look at all that, wouldya?"

Alex accompanied Robbie to the rear hatch. "What did he say?"

"I think he said 'fuckeroonie.'"

"Is he all there? Seriously."

"People react in strange ways to something like this," she said, handing him a rifle.

Suddenly her—what would you call it, *macha?*—bravado got to him. "You see things like this a lot? Because I'll tell you, I never have."

She caught his tone and winced, but didn't let it knock her off her stride. "Think you can use this?"

"If I have to."

"Okay, good." She closed the back of the Tahoe. "Let's go see what we can see. You can still stay here."

"I'm going."

"Let's go, then."

Robbie trudged through the snow. Alex followed, the rifle unfamiliar in his hands but somehow still a comfort. Could he shoot a wolf, if he had to? He thought he could. But that was something one didn't know, not for certain, until he was tested. He hoped he wouldn't be tested.

Approaching the slaughter, the ripe smell of death was thickest in the air, overpowering the rest. It was a stench he had never forgotten, though his earlier experience with it had been in a landscape of utter black, not pure white. This was like a negative image of that, except for the red. Blood was blood was blood, and when it fled the body it did so in crimson streams, scarlet rivers, pools so dark they were almost black in the center and pinkish toward the edges.

Everyone was out of the vehicles now, and they walked in near silence among the ruined flesh and spilled blood and jagged bone. Snow was falling, heavy and wet, soaking through Alex's jeans and encrusting the stocking cap he had donned, and the slow, steady pace of it was somehow funereal and fitting. He recognized the truck that Peter and Ellen had jumped into, and he went to it. Peter was on the ground beside it. His mouth was open as if stuck in a scream. His eyes stared unblinking at the falling snow. His throat had been torn away and one hand was gone. The video camera was close to him, as it always had been since Alex had known him. He still had the gear bag strapped across his chest. Alex was ready to write it all off—ready to write the whole project off, at this point, it had been a disaster from the start and had only gotten worse. But looking at Peter, or what was left of him, there on the frozen earth, he knew that Peter would have been filming until the end. Peter could be a pain in the ass and he was opinionated and full of himself but he was a filmmaker through and through, and he would have kept shooting and he would have wanted somebody, anybody, to view his footage.

Alex retrieved the camera, brushing snow off it with his gloved hand. He looked at the bag, but that would be harder to get to. Even if rigor mortis had not set in, the cold would have and Peter would be stiff. Never mind, he told himself, if you want it later you can get it from wherever they take the possessions of the dead.

Chief Deeds was eyeing him as he cleaned off the camera, and he wondered if he should explain that it belonged to him, that he had bought or leased all the equipment for this project, and Peter was only an employee. But Deeds moved on and Alex carried the camera back to the SUV and put it on the backseat, out of the weather.

Police officers were unloading body bags from the back of one of their vehicles. That was something he could help with. He had done it before, anyway. He went to the cops and someone handed him a couple of bags, surprisingly heavy even when they were empty, and he walked out with the others. On the way he saw that Robbie and some of the men had taken up positions along the perimeters, rifles in their hands.

Watching for wolves.

CHAPTER TWENTY-SIX

By the time they got back to town, the snow was falling harder, and winds whipped out of the north, driving it sideways. There had been no survivors, and some of those who had gone out on the trucks were still missing. Bloody drag marks in the snow showed where they had been taken, but the trails had eventually been obscured by yet more snow, and some of the bodies had been taken apart on the way, so there seemed little hope of finding anything identifiable, much less salvageable. Given their concerns about the weather and impending darkness, the people calling the shots had decreed that the search for those victims would be called off, in favor of getting the remains they had collected back to town by nightfall.

Alex and Robbie retired to her shop, where she dug a TV free from underneath canvas bags and paperwork and other things Alex couldn't even identify. She had a rat's nest of cables and Alex found the appropriate kind and plugged it into both devices, and in a few minutes they were watching the video Peter had shot. Even sitting in a moving truck, Peter had been a craftsman. He shot quick grabs of this and that—passing foliage and a bird in flight and a family of mule deer watching the trucks rumble past—as if they had been as artfully arranged and lit as big-budget studio footage. After a few minutes of that, the scene changed to a long shot of a ridgeline with something standing in the shadows of the trees.

"Is that a—?" Robbie asked.

Alex let the video run. Peter zoomed in on what was definitively a wolf. People were shouting, calling one another's attention to the beast. At about the same time that Alex noticed that the wolf had a chunk missing from its right ear, somebody in Peter's truck said they should call the animal "Notch."

"Good name," Robbie said. "Someone took a bite out of that guy."

The video didn't stop. Notch vanished behind the ridge, and the trucks gave chase. Peter turned—his balance was precarious but he kept the camera relatively steady, even though the truck left the dirt road and careened overland, up the slope and then down the other side. Alex recognized the landscape—the same course his group had taken earlier—and a chill set in as the vehicles in the video neared the canyon where he knew the recording would end.

Then they got deep into the canyon and the wolves attacked. They came from every direction—Peter was swinging the camera from side to side, giving up any attempt at art, but capturing the chaos and terror of the moment. Wolves jumped into open truck beds and blood fountained into the air and they climbed into vehicles through open doors or windows and dragged people outside, dismembering them in the just-fallen snow or sinking their snouts into torsos and bringing them up with muzzles wet and red, sometimes clutching organs in their mouths.

Throughout, Alex heard Ellen's screams sometimes, but from Peter he only heard muttered, occasional words. "Fuck. Fuck me. Oh, fuck." Then a wolf got Peter—his scream was long and piercing and the fear in it made Alex want to weep. He was trembling and watching the video—Peter had turned the camera toward the wolf that had his thigh in its mouth, blood shooting out around its teeth—and he didn't even realize until the screen went black as the video ended that Robbie had taken his hand in both of hers and was stroking his with a gentle caress.

"It's done," she said.

"Oh, God, that was ..."

"Shh. I know, Alex. He was your friend and it was awful. More than that. I don't even know the words. It was—you shouldn't watch it again. I have to show it to Morris and Alden and some others. Dr. Conklin. But you should—"

"You think I'm letting you leave my side?" he asked.

"I won't. You can come with. You can sit with me and I'll hold your hand, but you don't have to look."

He tried to gather himself. "I can deal with it, Robbie," he said. "I know I come across like a city-slicker with no experience of death or bloodshed or tragedy, and I wish that was me. But it's not."

"You do a convincing impersonation."

"Years of practice, that's all. The people I know, back in LA—they wouldn't want to be near someone who had done and seen the things I have. So I don't let them know, and they're fine with that and so am I. But when I close my eyes, when I go to sleep—it's all there. The things you most want to forget are the things that never let you go."

She held his gaze for a long time. He didn't think he could ever get tired of looking into those eyes. There was an expectant look on her face, as if she were waiting for him to say something else, or perhaps trying to formulate a sentence or question of her own. Instead, she shifted her attention to the TV, shutting it off. "I'm calling Dr. Conklin. He's got to see that video."

"Good idea."

"And after that, we should get something to eat."

Out at the scene of the attacks, Alex had not expected to ever have an appetite again. He was surprised to find, now that she mentioned it, that he was famished.

Alex had never been to a tactical operations center in a war zone, but when they walked into the Cup & Cow, that's what he thought of. There were people eating their dinners, and the wait staff was busy carrying plates and refilling coffee mugs and putting bottled beer down on table-tops where there were already empty bottles standing. Nearly every table was full, some more than, with extra chairs pulled up at the corners. People who weren't eating were talking in low, serious tones, some writing or sketching on scraps of paper or notepads or even tablecloths. By picking up snatches of conversation, Alex learned that Clara Durbin was still missing, as were the other women who had disappeared over the past few days.

They managed to find a table near the kitchen door, and a frazzled waitress took their orders. Conklin's face was still pale; it had blanched while watching the video, and his color had not returned.

"You haven't said much, Cale," Robbie observed. "I know it was grue-some, but when the wolves were on camera, could you get a sense of what's driving them? They can't all be rabid, can they?"

"I didn't see any signs of rabies or distemper," Conklin said. "I still haven't quite processed what I did see."

"I don't think human beings can make sense of something like that," Alex said. "It's just ... it's wrong. Like you said, it isn't natural."

"I would never have believed it. If you didn't have that video I still wouldn't. Wolves don't behave that way. There's this mythology around them—we think about places like Romania, back in Dracula's day, when your coach could be run down by a slavering pack of wolves. But that's fantasy, it doesn't happen in the real world. Only—"

He stopped as the waitress poured coffee for Robbie and Alex, then went away and hurried back with a small pot of tea for Conklin. "Your orders will be up in a couple of minutes," she said. "Sorry, we're kind of swamped. It's usually quiet this time of day."

"That's okay, Grace," Robbie said. "Today's not a usual kind of day. Whenever you can is fine."

A man in a blue work shirt and wheat-colored canvas pants that looked to Alex like something he might have taken off a farmer from the 1880s approached the table. He moved with the hesitation of a teenager, dared by his buddies to ask the prettiest girl in school to dance. "'Scuse me," he said to Conklin. "You the wolf guy?"

"Guess you could call me that."

"We had a question. 'Bout wolves."

Conklin nodded sagely. "Makes sense."

"Where do they live? Don't they have to have some kind of a, what do you call it? A den?"

"Wolves do have dens," Conklin said. "They're usually used by a pregnant wolf, to give birth in. The pups might stay in there until they're ready to face the world. The adult wolves will have a rendezvous site somewhere, and the den or dens might be close by. There's not much about these wolves that's ordinary, though."

The man turned back toward his companions. "A den, it's called. You were right, Bill!" He spun back to Conklin. "How would we find that? The, whatever, rendezvous site and the den?"

A woman seated at a nearby table joined the conversation. "If we could find it, could we kill them that way? Catch them all there and, I don't know, machine-gun them or something?"

"That likely wouldn't be much easier to do at the rendezvous site than it was out in the open," Conklin said. "More difficult, maybe, if some of them went into the den."

"What's it like?" the man asked. "Inside the den?"

"It could be a cave, a hollow in the ground, something like that."

"If we destroyed their site, somehow, would that make them move on?" the woman asked. She had a bandanna tied on her head, with long, dark hair falling from it. Her eyes were quick and lively, and she had big hands, rawboned and chapped and creased from hard work.

"It's impossible to say," Conklin replied. "You're wanting me to characterize what these animals would do based on what typical wolves might do, and I'm not sure there's any correlation."

"How would we find it?" the woman asked.

"Chances are, after the massacre the wolves would have gone back there. They had eaten their fill, from the sound of it. They'd leave the rest where it was and return to the rendezvous site, expecting to be able to go back for seconds when they got hungry again. Since the bodies were recovered, they won't have that option, so when they're hungry they'll hunt again. But I suppose the best chance of finding them all together and as relaxed as they'll ever get would be there."

A man sitting at the table with the woman looked out the big windows at the front of the café. Snow drifted lazily past the outside lights. Most people in the room were paying attention to their conversation; chatter at the other tables had died. "Too late to do anything tonight."

"Hell, yes," another man said. Alex recognized him from the search party. "I'm not goin' out there in the dark. Maybe never again."

"In the daytime, though," the man who had started the discussion said. "I'd be game in daylight."

"What do you want to do?" someone else asked. "Blow it up?"

"Would that work?" Alex asked Conklin.

"I suppose as well as anything. Blow up any dens and do as much damage to the site as you can. Make them understand that it's not a safe harbor."

"I'm in!" someone shouted.

"Same here!"

There was a chorus of assent, general but far from universal. The next thing Alex knew, another man was saying that he knew where to get a bunch of dynamite, from a storage locker at a mine site. "I don't have a key," he said. "But I can get it by morning and bring back as much as we need."

"Is it safe?" Alex asked.

"Safe as things that go boom ever are."

"I mean, is it old? You don't want to just throw old dynamite in the back of your pickup and drive it out into the woods."

"I don't think it's real old," the man said. "Mine was just closed about four months back. Not even closed, really, just temporarily."

"Just check it," Alex urged. "Do you know what to look for?"

"Mister, I worked at that mine for eight years. Don't worry, I know what I'm doing."

"We should meet up here in the morning," Robbie said. "And somebody should check in with Chief Deeds and the DOW folks, make sure we're not fouling up any other plans."

"I'll talk to Morris," the woman said.

"How about here at seven, Robbie?" the former miner said. "That early enough?"

"Should be fine," Robbie said. She took control of the arrangements, and within minutes there was a plan in place. Everybody in the restaurant seemed to know her, and they respected her as a natural leader. Alex had been impressed since he had met her, and seeing the way the people who knew her best responded to her only deepened his appreciation.

Once the details were in place, Alex paid for the meals that he, Robbie, and Conklin had eaten (Alex without really tasting any of it, his attention riveted on the discussion instead), and they bade the scientist good night. Then Alex walked with Robbie back to her shop. Snow coated the sidewalk like a sheet, crumpled where people had passed by, and formed a thick white blanket on the slanted roofs of the buildings across the way. The night was cold, and Alex zipped his coat against the chill.

"So," Robbie said as they neared her door. "Sounds like you've got some 'splainin' to do, Lucy."

"What do you mean?"

"All that stuff about dynamite? And earlier today, at the scene? There are layers you haven't shown me."

"I didn't know you wanted to see."

She put a key in the lock, turned it, and shoved the heavy glass door open. Then she put a hand on Alex's arm. "I've never been much good at subtle," she said. "I think there's something going on here. I mean, between you and me. Or there could be."

"Could be."

"But it's not going anywhere if I feel like we've got secrets. Big ones, I mean. Everybody has little ones. I feel like you're holding back on me, and that leaves me kind of groping around in the dark, wondering if I'm going to say something that offends or shocks or terrifies you. So, you going to tell me, or—"

"Well, if there's going to be groping involved, then I guess I ought to."

Robbie laughed and released him. He followed her inside, and she bolted the door behind them.

CHAPTER TWENTY-SEVEN

M y family owned a company that was called Converse Coal when it began, back in the post-Civil War era," Alex began. They were in Robbie's cluttered back room/office, she in her desk chair and he occupying an ancient gray chair in which the springs were either collapsed or trying to tear free of the fabric. She had turned on an old space heater, and its coils grew bright orange as he talked. "Now it's called Converse Energy, and is about a lot more than just coal. But it's not the family business anymore, either, it's a public company, and I own just enough shares to be completely ignored by the board."

"So that's where all the money comes from?"

"That's right. There was a lot of it, and for generations we kept it in the family. I'm not saying we were the Vanderbilts or the Rockefellers or anything like that, but we were definitely the one-percenters of the day. But we weren't coddled, like in some rich families. One rule was, every kid had to work in the mines. Every summer, from ages fifteen to twenty."

"That's not just a taste."

"No, it was a serious deal. You went in at the bottom of the totem pole. I mean, the other miners knew you were a Converse, but that was a mixed blessing. Sometimes they kept you out of trouble, and other times they targeted you. If you worked hard, you got promoted. The idea was that you'd have at least a good idea of what everybody in the company did, at every level. That way, the theory went, you could manage them wisely."

"Makes sense."

"The Converse family thought so. Anyway, the summer I was seventeen, I was still working underground most of the time, but as an apprentice foreman, so I was up and down, constantly moving between one shaft and another.

"One day at shift change, I was checking the miners as they went down, checking their tags and gear, making sure everybody had the required safety equipment. Coal mining has always been a dangerous job, and they all knew it. But they looked to the company to create the safest working conditions possible. And that was my goal, too. You want everybody who goes underground to come back out at the end of a shift.

"Anyway, on this day—it was the third of June, I remember—one of the miners was nervous. I could tell by the way he was kind of shuffling. His eyes were twitchy. I wondered if maybe he'd been doing speed or something, so I engaged him for a couple of minutes. I took my time checking him out and tried to get him to talk to me. Eventually I figured out that he was just scared. On the verge of panic, really."

"Why?"

"I don't know if it was a premonition, or a bad dream, or what. He wouldn't ever say, but I got the sense that it was something like that. He just had an awful feeling about going into the mine that day. His name was Jared Flannery, and he had these bright green eyes. He told me he had a bad feeling, and I calmed him down. 'Don't worry, Jared,' I said. 'I wouldn't let anything happen to you, would I?' 'I don't know, boss,' he said. So I said, 'Trust me,' and sent him down."

"Why do I get the feeling this doesn't end well for him?"

"Not just for him," Alex said. He hadn't talked about this in so long, he wasn't quite sure how to tell the rest of it. It was technical, and it was terrible, and he felt something akin to Jared Flannery's panic when he thought about continuing. He wondered if he could get away with making up some anticlimactic ending and going back to the motel.

But that wasn't necessarily any better. Charles Durbin might or might not be there, but it didn't sound like Clara would be. Paul and Ellen definitely would not be. He didn't want to face that, not tonight.

He looked at Robbie, waiting expectantly, her lips parted a little, her eyes clear and focused. He wanted, suddenly, to kiss her. He knew that was not a good idea, knew that her reaction could range from kissing back to throwing him across the room to unloading one of her many firearms in his direction.

He took a deep breath and let it out. "Jared Flannery went down, and so did twenty-eight other miners. Not me; I would be going down later, but had some paperwork to take care of first.

"I never got the chance. Because they had been down there about two-and-a-half hours when methane and coal dust exploded in the forty-seven section. Nine miners died right away. Two others were injured, but the explosion caused a cave-in, and we couldn't get to them for eight days. By that time, they had died. Four more were injured but were on the right side of the cave-in, and they got out okay, along with the remaining uninjured ones."

"Oh, my God, Alex. That's awful!"

"Yeah. It was pretty bad. Of course, the families of the missing camped out at the mine for all eight days, at the end of which we couldn't give them any good news. You hate to see miners trapped underground, but at least if they come out alive, there's a happy ending. Not in this case."

"I'm so sorry."

"So was I."

"What happened? Do they know what caused it?"

"Apparently there had been some bad decisions made earlier on—not while I was there—that resulted in stress on the coalbed and face. Those stresses and other factors caused an outburst of methane and coal dust. We had a machine going, called a continuous-mining machine, and it had a sealed compartment containing a light switch and switch control. Rather, the compartment was supposed to be sealed, but it had been closed with a wire hanging out of it, and that wire allowed enough of the combination coal dust and methane atmosphere to get to the switch. When it operated, it ignited the atmosphere. And boom."

"But that wasn't your fault, was it? That switch?"

"I wasn't the one who had closed it, no. But I was the person in charge down there. I should have checked it, should have seen that. I didn't. For those eight days—and weeks after that—I hardly slept. I was at the site nonstop, and when we finally were able to tunnel in to get the bodies out, I was the first one down. I learned everything I ever wanted to know about carrying bodies that day. So when I say I've got a passing familiarity with devastated corpses, I'm not kidding."

She moved then, off her chair and into his, putting her arms around him, drawing him into a hug. She was soft in places and firm in others, and when she spoke he could feel her voice as well as hear it. "What about that one miner? Jared?"

"He was the closest to the ignition," Alex said. "They told me he would have died instantly. A flash, a superheated blast, and he was gone. When I got to him, there wasn't much left but a blackened husk. His eyeballs had exploded and most of his flesh had burned off, and he was curled in on himself as if he had laid down to take a nap."

"I'm sorry I asked," she said again.

"It's okay." It wasn't, not really, but she couldn't have known, and given what he had already told her she couldn't have not asked. "Anyway, that was the end of me being underground. I never wanted to go down again, and nobody asked me to." He cast about for some safe ground, because otherwise he would be moving into treacherous waters, and he wasn't sure he was up for that. Maybe it would be easier with her sitting next to him, squeezed into the big chair, arms around him. But then again maybe it would not be. It would never be easy.

"That was the end of my grandfather's time at the helm," he said. "The public blamed him, not me. He was old, anyway, and close to retirement. My father was already running the company, but people still looked to the old man for direction. But it rained all that week, and we were out in it a lot, and he caught pneumonia and died thirteen days later. So that's another victim on my conscience."

"That wasn't your fault, Alex. You can't blame yourself for the weather."

"I can blame myself for him being outside, not sleeping. That's on me."

"I think you're too hard on yourself."

"You're not the first to tell me that. And thanks. It never really helps, but I don't mind hearing it."

"You're welcome. And I mean it."

"Anyway," Alex continued, "there were only three people who knew that the error was mine. My grandfather, my father, and the foreman I was apprenticing under, Mickey O'Bierne."

"Wasn't it really his fault? If he was the real foreman?"

"He had sent me down to do his job. He might have caught the seal that I'd missed. It's on me. They knew it. My grandfather died, like I said. Seventeen years ago—after the company went public, and we lost our majority share—my father died. Then six months ago—really, just as I was conceiving this project, the documentary—Mickey died." He laughed, a guttural sound, without humor. "I guess the documentary will never get made now. At the time, I thought it was some kind of sign, an omen. The only three people who knew I was at fault were gone. I thought that would be liberating, somehow, but it wasn't. Instead, knowing that I'm the only one living with the secret makes it worse somehow."

"Well, you've shared it with me, now. You're not the only one. Not anymore."

"Thanks for that. And for, you know, everything else. You don't know how much it helps."

"Not a lot, I'd guess. I'm just some small-town chick who hunts shit."

"Yeah," he said, chuckling a little and feeling it this time. "Just some chick, that's right."

He had to tell the rest of it, even though he was afraid. If he didn't spill it now, he might never say it. And the only thing worse than carrying a secret, he had learned, was carrying it alone. "I started having nightmares, after my father died. Bad ones."

"That sucks."

"More than you know. At first it was mine dreams, and it mostly still is. But it's not just that. And—look, Robbie, I know I've been kind of a basket case tonight, and you might wish you had never met me. I hope not. But after what I'm going to tell you, you might really wish that. In a big way."

Her hand was resting on his thigh. He liked it there. "I don't see that happening."

"Okay, well ... the dreams were ... I don't know, precognitive? Predictive? Something like that. Maybe that's what clairvoyant means, I don't know."

"How?"

"At first I wrote them off. They were just bad dreams. Sometimes I saw Jared in the dreams, and he tried to warn me about things happening, but I didn't connect them to anything in the real world. And look, I know this is impossible to believe, but I swear to you, it's all true. Every word I've told you is true."

"I believe you."

"Just keep thinking that. Anyway, then I had this dream where I was trying to get on the 405 freeway, only the freeway sign was in the shafts and Jared kept getting in my way so I couldn't see it. That day, I had a meeting in Burbank, and I was going to take the 405. But that dream kept coming back to me. The urgency with which Jared was getting between me and the sign. So instead of taking the 405 I took Coldwater, through the hills. It was pretty up there. Trees and birds and nature, instead of the grind of the freeway. I was listening to a CD. It wasn't until I got to the meeting that I learned that a sniper had opened fire on the 405, just when I would have been going over it. He caused a massive accident that killed six people. Finally a cop killed him."

He had felt Robbie stiffen up as he told the story. He didn't blame her, wouldn't blame her if she pushed him out of the chair, if she ran away.

But she did neither. Instead, she pressed herself against him and squeezed his thigh and wiped sweat from his forehead. A lock of her hair brushed his cheek, and it felt like a caress. "That is ... you must have been freaked out."

"That's putting it mildly. I was ... I can't even say. I still can't quite believe it. But then, after that, I tried to remember details of some of the other nightmares. I went back and did some research, and learned that I'd been lucky, that some of the other things he had warned me about had also come to pass. They weren't as disastrous, not as fatal, but they were bad and he had warned me."

"In your dreams."

"I told you. Impossible to believe."

"I'm not saying I don't believe you."

"Is this where you say, you believe that *I* believe it?"

"That would be patronizing. I hope you know me better than that."

"I think so. Think I'd like to know you better, too."

"So go on."

"Okay." Another deep breath. In and out. He felt like he was exposing himself, tearing off his clothing and his skin, showing her everything he was on the inside, and he kept being afraid at every moment that she would be repelled by what he offered. "I had another dream. Just a few weeks ago, maybe a month. I was deep into the planning then, for the film. Trying to figure out where to go first, where the effects of climate change could be demonstrated in a real, visceral, visual way. And I had another nightmare. I was in the shafts, and there was coal dust everywhere, so thick I couldn't breathe. I was lost, it was dark—this is essentially the same dream I've had almost every night since I've been here, by the way, with minor but significant differences. I was completely blind, choking, dying, but then Jared came and his eyes, those green eyes, illuminated the shaft, cut through the darkness, and he led me toward ... toward something. I was never quite convinced it was toward salvation, or anything like that. But it was a direction, and that was better than stumbling around until I fell down and died. And in this one a few weeks back, at one point in the shaft we passed a sign, and the sign said, 'Silver Gap.' After I woke up I did some research, found Silver Gap, Colorado, and learned that the trees, the pines, in the area were suffering from an intense bark beetle infestation. It was like he was telling me to come here. So I did."

"I'm glad."

"You think so now. Listen, Robbie, that thing when I was seventeen? Going into the shaft, hauling out those burned, destroyed bodies? That was the worst thing I had ever experienced. Worst thing I thought I would ever experience. I thought I was home free, after that. Nothing could top it, and anyway, I was rich, and the rich can inoculate themselves against many ills. But now, here—this is worse. Far more bodies, far worse injuries. And it was done by wolves, by animals that everybody says just don't act that way."

"They don't."

"See? But they did. I can't help thinking it's because I'm here."

"You didn't bring them. You didn't set them off. The first attack was before you even got here."

"I don't mean that directly. But still, somehow, my presence is ... connected to it."

"Because you saw a sign for Silver Gap in a dream?"

"I still haven't told you all of it," he said. "I'm still having the dreams. Like I said, almost every night since I got here. They're just as bad as ever. The other night I had one, and in it I saw these three women with silver mouths."

"Silver mouths? What do you mean?"

"I don't know. That was just the impression I had at the time. They were afraid, and they had silver mouths. And—"

He shivered. She held him. "Go on, Alex."

"And one of the women was Clara Durbin."

"Clara, who disappeared today."

"That's right."

"When did you have this dream, Alex?"

"Last night. Before she disappeared. And there's one more thing."

"I don't know, Alex, this is pretty creepy already."

"I know. But I have to say it now. You can kick me out when I'm done. Point one of your guns at me and send me packing."

"Not a chance."

"Before Clara disappeared, I was in the apartment she and Charles have. There in the lodge. And I saw a photograph there, that showed Clara and her brother, years ago. She was just a kid, really."

"And?"

"And her brother was Jared Flannery."

"He looked like Jared?"

"He *was* Jared. Charles confirmed it. Clara's maiden name is Flannery. She came from Kentucky, where the mine was. Where I knew Jared."

Robbie had gone white, and it was his turn to soothe her. He held her tight and pressed his cheek against hers and fought off the urge to do more, and after she had stopped trembling she swallowed and said, "That is strange, Alex. That's ... I don't even know. I just don't."

"I don't either. I know it's impossible. You probably think I saw the picture and then had the dreams or something, but I *knew* Jared. And I've been having the same basic dreams for years, long before I ever met Clara. It *means* something, Robbie. It has to. But I don't know what it is, and I don't know if I can figure it out. And if it has to do with Clara's disappearance, then I have to, and fast. She's been nothing but kind to me, and if there's something I can do, I have to do it."

"Because you're a good man," she said.

"I don't know about that. Maybe. I have my moments, I guess. Right now, though, I feel like a failure. Like if I can't find out what this is all about, and something happens to her, that'll ... well, it'll be the last straw. I don't know what it all has to do with me, but it has something, and I have to find that answer. I just have to."

CHAPTER TWENTY-EIGHT

She had a house less than a block from the shop, out the back door and through the alley and then through a gate in her fence and up three stairs and they went in the kitchen door. The house was small but it was neat, surprisingly so considering the shop, but she said that was because she spent most of her time in the shop or in the field and mostly went home to shower, eat, and sleep.

They didn't eat, and it was a while before they slept. When his lips met hers for the first time, it was like coming home after a long absence. They tore off their clothes, and he was enthralled by her muscular arms and shoulders and the lush, heavy terrain of her breasts and the blonde patch of her pubis. He didn't think he was much of a specimen, comparatively, but she seemed to like him and he was glad that she did. They held each other on the bed and then moved closer, grasping and clawing with ferocious urgency, and their lovemaking was frenzied, as if by moving together in a fevered heat they could burn away the terror that gripped him when he thought about what had happened, and what would have to happen tomorrow.

After a while, they dozed, and then they showered and then returned to bed and this time the sex was slower, almost stately in its pace, as he explored her body with hands and mouth and then plumbed its moist depths until he exploded in her, and after some rest she explored him, with ultimately the same result. Then they slept, really slept, and his sleep was largely dreamless. One time, the nightmare started; he found himself in the dark tunnel, but he moaned and shifted a little in the bed and Robbie turned against him and nuzzled into his cheek and the dream vanished like a soap bubble popped on a fingertip.

Reverend Calderon was alone in his office. The church was closed, the front door locked because of the strong winds and snow, and his office door was locked. A space heater buzzed near his desk, blowing warm air across him. He had a glass of brandy on the desk, just a small one because Dr. Steinhilber said alcohol was probably not a good idea, not just that it might make his vision worse but even under optimal circumstances, excessive use could affect the vision, and he couldn't afford that. He needed clarity on this night. He needed to be able to see, and he needed to be able to think.

What he had done with Christy Deeds—what he would, apparently, continue to do, as long as she lived and he lived and they were in any kind of proximity at all—was wrong. That much was easy to discern. It went against the teachings of the Bible and of Jesus Christ and of everything he understood about God the Father. She was married to another. Even if she had not been, she was not married to him.

Honestly, he was pretty sure that Jesus wouldn't have cared whether two people who loved each other were married, but all the teachings of his faith told him that marriage was a covenant in the eyes of the Lord and that covenant was what made the rest of it, the things he and Christy did when they were together, okay. Without that sacred bond, it was sinful, and they had performed what he believed was a truly impressive catalog of sinful acts in any number of imaginative, erotic positions and places. The woman had a delightfully creative imagination, one that she claimed her husband had never appreciated.

It had to end, but he was a weak man, not worthy of his position, and he knew he would not end it. Christy needed to be strong, she needed to call quits to it. For a while she had, but then she had backslidden, as they said at seminary, and he had been happy to see the backside that appeared before him as a result of that backslide.

But he loved her. He wanted her. He wanted her to vanish, to never step into his church again, to remove the temptation he could not resist. And he wanted Chief Deeds to vanish so there would no longer be that obstruction coming between them. He sat down at his desk and started to write a letter to Christy, to tell her the things he couldn't say in person, that he loved her but that he could never be with her again, and if she didn't keep her distance he would have to leave town. But then he changed his mind and tore the letter up and threw the scraps in his wastebasket, and then he decided that he should burn them instead.

He was reaching for them when he saw headlights outside. A vehicle—a police department SUV, he realized—came to a stop in the parking lot, but the headlights stayed on, burning through his window like the eyes of the Lord.

So he didn't need to write a letter at all. Chief Deeds had found out, had come to confront him. There would be words, there might even be physical violence. Then he would have to leave town. Morris would give him no choice.

He went to the door, shaking with fear of the coming confrontation but feeling his heart lightened at the same time. It was over, temptation was gone. He would leave Silver Gap, at Morris's insistence. He would never be alone with Christy again, or any of the other women in his congregation who had made themselves available to him. He would start over in some other place, and he would get a better handle on his urges there. He would seek the counsel of someone older and wiser, another priest, to help him be strong.

He unlocked the door, threw it open. "Morris," he said. "Come in."

"It isn't Morris, Reverend Fuckbuggy," someone said.

Calderon was confused. He was sure the vehicle belonged to the police department, and though he couldn't see the man clearly, he appeared to be in uniform. He definitely had a belt with a holster and other equipment hanging from it.

"Who—?"

"I know what you've been doing. I know where you've been dipping that fuckstick of yours, that holy rolling fuckstick, and I'm here to tell you that it's got to stop!"

"I know," Calderon said. "That's what I've been thinking about all night. But I'm sorry, you are—"

"Don't pretend you don't know me, Fuckbuggy. You've been busy with the chief's wife, and he's ten times the man you'll ever be."

"Honeycutt?"

"Don't say my name! You don't deserve to have it in your mouth. Don't say the chief's name, either, or I'll kill you where you stand."

"Honeycutt, this is absurd, why are you—"

And then he stopped, because he couldn't see well but he could see that Honeycutt had drawn his pistol, and he assumed, though it had vanished from sight, that it was pointed at him.

"You are *filth*! Fucking fuckeroonie of filthy filth!" Honeycutt took a few steps toward him.

Calderon raised his hands, then brought his palms together. This, he decided, was no time for reason, it was a time for prayer. "Our heavenly father," he began.

Honeycutt fired, twice.

Calderon heard the reports, felt the hot missiles penetrate his clothing and his sinner's flesh, felt his insides as the bullets tore through. He fell to his knees, and opened his mouth to ask forgiveness, but the words would not come. And as he pitched forward, knowing he had reached the end; he knew also that soon he would meet his Lord or not, but even if not then at least the question that hovered at the edge of consciousness, always, for every believer, would soon be answered.

Honeycutt was still muttering, nonsense words, and Calderon felt himself being dragged out into the gravel of the parking lot. He didn't feel the man's hands on him, but he felt the small rocks as he scraped across them. He could hear the words but could not make them out. He could see Honeycutt, more clearly than ever, with a glow around him that might have come from the headlights but he thought not.

"The ravens," he heard Honeycutt say, and he understood that. "And the wolves. They'll get you here. No one will know a thing, Right Reverend Fuckeroonie Fuckbuggy, and you'll never—"

And then the voice faded out again, the words whisked away by the wind that wafted snowflakes through the headlight beams, and Honeycutt dropped him there, and there he stayed.

CHAPTER TWENTY-NINE

The gathering at the Cup & Cow in the morning was smaller and more solemn than the one the night before. The people who showed up seemed to understand that they were heading out on what could easily be a suicide mission, and they were appropriately subdued. Morris Deeds paced the front of the room and a couple of his cops, Jones and Honeycutt, sat at a table close by. The snow had stopped for a while during the night, but it was falling again.

Alex and Robbie had a table at the side, close to the bakery counter, and though people stopped by to share a few words with Robbie, no one else sat with them. Alex was on his third cup of coffee for the day. He was tired, but it was a good tired. His relationship with Robbie was in a state of flux, new and uncertain, and since they had arrived in a public place, she had been strictly hands-off. He accepted that—she knew these people, lived with them, and once he was gone, back to LA, she would still be here.

When Cale Conklin came in the front door, he looked around for a moment, then cut a straight path toward their table. Alex shoved out the chair opposite him with his foot. "Sit," he said. "They're serving, if you want coffee or breakfast."

"Glass of water would be good," Conklin said. He sat and scooted the chair back in close. "Been on the phone since five."

"With who?"

"Couple of colleagues I sent data from our necropsy to. They still have to get the tissue samples tested, but I was able to email photos and measurements and observations, and we had a conference call this morning."

"Did you reach any conclusions?" Robbie asked.

Conklin lowered his voice, to the point that Alex could barely hear him across the table. "Just tentative ones. Until we have the tissue results, that's the best we can do. And, honestly, I don't even like to say what we decided out loud."

"How bad can it be?" Alex asked.

"It can be pretty far out there. Look, I'm a scientist. And not one of those theoretical types. I'm a naturalist. I work with the real world. I observe and study and report. The work I do, it's not as much about testing hypotheses as about recording and reporting on the world around us."

Alex felt a familiar tingle of fear on the back of his neck. Conklin's disclaimer sounded like the kind of thing he had told himself, thousands of times, when he started to accept that his nightmares actually had some connection to reality. "Granted," he said. "Don't worry about us, we're not judging."

"Okay." Conklin reached over and took Alex's untouched water glass, downing half of it. "Here's the deal. Trust me, I know how impossible it sounds. Your wolves—at least, the specimen you guys brought in, and judging from the video the others as well—they're not normal gray wolves."

Robbie smiled. "We kind of figured that."

"Yeah, well, I doubt that you figured out just *how* not normal they are. I have a hard time saying this out loud. Even after a couple of hours on the phone with people who know this stuff far better than I do. But what it looks like is these wolves are a hybrid. Gray wolf, plus something else. And what the something else is is what makes it so nuts."

"You're killing me here," Alex said.

"Sorry. Okay, here it is. The wolves appear—emphasis on that, until we get some good DNA evidence—they *appear* to be a hybrid of the gray wolf and the dire wolf."

"No way," Robbie said. "That's impossible."

"That's what I'm saying."

"Fill me in," Alex said. "What is that? A dire wolf?"

Conklin took another big swallow of water, then continued. "Dire wolf. *Canis dirus*. A carnivorous mammal at one time relatively common in

North and South America. In fact, while the gray wolf is a European or Eurasian transplant, the dire wolf evolved here in North America."

"*Once* common, you said?" Alex looked from Conklin to Robbie. She was nodding her head as Conklin answered.

"Oh, yeah, once. For probably just under two million years. Right up until ten to fifteen thousand years ago, when they became extinct."

"They're extinct?"

"For a long time now."

"They were huge, right?" Robbie asked.

"A lot bigger than the gray. The two coexisted in North America, for maybe a hundred thousand years. Eventually the gray succeeded, where the dire didn't. But yeah, they were big. You can see it in the skulls, in the teeth. The dire had shorter legs, proportionate to its body size, than the gray. Short but sturdy."

"Like the one we found," Alex said.

"Right. The dire wolf is a prime example of North America megafauna, the big animals that lived during the Pleistocene but died out around ten thousand years back. They've been studied extensively—for one thing, the La Brea tar pits held a lot of specimens, in relatively whole skeletons, for us to look at. That's why we're pretty convinced of our theory, even before we have DNA to back it up. We know what the dire looked like, we know what gray wolves look like, and we can extrapolate what a hybrid would look like. And that would be the one sitting in Doctor Steinhilber's freezer."

"But ... I'm not following. If the dire wolf is extinct, then how did it crossbreed with gray wolves? The ones we're talking about are clearly still alive."

"That's something else we're not sure about," Conklin said. "My colleagues are working on that question while they wait for the tissue samples to be analyzed. They'll get back to me as soon as they have something."

"This is a little hard to swallow, Cale," Robbie said. "I mean, if you say it's so, then I believe you. But I don't know that you should spread it around until you have that confirmation. Bad enough that these folks think they're after some sort of wolves gone mad. But if they find out they're, I don't know, superwolves? That's going to make things that much tougher."

"Yeah, I'm with you," Conklin said. "I was planning to go up today, with the search party, but I think I'll stay here instead. I've got a couple of theories I want to check out, and it'll mean spending a lot of time with my laptop and a pencil and paper."

"That's fine," Robbie said. "I mean, it would be great to have you with us. But it sounds like you have more important work to do."

"That's what I think," Conklin said. The words were barely out of his mouth when Morris Deeds called for the room's attention.

"I expect we're all here that's coming," he said. "From the looks of the street, there's enough vehicles that everybody could take their own and we'd still have some left over. I don't want anybody driving alone, though. Let's buddy up, two to four to a truck. Four-wheel drive only. The state DOW has decided they don't want any part of this, so it's just us. Anybody got a problem with any of it, now's the time to walk."

He let that sit in the air for a minute. Nobody budged. "All right then," he said. "Let's go find us a wolf den."

Once again, Chief Deeds insisted that Robbie ride with him, and she insisted that Alex be included. Honeycutt drove, and the backseat was a little crowded with Jones in there, too. They were barely out of town when Deeds took a call on his cell phone. He mostly listened for a couple of minutes, then ended the call. "Well, shit," he said. "That's not a good way to start the day."

"What's up, Chief?" Honeycutt asked.

"Reverend Calderon's dead."

"What?" Robbie said.

"He is?" Honeycutt asked.

"That's what I *said*, goddamnit! Charles Durbin went out to the church this morning, said he wanted Calderon to call some of the congregation in, get a bigger search party going. When he got there, Calderon's office door was wide open but nobody was around. He looked inside, then saw blood in the parking lot. He followed the trail and found Calderon's body at the edge of the woods. Some animal got to him, don't know yet if it was wolves or what. He called Norman—that's Doctor Steinhilber, Mr. Converse—who took a look and said that maybe wolves or something munched on him postmortem, but there are a couple of bullets in him, too. That's when they called Althea. Ortega's on his way over there."

"This town," Honeycutt said. "No killings for I don't know how long, and then all of a sudden. Women vanishing, people getting eaten up. Man alive."

That final comment seemed the height of inappropriateness to Alex, but he was a guest in a police vehicle, and so held his tongue. They rode back out to the site of the slaughter mostly in silence, with Honeycutt making a few conversational overtures that quickly petered out. Nobody, save him, was in the mood for chatter. Robbie's thigh pressed against Alex's, but that might have had more to do with the full backseat than her intentions. Her hands stayed on her own lap.

At the site, people piled from the vehicles and spread out, looking for tracks. They'd been everywhere, of course, wolf and human alike, a chaotic mess of them overlapping each other. Alex remembered that from yesterday. But the snow had fallen for long hours since then, obscuring everything. Alex couldn't look at the canyon without remembering the way it had looked and smelled, but now, even though the abandoned trucks had been left in place, the snow covering it all lent the scene an illusion of virginal innocence it didn't deserve.

He stood back and let the practiced trackers do their thing. In a little while, someone waved the others over. Robbie got there first, and when she confirmed that the man had discovered something useful, they began the laborious challenge of tracking the animals through the snow while others followed in the vehicles. Honeycutt had a hard time getting the police department Tahoe—its cargo area loaded with guns, boxes of ammo, and crates of dynamite—through the thicker drifts and up over hidden rocks and dips.

Fortunately for Alex's sanity and the health of those doing the legwork, the wolves beat a relatively direct path, always rising toward the tree line. The pines at the higher elevation were mostly dead, their branches bare and hung with snow, red-brown needles showing only occasionally through the white.

They were just approaching the tree line when they found the rendezvous site.

It was just below a ridge. There was a hollow there, a kind of depression in the earth ringed by boulders, somewhat protected from the elements by the trees and rocks surrounding it. A stream ran through it, half-frozen but still trickling, and a few pines yet lived. The snow was beaten down and discolored by the presence of many animals and mottled with pine needles. Set into the hillside were a series of openings, with diameters anywhere from eighteen inches to three and a half feet. Trails cut this way and that from the openings. There were no wolves here, at least none visible from outside. That fact made Alex nervous, and he kept looking behind them, scanning the near distances.

They had reached it on foot, parking below the ridge, about twenty yards downhill. Almost everybody carried a gun. "That's got to be the place," Deeds said.

Robbie agreed. "Looks like it to me."

"Coast looks pretty clear, too."

"No way to know what's inside those holes," Alex pointed out.

"There's one way," Honeycutt said. "One sure way."

"Somebody's got to go in there," Deeds said. "Plant the dynamite."

"I'll do it, Chief," Honeycutt said eagerly. "Glad to."

"It's got to be me," Alex muttered.

"What?" Deeds said. "You say something, Mr. Converse?"

"It's got to be me," he said, louder this time.

"I hate to say it," Robbie said, "but he's right."

"He is?"

"I have experience," Alex said.

"With dynamite?"

"With dynamite *and* tunnels," Alex said.

"Alex," Robbie said, "these are not going to be like mine shafts, you know. No support beams, no lights. Not big enough to stand up, much less turn around in."

"I know that."

"What kind of experience are you talking about?" Deeds wanted to know.

"Coal mining."

"I thought you made movies."

"I come from a coal family. I've spent plenty of time in the mines. I've planted charges. I know how to do it, how far apart to set them, how to attach the blasting caps and feed out the fuse. You got anybody else on this hill who's done more of it and more recently than me, we can talk. But I know I can do it safely and get out."

Deeds raised his voice. "Anybody here work in the mining industry?"

One man raised his hand, the one who had said in the restaurant that he had put in eight years there. "What'd you do?" Deeds asked him.

"Accountant."

"Never mind." He looked at Alex. "Guess you're it."

"You sure about this, Alex?" Robbie asked.

He was afraid his voice would quake, betraying the panic bubbling just beneath the surface. "Hell, no. But I don't see any better options, do you?"

"We don't even know for sure if this will work."

"We don't know that it won't. I guess we ought to try."

"Look, Robbie," Deeds said. "The man says he can do it. Let's let him do it. Honeycutt, Jones, bring up that dynamite and stuff!"

The two officers hustled back to the vehicle. Alex had checked everything out earlier. They had about twenty-five sticks of dynamite. It had been kept cool and dry, and there was no nitroglycerin seepage, which was a good sign. He hadn't tested the blasting caps, but they looked well cared for. There was a good length of fuse, and a detonator, though a truck battery would have done the trick in a pinch.

He wasn't worried about his materials. He was worried about himself. Would he be able to do it? He hadn't been underground since that last day at the mines, bringing out the bodies. He had never been inside what he assumed the dens would look like. As Robbie had pointed out, these would not be professionally excavated shafts, but natural caves and animal tunnels. He might have to squeeze through them on his belly, then back out the same way, knowing that there were blasting caps attached to the dynamite and having no control over who on the outside might be holding the fuse to the detonator.

The cops carried two crates back up to the ridgeline. One held the dynamite and the other the blasting caps, in their own separate container, and the fuse and detonator. Alex gave the chief and everybody else watching a quick lesson in how it worked, and he stressed that the fuse should not be allowed anywhere near the detonator until he was back out of the den and everybody had moved well away from the area. "This hillside is going to go up in the air and come down again," he said. "We don't have time for me to take a lot of care with how I plant the stuff, so I won't have a lot of control over what direction it's going. Everybody's going to have to move back a good distance, and get under cover if you can. And nobody uses the detonator but me. Is that understood?"

Deeds didn't like being ordered around, but he nodded his head. Alex told the cops to put the crate with the dynamite down near one of the larger entrances, and to put the blasting caps and fuse with it. He handed the detonator to the chief, who traded him a Maglite for it, and he started down the slope. Someone grabbed his arm. He turned, startled, and Robbie was there, pressing a pistol into his free hand. "You don't know what's in those holes," she said. "And nobody can be in there to watch your back."

"If there's a bunch of wolves in there, I'll be back momentarily."

"I bet. Still, use this if you have to."

"Thanks," he said.

"And, Alex."

"Yeah?"

She leaned into him, brought her face near, and planted her lips on his. She held them there for a long time, her hands pressing against his back, holding him against her body. When she broke the kiss, she said, "Come back soon. I thought of some more things I want to try."

There were good natured whoops and hollers from the assembled people, most of them men. Alex was sure he was blushing. He took another step down the hill, then stopped again and picked up a fallen branch, snapping off a section about two feet long. "Chief, your men have to turn their radios off. Anybody else who's got one, get it off. Radio signals can set off blasting caps."

"We just rode all the way up here with the caps in the back and the radio in the Tahoe on, plus our personal radios," Deeds said.

"I forgot."

Deeds grinned. "Turn 'em off, boys," he commanded. He switched his off, and the others did the same.

Alex did the easy part first, digging out narrow holes around the roots of the pines inside the rendezvous site and planting dynamite there. It helped him to remember how to do it all, how to attach the blasting caps and tie on the detonation cord, there in the daylight. That done, he turned to the more difficult task—the dens.

The smell of the wolves came from the entrance on puffs of air, as if the earth itself was breathing. It was pungent and smelled like life.

He hesitated there. He had a flashlight and a length of branch in one hand and a gun in the other. He bent over and shined the light in the hole, revealing a passageway that didn't contract much as far as he could see down it. He couldn't walk in it, even hunched over, but he could easily go on hands and knees. But not with the gun and the flashlight and the crate.

And he was afraid. He didn't like admitting it, even to himself, but fear was locking his joints up. Despite the cold and the snow that still fell, sweat ran down his sides.

But he had to do it anyway. He knew that as surely as he knew the cold and the snow and the smell, the dampness seeping up through boots not meant for this kind of punishment, the unfamiliar hard shape of the pistol. He had been afraid since that summer week of his seventeenth year. Afraid that someone would realize that the fault was his, afraid to be underground, afraid of the dark, sometimes, because it reminded him of what those trapped miners must have felt as their lamps blinked out and the coal dust filled their eyes. Fear had been holding him back, he thought. He had spent his whole life without a real job, any accomplishments of note, a successful relationship. He had been skating on the surface of life.

He was under no illusions that crawling into a tunnel and planting sticks of dynamite would solve those problems, turn him into a new man.

But it might be a start.

He liked Robbie—*really* liked her, in a way he hadn't liked anybody in a long time. He didn't know if he could love her, or if she could love him, or if they could make it work even if both unknowns proved true. They were so different. He might, he thought, like to make a life with her, or try to.

To do that, he would have to do *this*.

She was watching. She would require courage from a man, would need him to live up to his promises. He resisted the urge to look back at her. He knew she was there, knew she wanted him to go in and to come out again.

He went to his hands and knees, tucked the gun into his waistband at the small of his back, laid the piece of branch across the top of the crate and shoved the crate in ahead of him. He played the flashlight all around. The area around the opening was worn smooth, and there were tufts of fur here and there, but it was mostly clean. Apparently, wolves didn't shit at home.

He pushed the crate farther and went in behind it.

The interior was slightly warmer than outside, because there was no snow falling on him, no wind. He knew temperatures underground could be remarkably consistent, summer and winter, but he didn't know if that applied to as shallow a tunnel as this seemed to be.

Progress was slow. He had to shine the light ahead and push the crate and then crawl up behind it, watching the tunnel's height because he didn't want to scrape the gun in his pants against the ceiling. There was fur everywhere, matted on the ground, stuck to the sides, and the smell of their musk was strong. He saw bone fragments, pine straw, sticks and leaves the animals had carried in.

He didn't have a drill and didn't want to spend that much time anyway, nor was the result of his efforts required to be as precise as if he had been blasting in a mine. All he wanted to do was to bring these tunnels down, collapse the dens. Not a lot of specificity was needed.

As he went, he bored into the sides with the length of branch, then attached a blasting cap to a stick of dynamite, twisted the detonation cord on, and pushed a stick of dynamite in as far as his fingers could reach. He tamped it deeper with the branch. You didn't want to use anything metal, not at that point. Wood was the way to go.

The tunnel got smaller, though not prohibitively so. But then it connected with another one, and this one he would have had to pass through on his belly, dragging himself along on his arms. He went in less than one body length and felt panic return. With shaking hands, he clawed away a depression barely deep enough to shove the dynamite in sideways. He put on the blasting cap, knowing that because the dynamite itself was relatively stable, the blasting cap was the real danger; he had seen men who had lost fingers or hands or, in the case of a retired miner he had met, one eye and most of his nose and his upper lip, because of a blasting-cap accident. He put one stick on each side and backed out of the tunnel, back into the main one.

He didn't know how much time was elapsing, didn't want to start looking at his watch because then he would never stop. At some point the wolves would return, and if he was still inside, he would die. The people outside, Robbie and Chief Deeds and the rest, would shoot, but the wolves had already proven they could not be defeated by people with guns. There had been more people and more guns with the DOW group that had been torn to shreds than there were defending the rendezvous site. So even if he heard a cacophony of gunfire, some wolves would get past them. And he would die.

There were more side tunnels, and he could see that some of them connected to the other openings he had seen from outside, but others seemed to go ever deeper into the earth. This den was a maze, and he wondered how long these impossible wolves had used it. He couldn't explore every avenue. He didn't have time or energy or enough courage for that. So he planted dynamite where he thought it would be most effective and he twisted on the cord and he played the spool out.

Finally, he was out of dynamite. There were blasting caps remaining, but he didn't care. He left the branch and the caps and he unrolled the spool as he went, hurrying from the tunnel as fast as he could go without hitting something and injuring himself. For a moment he was afraid he had made a wrong turn, but then he realized that he was headed the right way, but the sky had grown darker and the snow was falling more heavily and the sun had ceased to break through the layer of clouds.

Then he was outside, and a small cheer erupted from the watchers, led by Robbie. She met him halfway up the hill and she kissed him again and she whispered, "You will get the fucking of your life tonight, mister." He wanted to say something in return, something clever and flirty and funny, but his voice had left him.

Chief Deeds took over, anyway. "Okay, everybody, move back!" he called. "Way, way back. Jones, take the spool from Mr. Converse. He looks plenty tired, and he's done everything so far."

Jones did as his chief ordered. "Thank you, sir," he said as he took the spool from Alex's hands. "You've done a good thing here."

"Hope so," Alex managed. He was wasted, he realized. All the strength seemed to go out of him at once, and he wasn't sure he would even be able to stay awake for Robbie's reward. He showed Jones how to keep unspooling the fuse, and they took it out as far as it could go, about eighty feet from the tunnel. He wasn't sure that was far enough, but he had used a lot of it inside, crisscrossing all the various paths he had taken. It was what it was.

"Everybody take cover," he said. "On the ground, arms over your head. I have no idea how far this stuff is gonna blow."

Deeds watched to make sure everybody had obeyed. When they had, he said, "Okay, Mr. Converse. Show us how it's done."

Although Deeds had assured him that everyone was safe, Alex made a quick visual check for himself. Mostly he was looking for Robbie, but she was close by, a dozen feet away, with her knees and head on the ground, arms protecting her skull. Satisfied, he connected the wire to the control box. He wished he had one of the old-fashioned plunger detonators, because for such a primitive task it seemed more fitting. But he had a modern electronic control box instead. Certain that he was breaking all manner of laws and OSHA regulations, he called out, "Fire in the hole!" Pressed the button labeled "Charge" and held it down, building up the power. When the indicator light came on, he kept that button depressed and pushed the one marked "Fire."

Then he set the box down in the snow and assumed the position.

The blast shook the earth. The den's tunnels had not been far enough below the surface to contain the force of the explosion. Dirt and mud and snow and roots and bits of trees and shrubs flew skyward, reached their apex, and then turned back toward home. The rocks hit first, slamming down like the devil's rain, and then dirt in clods and brown snow and the rest of it all at once, thumping and pattering and crashing to the ground. People shouted and a couple screamed, and when it was over there were bloody scalps and cut hands and no doubt a lot of bruises under coats and down vests and sweaters and the like. But nobody was seriously injured, and most of them were laughing at the sheer spectacle of it.

Robbie came to Alex and hugged him again and then held his left hand as they walked up the hill. People were coming up to them and congratulating him, clapping him on the back, shaking his hand. Were they cheering him for his demolitions expertise, or for getting Robbie to hold his hand? Even that strange cop, Honeycutt, shook his head, a huge grin on his skinny face, and said, "Fuck if that weren't the fuckingest fuckeroonie I ever seen!" Alex wasn't exactly sure what he meant by that, but he chose to take it as a compliment.

The den was history. It was a collapsed ruin, with most of its roof gone and whatever tunnels might have been left filled in by the debris. The pines had been felled, one all the way and one leaning precariously. Sections of the stream's banks had tumbled into the water. Alex felt a moment's sorrow for the wolves that had used this place. He was glad there hadn't been any pups inside, as Conklin had suspected there might be. He didn't know if he would have been able to pull the trigger on a pup, and he would have hated to see wolf parts falling from the sky.

He had been described as a rabid environmentalist, and yet he had just performed what was probably the most environmentally destructive act of his life. With luck, one he would never surpass. He had torn the top off this hill, just as surely as his ancestors had blown the tops off mountains throughout Appalachia. Same idea, smaller scale.

That these wolves had attacked and killed human beings, including people he had known, made it a little better.

Not a lot.

While he stood there looking at his handiwork, Morris Deeds approached him with his chest puffed out and his right hand extended. "I guess maybe I've been wrong about you, Mr. Converse. A cop has to size people up in a hurry, and most of the time we're right. But a man's got to be able to admit when he's not. That was a good thing you did here.

Denied those wolves their safe haven. Don't know if it'll be enough to make them relocate, but it can't hurt."

"All I did was plant the charges," Alex said. "But thanks just the same."

"You didn't see any inside?"

"No. Lots of fur. They've been here, for sure, but they're not here now."

"Hmm," Deeds said, gazing off into the distance. "Wonder where in the hell they are."

CHAPTER THIRTY

Clara Durbin understood that panic would only work against her.

Her hands were tied behind her back and her legs were bound and she had something draped over her head, a rough, scratchy fabric of some kind, loose-fitting but impossible to shake off. Her mouth was sealed with tape and she was inside some kind of building, but it was cold, wickedly so, and the floor was uneven, raw wood. She could hear the wind howling outside and every now and then the sound of something, probably snow, pelting against a window. It had been dark but now it was lighter, she could tell that much through the hood. And wherever she was stank like nothing she had ever known, like she imagined it would smell if she were inside a sewer underneath a meatpacking plant.

Howie had brought her here and he'd stayed a while. She had heard him moving around, eating something, she thought, and making other noises she couldn't interpret. Sometimes he spoke to her, but of course she couldn't answer. Once he hit her in the side of the head, hard, with what felt like a balled fist. There was a bruise there, she was sure, and probably swelling but she couldn't put her hand up to check. Once he had groped her left breast, under her coat but through her sweater. She didn't know if he had found it not to his liking, but he had let go after a few seconds and had not tried it again. She had tried to kick him, but her legs were tied together and she was sitting and had no leverage or freedom of movement.

But now daylight had come. She had spent some of yesterday and all night here, and she knew Charles must be frantic. The town had probably organized a search party, as it had for Marie Hackett and Barb Johnston. In those cases, she knew, the searches had been unsuccessful.

During the long hours of darkness and stillness except for the wind, she had despaired. She would never see Charles again, never set foot in the lodge. She would die and the flesh would rot off her bones and she would never again walk in the sunshine or sit in a window watching snowflakes or drink wine or taste her husband's salty cheek after he had painted one of the rooms. She was as certain of these things as she was of her own name, of her love for Silver Gap, of her faith in the Lord and her delight in the way that Reverend Calderon interpreted His teachings.

But daylight had come and with it, hope.

Just a glimmering, so far. She had always been an optimistic sort, always believed that after each storm, the sun would shine again. And here in this cold room, bound and hooded and gagged, that optimism only carried so far. She had been sitting on the floor in more or less the same position all these hours—once, she had shifted so that she was lying down on her side, hoping that she would be able to sleep that way, but then she panicked, afraid she wouldn't be able to sit up again. She managed, but the process had been long and full of pain she wouldn't willingly endure again. So she sat against the wall and even slept that way a few times, not for long but for minutes or perhaps an hour at a time.

And shifting uncomfortably, trying to ease the aches that had settled in, she had discovered a large splinter on the wall behind her, a section of wood sticking out from the planks forming the wall, and she had caught her head covering on it, and only hours later did it occur to her that if she snagged it just right, maybe she could peel the hood off and she would be able to see where she was. Seeing, she was certain, was a precursor to finding a way out. First one, then the other. Logical.

Logic helped fend off panic. So did prayer. So did action.

So—praying for forgiveness and for salvation of the physical as well as spiritual natures—Clara set to work, trying to snag the hood she wore on the dagger of wood.

With no way of measuring the passage of time, she didn't know how long she spent at it. Judging by the number of times her stiff muscles cried out in protest, it must have been hours. The daylight grew brighter, even filtered through the fabric, and the place she was in warmed slightly, and the wind changed from a howl to a high-pitched whistle.

And then she heard something else on the wind. A new kind of howling, made by throats instead of air currents.

There must have been ten of them. No, more. They were far away still, and she went on trying to catch the hood with renewed urgency. She almost had it once, had it well snagged, and she began the even more awkward process of trying to peel her head out from under it, but then she heard the animals howling much, much closer and she started and the hood pulled free of the spike.

The approach of what had to be wolves made her heart pound. She could hear the rush of blood in her ears and her muscles, already weak and cramped, became even more reluctant. Clara was trembling as much as she had during the worst moments of the cold night, and as she tried to hook the fabric again her head drummed against the wall.

Outside, the wolves came closer still.

Then she got the hood caught, a good, firm connection. She heard the fabric tear as the wood speared through it. She prayed aloud as she struggled once again to pull her head free. The head covering caught on her chin, so she clamped her mouth shut—He could hear silent prayers just as well as those spoken aloud, she believed—and tried again, tilting her head to press her chin toward her neck. This time, the hood slid easily past that obstacle.

She had to shift her bottom on the hard, wooden floor in order to get her head lower than the splinter, which she had to do or else risk moving her head away from the wall—and therefore releasing the caught fabric—as she tried to pull free. That shift almost did it anyway. She felt the fabric tug and was certain it would release, but she froze in place and it didn't.

Her back screamed with the agony of the angle, shoulders against the wall, bottom well away from it. But she was able to continue the progress she had made, easing her head down and down, then another shift of her rear—pain lancing through her—and she felt it slip past her ears. A final tug, and she collapsed sideways on the floor. The hood, a brown piece of something like a burlap bag, fluttered down on top of her. She shook it off.

She was in a cabin. The knotty pine walls were unfinished, as was the floor. It was small, although from her position she could see an upper corner of something that might have been a door to another room, perhaps a bathroom. By tilting her head slightly she could see a front door of heavy planks with crossbars and iron hardware. There was what looked like a bed against one wall, beneath a curtained window, and a small kitchen area with a table and two chairs.

Getting the hood off intensified the stench surrounding her. She could see the ropes that held her fast, now, but with her hands behind her back she still didn't know how to get herself untied. She would think of something, though. Getting her eyes back was critical. What she needed now was a broader view of her surroundings.

She needed to stand up.

Given the shaky status of her muscles, that looked to be considerably harder than getting the hood off.

She started by wrenching herself back up to a sitting position. Spear-points stabbed her from every direction, especially at the small of her back, her shoulders, and between the shoulder blades. She did her best to ignore them and reasoned out her next step.

Outside, a wolf howled. Others answered it. She wondered when Howie might come back. She wondered what that smell was.

She planted her feet firmly in front of her and raised her bottom off the floor a few inches, then leaned back against the wall. It hurt, but it worked. Slowly, her legs straining, every muscle she had complaining, she pushed up with her legs and used her hands to help make her way up the wall. Inch by agonizing inch she rose, until exhaustion overtook her. She still wasn't entirely upright, but she was close. She waited there, panting and sweating inside her coat and sweater and flannel-lined pants, and took another look around the cabin.

Barb Johnston was lying on the bed, faceup. She was nude, her legs spread, and she had been opened up in the middle. The bedding was soaked with blood and who knew what else, and Clara could see coils of intestine at the opening. Barb's head was on a pillow and her eyes were open and she was looking at Clara. Her mouth was taped shut, as was Clara's.

Clara turned away from the sight, and saw that on the floor in the kitchen area, where she hadn't been able to see before, lay Marie Hackett. She was curled on her side, but her abdomen gapped darkly as well, from between her breasts to just above her pubis, and the skin around the opening was brown with dried blood.

And then she saw that on top of the stove was a shallow pan, with something grayish-pink inside it, except it was writhing in the pan, maggots like animated grains of rice squirming everywhere, and on the counter near it was a dinner plate thickly coated with what had to be congealed blood. And she thought, *don't throw up because your mouth is taped shut and you'll choke to death*, and she thought, *stay calm and you'll figure a way to untie yourself*, and she thought, *pray, keep praying, dear Lord deliver me from evil*, and she thought, *and even if I do get untied and can get outside, the wolves ...*

CHAPTER THIRTY-ONE

Althea had called from police headquarters to let Christy know about Gil Calderon's murder. In the hours since then, half a dozen other friends had called, some of them doubtless aware—in principle if not in fact—about her relationship with the reverend. She felt like Hester Prynne, only in modern America, electronic and telephonic communication stood in for the scarlet "A" buttoned to Hester's dress. Their crimes, after all, were the same: adultery, and with a man of the cloth.

Morris was out, and she had spent the day weeping and pacing and sitting until she could sit no more, whereupon she resumed her pacing. The weeping was pretty much constant, with intermittent breaks during which she blew her nose raw and pawed her eyes dry and promised herself that she would get over it, had to, and before Morris got home (although she also made up a legitimate excuse—it wasn't just Gil's death she was mourning, it was everything, the last straw, the disappearances and the wolf attacks and now Gil). He would buy it, because it was largely true. And he knew that she and Gil were close. He didn't know how close, but that was the point of an affair, wasn't it? One of them, anyway. The attraction to the other was real, as was the white heat of forbidden love, of illicit sex acts performed in stolen moments. But part of it was the betrayal itself, the self-congratulatory certainty that she was smarter than her spouse, because she could get away with it and he—a decorated policeman, no less—was none the wiser. That made the betrayal more acceptable, somehow. If he had paid sufficient attention to her, he would have known. If he had cared enough, he would have found out.

In the hours after she learned about Gil, with snow battering at the window and a cup of tea going cold on the kitchen table and her nose chapped and sore from tissues, she knew that was all nonsense. It was about her, not about Morris at all. It was selfishness, a desire to have the stability and security of married life, a dedicated husband, a steady paycheck, standing in the community—but at the same time, to experience the visceral thrill she felt in Gil's arms and in his bed.

Only after hours had passed and the pale circle of the sun started its descent did she wonder about the church itself. Gil was dead and Clara was missing, and most of the town seemed to know about both. If the doors were unlocked—or worse, left open, in this storm—the church was vulnerable to vandals, to animals, to snow and wet.

She tried calling over there, just in case, but when she lifted the receiver on the landline phone, silence greeted her. She tried her cell phone, but the church number and Gil's office line just rang and rang. She couldn't tell if the lines were down everywhere or if there was just no one there to answer. She pulled on an overcoat and stepped into boots and grabbed her purse and the keys to her Camry.

The snow was falling harder than ever. The roads were slick and in spots the snow was inches deep, trackless but for the dotted lines made by the occasional passing animal. Visibility was almost nothing; the wipers swatted away the snow as it blew against the windshield, but even so she could barely see past the hood. Headlights didn't help, but she left them on in case they made her easier for others to spot.

The ten-minute trip took thirty-five.

When she arrived, she parked in front of the church, buttoned her coat, and dashed to the big door. She gripped the handle in her bare hand, wishing she had thought to bring gloves. It was icy, but the door didn't give. She ran around to the back. Gil had given her a key to his office once, and had apparently forgotten about it, or forgotten that from the office one could access the residence and the church.

She slipped the key in the lock, turned it. The door opened and she went inside, shutting it.

He had left the heater blasting; it must have been ninety in the small office. She went to it and twisted the knob, almost burning her fingers. For safety she also went to the wall outlet and unplugged it. *It's a good thing I came,* she told herself. *The whole place could have burned down.*

She went first into his residence, walking through quickly as if on some vital mission, until she got to his bedroom. There she stopped and inhaled, taking in the scent of him, and the fingers of her left hand traced a line on her cheek until she realized that's what he used to do. She stopped, steeled herself. Was there anything here that could give away the affair, she wondered. Photographs, emails? A diary?

She didn't think so. She had been careful to keep her text and email correspondence with him focused on church and community matters, for just that reason. She'd had no reason to think that Morris spied on her accounts, but knew he would be able to if he wanted. The only photos she and Gil had ever been in together had been taken at church functions, picnics and weddings and the like. He had suggested once that they take pictures of themselves making love, but she had been feeling heavy, water-logged, and turned him down. He had never brought that up again. If he'd been with other women in town—and sometimes she felt sure that he had —she didn't know if he would have made the same suggestion, or if they would have gone along with it. But she didn't know where to begin looking.

Same thing went for a diary. She checked inside the nightstands flanking his double bed, but found only a Bible and a laminated eye chart. That struck her as tragic, and the tears flowed again. "Oh, Gil," she said softly. She went into the bathroom, but the tissue box was empty, so she unrolled some toilet paper and held it to her stinging nose.

Through the sound of the wind outside she heard another noise, snapping her attention back to her present situation. Though it had been out of unselfish concern, at least for the most part, she was trespassing on what was probably still considered a crime scene. No tape marked it as such, and the door hadn't been sealed, but she knew that Gil's death was being treated as a homicide. She was here leaving fingerprints all over the place, and DNA in the form of scraps of toilet paper. She pocketed them and listened.

The sound outside had been a vehicle's engine, and now the heard the familiar staccato triple-beep of a horn. Morris's signal. She pushed at her hair and went to the office window, shutting the door to the residence behind her, and outside, in the back lot, was a department Tahoe with Howie Honeycutt at the wheel. As she watched, Morris climbed out of the passenger side. She opened the office door into a gust of wind and snow and started toward him.

"I thought that was your car out front," he said. "We're just on our way back into town."

"You heard about Gil?"

"Yeah, this morning." He shook his head. "This town, I just don't know."

She half-expected condolences. But if he didn't know, he wouldn't say anything, and if he knew he certainly wouldn't. "It's a frightening time. I just thought, with Gil gone and Clara missing, someone should check and make sure everything was locked up tight here."

"Was it?"

"It will be now."

"Let's go, then. The Tahoe's a little crowded, but I don't trust that Toyota to get you home in this storm. It's just about turned into a full-on blizzard."

"I got here okay, just a little while ago."

He waved an arm at the sky. "Look at how it's coming down now. The Tahoe's got four-wheel drive. You can come back for your car tomorrow."

She couldn't see any way out of it. In the backseat of the Tahoe she could see figures, but couldn't make out who they were. "If you're sure you have room."

"We'll make room. You can sit on my lap." He barked a laugh. "Maybe better yet, Robbie can sit on Converse's lap."

She closed the office door and locked it with her key, which she quickly dropped into her purse. "What? Robbie Driscoll?"

"Seems she and Mr. Converse have a little something going."

"Who's Mr. Converse?"

"The movie maker."

"A tourist? And Robbie?"

"Come on, Christy, get out of the snow and I'm sure they'd love to tell you all about it."

She could hardly believe it. Plenty of men had gone after Robbie Driscoll, and she had dated enough of them to get a bit of a reputation around town. But never for long, never very seriously. And never, ever a visitor.

She squeezed into the front passenger seat with Morris, and as Howie steered the Tahoe toward the highway, she craned around and caught Robbie's eye. "So, introduce me to your friend," she said.

Robbie laughed. "Christy Deeds, meet Alex Converse."

"It's a pleasure."

"Pleasure's all mine," he said, putting out a hand. She gave it a quick shake. He was handsome enough, and his clothes looked to be expensive. She'd heard he had plenty of money and didn't mind spending it.

"I'll bet it is," she said. "Robbie's considered quite a catch around here, Mr. Converse. I imagine she would be anywhere, even Hollywood."

"I'm not exactly from Hollywood, Mrs. Deeds. But yes, I'd have to agree with your assessment. She'd be a catch even in Hollywood."

Robbie touched the scar on her cheek. "Because I hear they love *Scarface* there."

"That old thing?" Christy said. "It's practically invisible."

"I don't mind it," Converse said. "In fact, I keep meaning to ask how you got it."

"It's not much of a story," Robbie said. "It's stupid."

"I bet it's a great one."

Christy turned toward the front again, because looking back was straining her neck. But she imagined Robbie turning pink.

"If you must know," Robbie said, "I got it hanging a picture. For my dad."

"Really?"

"Really. He had this old rodeo poster, and he wanted it up behind a piece of glass that had been cut to size. No frame around it, just the glass, clipped at the top and bottom. It was modern, and he liked that, the contrast, I guess. Antique and modern. Anyway, I was putting it up for him, and I thought I had it hooked, but the hook was barely on. When I let go the thing fell. I caught it, but a corner sliced me open."

"I thought it was a bear attack or something like that."

"I told you," Robbie said. "Maybe next time I tell you something is stupid, you'll believe me."

"Maybe," Alex said. "I wouldn't count on it, but maybe."

Howie had been silent the whole time. He had always been a little shy in Christy's presence, though, so that wasn't surprising. Now, though, when the conversation lagged, he spoke up. "We all going to the same place?"

"Just go to Town Hall," Morris said. "Christy, I've got at least an hour or two ahead of me, and I'll take you home after that. Or if I can't get away, Howie will."

"Fair enough," Howie said. "It's a pleasure to see you, Mrs. Deeds. A real, true pleasure."

"Why, thank you, Howie," Christy said. *Something about that man isn't quite right,* she thought. She often caught him staring at her, when he thought she wouldn't notice.

"Yes, ma'am," he said. "It's been a grim day, I guess, but this is a real nice way to end it." Then he turned his attention to the road and the ice and snow, and he didn't say another word all the way back.

CHAPTER THIRTY-TWO

Charles Durbin had not given up on Clara. *Could* not.

He knew the odds, the situation in Silver Gap. Wolves on the prowl. Women going missing. There was no way to know if the disappearances were related, or if they had to do with the wolves, or what. At least not until the women were found.

The police and various community members had turned the town upside down looking for Marie Hackett. A similar party had been organized when Barb Johnston went missing. By the time of Clara's vanishing, the townsfolk had grown weary of the whole thing, and were already dealing with tragedy piled upon tragedy. Enthusiasm for yet another search was hard to muster, and between the folks who had died in the wolf attack and those who had gone out looking for them, the pool of potential searchers had shrunk.

Nevertheless, he had pulled together a few hardy souls. They had searched in town yesterday, not knocking on every door there was but hitting every street, every block. No sign of her anywhere. Given that the other women had not been found, that was to be expected. If finding them would be easy, it would already have been done.

Today they had tried a different approach, checking some of the outlying homes and properties flanking the town. Although they were harder to reach, it made more sense to him that whoever took the women —if indeed it was humans, and not animals—would hide them someplace away from town, someplace isolated, where screams wouldn't be heard.

Thinking that way made Charles's stomach clench, and he had spent most of the night awake, praying and pacing and vomiting. He believed that he would know if Clara had died, that somehow the world would become a different place in a way he would understand. That had not happened, so he still tried, and he dragged everybody he could convince to go out with him, to cover more ground than he could on his own.

As the weather worsened, people peeled off. Some had legitimate excuses, others were simply tired, or had quit believing. Late in the day, the snow had grown deep out in the country, and it was still coming down, heavier than before. They were several miles east of town, where they had hit a few farm properties. Buster Glenn had convinced Charles to head back before they were trapped by drifting snow, and Charles had only reluctantly agreed. He was driving a borrowed Jeep Cherokee with four-wheel drive. He knew it could deal with weather, but he wasn't confident enough in its capabilities to overrule Buster and the other guys with them, Harry Howell and Brad Cox.

Driving toward town, Charles spotted a dirt road he had noticed on the way out. "Anybody know where that goes?" he asked.

"I've seen it forever," Buster said. "Don't think I've ever taken it, though."

"If it's the one I think it is," Brad said, "there's a couple of old hunting cabins up there."

Charles decided and spoke in the same instant. "We're checking it out."

Buster objected, but Charles had the wheel. He slowed, fishtailing a little on the snowy road, but made the left onto the narrow dirt lane. It weaved up between stands of trees, cutting through hillsides that left steep, rocky embankments. The snow was thicker here, with less traffic to push it to the sides, and it made seeing the roadway difficult. "How far up, Brad?"

"I don't know. Half mile, maybe."

"Look, Charles," Buster said. "Even if we see a cabin, it's thick enough out here that we'll need snowshoes to get to it."

"It's not that bad, Buster," Harry said.

"And if we get stuck here, there won't be any cars passing to flag down. It could be days before we get out."

"I can drop you by the road," Charles suggested.

"Dude, you know that's not what I'm saying. I'm with you on this. But I don't want us to get snowbound looking for her."

Charles couldn't face going back yet. If they gave up, he was convinced —even in the face of a daunting storm—he would never be able to get anybody to go out looking with him again. He wasn't even sure he would have the energy, though he didn't think he could stop, either. He might just wander the roads of Silver Gap until he collapsed from exhaustion. "We'll just go a little farther. If we don't see anything, we'll turn around."

"Okay, cool. Whatever."

Buster was almost fifty, and he had a wife at home waiting for his return. She had called four times today, while they were out. Each time, Charles had wished she would stop. It hurt to know that she could call, when Clara couldn't.

He pushed everybody's patience longer than he should have, driving deeper into the backcountry. Buster grumbled, and Brad and Harry stopped coming to his defense. When they finally spotted the first cabin, even Charles knew he had gone too far. The cabin was on the far side of a deep hollow, and the road was completely obscured by snow. With no way to tell how high it might have drifted, he wasn't about to drive the Jeep into it.

"There it is," he said, braking the vehicle to a stop. "I'm not driving down there, but I'll walk over and check it out. You can go with me or wait here, either one."

"Looks pretty deserted," Harry said from the backseat.

"It's not like anybody would put out a sign," Brad countered. "'Abducted women here.'"

"I'll come with you," Buster said. "But then we go home, right?"

"Yeah, Buster. If she's not in there, we'll go home."

He killed the engine and opened his door. A blast of Arctic air struck him; the outside temperature had turned a lot colder just in the last forty-five minutes or so, and without the vehicle heater blasting it was a shock. He steeled himself against it. If Clara was in there, she was cold, too.

The other guys got out and followed, exhibiting more or less reluctance. Buster grumbled about the cold, but that was just Buster doing what he did. The snow was deep, reaching past Charles's knees, and he walked with big, awkward steps, lifting his feet high.

"Hey, Charles," Brad said.

"Yeah?"

"Look at the snow around the cabin door."

Charles looked. It took a few seconds to comprehend, but then it seemed obvious. The snow had been disturbed; even though it had clearly been some time since anyone had been there, and snow had filled in any tracks left behind, it was not the even, unbroken expanse that it was elsewhere.

"Someone's been here," he said.

"I think so."

Charles cupped his hands around his mouth. "Clara! Clara, are you there?"

He waited, but heard no response. "Clara!" he called again. The others joined in, calling for Clara, but also calling Barb's and Marie's names.

No sound issued from the cabin.

They kept walking toward it, pushing through the snow, down the long slope. As he had expected, it was deepest at the low point.

"Charles!" Buster said. He was a few paces behind, not yet all the way at the bottom.

"What?"

"Dude ..."

Charles looked at him. He was pointing to his right, and slightly ahead, up the opposite slope.

Where the wolves had gathered.

A voice woke Clara.

She tried to sit up, but dizziness overtook her and she slumped to the floor again. Her head was throbbing, and she saw a bloody spot on the planks where she had lain. She tried to put the pieces together. She had seen the mutilated bodies of women she had known, Barb and Marie, and had fought to keep from throwing up. Then the world grew dark at the edges, and she must have passed out. From the look of it, she had landed on her forehead, cutting it open.

The quality of the light filtering in through the curtain had changed. Hours must have passed while she lay unconscious on the floor.

She heard the voice again. It called her name.

Charles?

She tried again to sit up, managing this time, though the pain that wracked her every muscle was nearly unbearable. She heard other voices outside, coming closer, and she tried to call back to them, but the tape snugged tight over her mouth meant she could only whimper.

If she could reach the window, maybe she could break it. Even with her hands tied behind her back, she could toss something heavy through the glass. That would get Charles's attention.

But it was all the way across the cabin from her. Sitting had been agony. Could she stand again? Somehow hobble all the way over there?

He was just outside, though, not far away. Surely he could see the cabin, and if he saw it, he would come to it. Once she heard him right outside, she could pound on the floor, the wall.

He would hear that. Then he would come in and untie her, and—

She didn't want to think about Marie and Barb, about what had been done to them, what they had suffered.

For all the terror she had felt, she had hardly been hurt. And her deliverance was so near.

But then the quality of the voices outside changed.

"Shit!" Brad said. "Who's got a gun?"

"Mine's in the Jeep," Harry said.

"I think they all are," Charles said. You didn't leave your house these days without one, not in Silver Gap. But he had been so tired, so anxious to check the cabin and get home, he hadn't thought to bring them.

"What do we do?" Buster asked.

The wolves eyed them from the top of the slope. There were five of them. One was already starting down, muzzle open and twitching as it tasted the air. The biggest one stood behind the others, mostly black with some gray streaks and lighter patches under its eyes. Its right ear had a chunk missing from it.

"Maybe they'll back off," Charles said. "They barely outnumber us, and they can't know we don't have guns."

But a second one started down, just behind the first.

Charles looked toward the Jeep. Could they run, uphill and through the snow, and make it in time?

Then from the other side—between them and the Jeep—three more started their way.

Their heads were massive and golden-eyed, with thick, snow-laden fur and pink tongues and teeth that looked, even from a distance, like they could crack concrete.

"Make for the Jeep," he said. "It's not locked. Whoever gets there first, get a gun and start shooting."

"Shit, Charles," Buster said. "Amelia's gonna be pissed."

"I know, Buster."

"You think a loud noise might scare 'em?"

"You can try."

"Boo!" Buster shouted. He had a deep voice, *basso profundo*, Charles thought. One of the wolves twitched an ear at his cry, but that was the only visible reaction. "Shit," he said again, his voice considerably softer.

The wolves kept coming. He had thought they would charge, but so far, they hadn't. Their approach was almost cautious, as if—

—as if they were waiting to see what the humans might do.

Could they be that smart?

The wolves came closer, then paused, all at the same time, tense and focused.

"I think we better run," Charles said. "They look like they're gonna come at us."

The other men didn't speak. They broke and took off in different directions, each one pushing through the thick snow as fast as they could, more or less angling for the Jeep.

The wolves fairly glided across the snow, moving fast and with unerring accuracy. Brad was out in front, but a pair of wolves figured out where he would be before he got there, and when he did, they met him, leaping up and pulling him down. His screams had just started when Harry went down. The disturbed snow was painted with red.

Buster made it farther. Charles, panting with effort, thought for a moment that he would reach the Jeep. He took huge strides, lifting his feet from the snow and dropping them again, and he was making steady progress until a wolf got in front of him, snarling and snapping. It planted its feet squarely in his chest, shoving him backward. Buster fell and the wolf stood on him, lowering its muzzle and then raising it again, dripping now with Buster's lifeblood.

Then one was on Charles, tearing at his arm. "Clara!" he called out, in case she could hear. "I love you, Cl—"

Before he could finish the name, another wolf caught his knee in its huge maw and crushed it. He fell in the snow. A third one appeared, and this one went for the throat.

CHAPTER THIRTY-THREE

"You don't want to see him," Dr. Steinhilber said. "He's pretty messed up."

Robbie and Alex had arrived at his office just after he and Cale Conklin had finished up Gil Calderon's autopsy. He had sent his nurse and medical assistant home for the day, hoping they would make it there before the storm made travel impossible. But, he told them, Conklin had been helpful, and the two men seemed to get along well. They had just put the corpse into a freezer drawer and were washing up when Alex and Robbie arrived.

"It's good to have another doctor to talk to," Steinhilber said, settling in behind his desk. "Even if he is the wrong kind."

Robbie had taken one of the guest chairs, Conklin the other. Robbie laid her rifle across her lap. Alex leaned against the wall, arms folded over his chest. "The only real difference," Conklin said, "is that I was able to repay my student loans after twenty years. I imagine you're still paying on yours."

"If only I'd gone into neurosurgery, like my mother always wanted."

"Hey, the country needs as many rural GPs as we can get."

"Seriously," Steinhilber said. "I wouldn't change a thing."

"What brought you over here today?" Alex asked.

"Actually," Conklin said, "something we wanted to talk to you about."

"We?"

"Had another conversation with my wolf-expert friends, and I wanted to talk over a theory with Norman. I think we've settled on a conclusion —a tentative one, at least. But the evidence all points in one direction."

"What is it?" Robbie asked.

"It'll seem like a pretty far reach," Conklin warned. "But it explains some longstanding holes. So maybe it's a good thing."

"Are you ever going to tell us, or just keep issuing disclaimers?" Alex asked. He said it with a grin, but the day had already been a long one, and he was tired of standing.

"Okay," Conklin said. "Well, almost. Gotta tell you first that these are still just theories, and still in the formative stages. I know, another disclaimer. It's just that we haven't yet had a chance to confirm any of this."

"Just tell them, Cale," Steinhilber advised. "I think they get it."

"Okay," Conklin said again. "Here's the hole I mentioned. Up in northern Alberta, in Canada—up in the Pelican Mountains not far from a place called Horsetail Lake, a hiker found a bunch of old bones. Anthropologists studied them and determined that there were dire wolf bones and gray wolf bones, all mixed together. Also some they couldn't definitively say came from what. This was about twenty-five years ago, so they were working with fairly current science but not the most up-to-date. The bones seemed to be from the same period, which didn't make sense, because nobody thought dires and grays would hang out. Same place, same time just wasn't likely. And then there were other issues, leading to the conclusion that the samples had somehow become hopelessly cross-contaminated. The DNA seemed to imply part dire, part gray. And of course, that was impossible. So cross-contamination was the agreed-upon conclusion. The matter was set aside, never to be resolved."

"Or so they believed." Steinhilber said.

"Right. What we seem to have here—hybrids, dire/gray crossbreeds—could account for what they took as testing errors."

"Makes sense," Alex said.

"But how did they get here?" Robbie asked. "Northern Alberta is a long way off."

"It is indeed," Steinhilber said. "And isolated. That's key."

"Very remote. They could've survived there for a long time without ever encountering human beings," Conklin said. "Or if they were seen, they were taken for ordinary gray wolves. They were shy, like all wolves, rarely spotted. If someone came across one of their kills, he would assume it was a gray. If you saw one in the distance, through binoculars, whatever, you would just tell yourself that it was a gray. Until we saw one close up, and dead, till we were able to weigh it and measure it and take samples, we thought it was a gray. A strange-looking one, maybe. But nobody would catch a glimpse of one of those animals and think, my God, that's a cross between a dire wolf and a gray wolf! Just wouldn't happen. So geography isolated them and simple human nature allowed them to remain undetected."

"Which still doesn't answer the question of why they're here," Alex observed.

"That's where global warming comes in," Steinhilber said.

"What?" Robbie asked, sounding shocked. "Not you too, Norm."

"What do you mean?" Steinhilber asked. "Are you a denier?"

"I don't know, it's just ..."

"I prefer the terminology 'climate change,'" Conklin said. "Warmer overall, but some places will be colder. Some drier, some wetter. More extreme weather events. Global warming is just too limiting."

"But it is happening, Robbie," Steinhilber said. "More and more carbon in the atmosphere. There are lots of reasons, including deforestation, automobiles, industry—"

"There have always been warmer and cooler cycles though, right?" Robbie asked. "Ice ages and so on?"

"Oh, without doubt," Steinhilber replied. "The difference this time is that the warming cycle that used to take thousands of years is happening much, much faster—over the course of a hundred or so years. People have turned it—nonsensically, I think—into a partisan issue over the past few years. But really, the science is settled."

She smiled at Alex. He liked the way that looked. "I guess you have reinforcements," she said. "How's it feel?"

"Appreciated," he said. "I've been kind of an odd man out in this neighborhood." The conversation made him think about his movie, which reminded him of Peter and Ellen, and the unbearable cost, beyond the financial, of the project. He hadn't made up his mind how to proceed from here, if at all. Hadn't had time to even think about it.

"All right," Robbie said. "Say I accept global warming. Climate change. How does it apply to the wolves?"

"Let me take a crack at that one," Alex said.

Conklin made an offering gesture with his hands.

"You're postulating that they were up in Alberta, but we don't know that they weren't elsewhere as well."

"Good," Conklin said. "Keep going."

"Well, everything you already said still applies. They stayed in the high country. Cold country. They weren't seen often, and when they were they were mistaken for gray wolves. By keeping to themselves, keeping away from people, they survived for thousands of years, a separate, unknown breed."

"We think they mostly stayed in Canada. Maybe remote parts of Montana, but for the most part, well to the north."

"And then," Alex went on, "things started to warm. Here we're seeing it reflected in the devastation caused by bark beetles. Farther north and at higher elevations, we've got glaciers melting, streams running faster. At any rate, what seem at first to be small changes can have big consequences."

"Such as?" Robbie asked.

"Well, take here for example. Various animals depend on the trees for nutrition, for protection. The trees die, the animals have to move. If they're already at the tree line, they have to move down the mountains. These critters are the bottom of the food chain, but when they relocate, so do the larger ones that prey on them. And the ones that prey on those, and so on, all up the chain."

"And wolves," Conklin said, "are the ultimate predators. They go where the food goes."

"As they're forced to lower and lower elevations," Steinhilber added, "it was inevitable that they would encounter human beings at some point. We live at these elevations. Conflict was unavoidable."

"You really think there are a lot of these crossbreeds?" Robbie asked.

"As I said, it's all a theory," Conklin answered. "Maybe not, maybe there are only a couple of packs. One up in Canada, another here. Maybe the rendezvous site you visited today has been used for a hundred generations."

"And I blew the hell out of it," Alex said, guilt settling in on him again.

"You did what you had to do. Like the good doctor said, conflict between man and wolf was bound to happen. It's unfortunate, but climate change is having a lot of unfortunate effects and they're just going to increase."

"I'm a wolf guy," Conklin said. "I love 'em. Literally. But I'm also a human being. When wolves and humans are up against each other for survival, I have to root for the humans."

"You make it sound like a war," Robbie said.

"Only halfway," Conklin replied. "Wolves kill to eat, and sometimes for other reasons. The protection of the pack. They don't know the concept of war. But self-defense? Oh, trust me, they get that. They completely understand that."

CHAPTER THIRTY-FOUR

Doctor Steinhilber said he had more to do at the office. He expected, given the worsening storm outside, that it would be closed for a couple of days, unless emergencies demanded otherwise. He would meet the others later at the Cup & Cow, weather permitting. "Weather," he added with a chuckle, "and wolves."

"Don't even joke about that, Norm," Robbie said. "We're going to get started on that meal. Join us when you can."

Cale Conklin accompanied them. It was a short walk, a block back to Main and then six down to the restaurant, passing Robbie's shop on the way.

But the wind howled with renewed ferocity and it blew stinging snow into their faces. They walked with eyes downcast, heads into the wind. There weren't many people out, but they saw a woman Robbie called Mrs. Kuchar, sixty-something and pear-shaped, out walking a once-fluffy Keeshond, its fur matted with snow. Robbie waved, and the woman waved back, tugging on the dog's leash. The dog had frozen, nose to the wind.

Robbie must have noticed the tremble in the dog's legs at the same instant that Alex did. She unslung the rifle from her shoulder and aimed it, cool and steady.

Mrs. Kuchar was looking at the dog, saying something to it, but then she looked up and saw Robbie pointing a gun in her general direction. Her mouth dropped open and she released the leash.

As soon as it felt the slack, the Keeshond unfroze. It barked once and took off—running not with the wind, but against it, which surprised Alex. He called to the woman, beckoned her. She was staring after her dog, though, and her dog was charging toward the wolf coming in from that direction.

Robbie swung the rifle around and squeezed off a shot. The wolf bucked, staggered. The brave Keeshond attacked it. The wolf fought back, injured but still upright and fierce.

"Where are the others?" Conklin asked.

"What others?"

"Coming in from upwind? That's a distraction, not an attack."

The words were barely out of his mouth when they saw the rest. Robbie brought the gun about, sighted quickly on the first of three.

"Mrs. Kuchar!" Alex called again. "Get inside the house!"

This time she looked at him, confusion on her face. He pointed behind her. The Keeshond was already dead, and the wolf Robbie had shot was down as well, regaining its feet and then stumbling again, finished though it had not given up.

Robbie squeezed the trigger again, shifted the gun, fired, shifted, fired. A red mist sprayed from the lead wolf's skull and it collapsed, sliding in the snow. The wolf behind it jumped over without breaking stride, and that sudden movement saved it from Robbie's second shot. Her third caught the back wolf on its right rear haunch, driving it sideways and down. She held the weapon steady, instantly recalculating her aim. The remaining wolf launched itself toward Mrs. Kuchar, whose legs seemed to have locked her into place.

Robbie fired.

The wolf's head exploded, spraying Mrs. Kuchar with blood and brains. The animal collided with her, knocking her down, but it was already dead.

The wolf Robbie had wounded regained its footing. Blood bubbled from the injury, but it ignored the pain, drawing back its lips, snarling and advancing on the woman still trying to coax cooperation from her hands and feet. Robbie fired twice more, and the beast went over with a grunted exhalation.

Alex and Conklin ran across the street toward Mrs. Kuchar while Robbie held back, surveying, making sure there weren't more wolves on the way. Alex reached the woman first. He extended a hand, helping her to her feet. She was as white as the snow around her, with red splatter on her coat and legs and face.

"What in heaven's name is—" she began.

"You should get inside your house, and stay there," Alex said.

"But, what about Ferdie?"

"The dog?"

"Yes!"

"Ferdie's gone. He tried to save you from the wolves."

"They killed him?"

"At least they didn't kill you," Alex said. "But please get inside, before they do."

"He's right," Robbie said, crossing the road now that the coast was clear. "You've got to get in your house, Mrs. Kuchar. Lock your doors and close the shades and don't come out again."

The woman stood, indecisive, for several long moments. Tears had started to well from her eyes. Robbie made a little shooing motion, and then she responded, turning away from them and waddling up her snow-packed walk. Her door closed and Alex heard the sound of locks being shot.

Conklin was crouched over one of the wolf carcasses. Tracks in the snow showed that he had examined all three. He rose, nodding his head. "They're the same," he said. "Dire/gray cross."

The news was no surprise, but it was a confirmation.

Things had changed. The world was not what Alex had thought.

There were unknown creatures, large predators, among them. They were marvels, and they were deadly.

The next few people they saw, they could not save.

Robbie was reloading her rifle when a man came out of his house, two blocks down, probably to see what all the shooting was about. Alex and Conklin tried to wave him back inside, but he was standing there trying to understand when the wolves darted from between houses, just a blur through the snow, and they took him down. For an instant, Alex saw red, and then they were gone again. On the hunt.

They headed back to Main, where a couple of people driving too fast passed them in a little Nissan coupe. The car didn't make a turn and slid out of control, coming to a halt halfway up on the sidewalk. The people, too distant to hear shouted warnings, got out of the car to survey their situation, and wolves manifested from the shadows and struck, swift and efficient, and they were gone by the time Robbie got off a shot.

Another man wore a blaze orange vest over a down coat and carried a rifle of his own, and he cut through the snow like a man on a mission. He saw something off to his right and stepped between two buildings, out of sight. Alex couldn't see the wolves, but he heard the man's cries, heard the terror in them, and then he heard the silence.

They walked faster, the knowledge that the wolves were in town—and attacking—lending urgency to their pace. "I thought you said they didn't know the concept of war," Alex said.

"They don't," Conklin said. "But they know self-defense. You blew up their home."

"Yeah, I guess I did."

"If it hadn't been you it would have been someone else, Alex," Robbie reminded him. She glanced over her shoulder. "It wasn't your idea. And they were killers long before that."

"They do what they have to do," Conklin said. "At least, that's true of regular grays. I don't know about these things. They seem more—"

Robbie cut him short. "Run!" she said.

They ran.

"Behind us," she said, panting. "A few blocks, but coming fast."

They ran faster. Conklin started to pull ahead, his long legs eating up the ground, arms pumping. Robbie kept looking back, which slowed her down. Alex grabbed her hand and tried to hurry her along. They were less than a block from her shop, but the door would be locked. He didn't know how far back the wolves were, or how many, but he guessed enough that Robbie didn't think she could shoot them all or she would be doing it.

Much of the snow had been shoveled or scraped off the sidewalk, but new snow had fallen and ice glazed it in spots. One slip and he would never get up again.

Then he was at the door and Robbie was shoving her keys into his hands. He fumbled one into the door, but it was the wrong one. "Which key is it?" he asked. But Robbie was down on one knee, aiming the rifle back down the street. She fired and the acrid scent bit at his nostrils and he pushed another key into the lock, turned it. The door gave under his push.

He yanked the key out and went inside, followed by Conklin, and finally Robbie. Once she was through, Alex slammed it shut and locked it again. He was still standing there, hands on the door, when a wolf lunged against the glass. The impact made Alex jerk his hands away from the door, as if it had suddenly turned electric, and he let out a cry of surprise.

"The back room!" Robbie shouted. "Quick!"

She was already on her way. Alex followed. Conklin was standing by the window, watching the four wolves that had gathered on the sidewalk. The one that had tested the door slammed against it once more. It rattled but held.

"Cale!" Alex cried.

"Come on!" Robbie said. She grabbed Alex's shoulder and hurled him into the back room. He fell against a shelf unit and rolled-up maps fell out around his feet.

The wolf tried the door again. This time, glass shattered and crashed inward. The wolf yelped but kept coming, struggling over the jagged remains of the pane, rear paws scrabbling for purchase. The other wolves were growling and crowding the first.

Conklin was still halfway across the shop, his attention riveted on his beloved creatures. Robbie and Alex both called him, but he didn't seem to hear. Then the first wolf was inside. Blood slicked the doorway glass and pattered on the floor. The other wolves charged through the opening and finally Conklin seemed to realize that he was in trouble, but he still couldn't pull himself away. He glanced over his shoulder at Robbie and Alex and took a step backward, then another. Robbie fired into the furry mass at the door, two shots echoing in the small space, and then her hammer fell on an empty chamber.

Alex started toward Conklin. "I'll get hi—" he began. But Robbie caught him and drew him back into the room and as the first wolf reached Conklin—the scientist's hands extended toward it, as if in greeting, in invitation—she shut the steel door and threw the deadbolt.

Conklin's screams were loud and seemed to go on for a long, long time. The tearing and growling and snapping and chewing went on for much longer.

CHAPTER THIRTY-FIVE

Wolves huffed at the bottom of the door. One of them must have gone up on its hind legs and pushed against it—it shook in its frame and Alex heard the clicking of front claws against it, as high as his head or a little higher.

Robbie looked through a peephole. "Eight of them in the store now," she said. "This door will hold them off, but at some point we'll have to make a run for it."

"Can we go out the back?"

The shop's back door was also steel, a double door with a deadbolt lock and a length of two-by-four held in place by steel braces. There was a second fish-eye peephole in the left door, and he went to it, looked out. At first the alley behind the store appeared clear, but then he saw a fluff of tail pass by at the bottom edge of his field of view. "They're out here, too," he said, answering his own question.

"Let's give it a little while," Robbie said.

"We could call the cops."

"I imagine they're a little busy."

"The Marines?"

"That might be better."

Another impact against the door into the shop jolted it and startled them. Robbie grabbed a corner of her desk and started to slide it in that direction. Alex joined in, and when the heavy piece was solidly against the door, Robbie gave him a smile. "Those guys are strong," she said.

"Let's hope they're not real patient."

"We can hope," she replied. "I wouldn't put a lot of money on it, though."

Chief Deeds looked out Alden Stewart's second-floor window. Four wolves passed silently by, claiming the middle of the street. They were almost obscured by thick, wind-whipped snow. He knew there were many more out there. He'd finally ordered every phone in the building disconnected because they had been ringing so steadily he couldn't think.

Alden had refused to turn off his own cell phone, but he had at least silenced it, after a couple of frustrating conversations with the governor's office. The storm was too powerful, the governor said. Helicopters couldn't get airborne and trucks couldn't get up the mountain. Until the weather cleared, the people of Silver Gap were on their own.

Since then, Alden had been sitting in his desk chair, staring into space. The town was in Morris's hands, and he didn't know what to do.

Most of the calls were from downtown. Judging from that, he guessed the wolves had decided to attack where the most people were massed. Homes on the outskirts hadn't seen any sign of them. To make sure, he had called the neighbors on both sides of his own place, way on a hill on the western edge of town, and the neighbor across the street. No wolves reported there.

That was good, because Christy had been complaining for the last hour. He couldn't unplug her or set her to vibrate. He had come to Alden's office to escape her, but if he stayed much longer, she would follow him up. She wanted to be at home, and from all reports, she would probably be safe there.

He couldn't leave, and Jones and Ortega were out in one of the department's Tahoes. He had sent them to the motel to gather up whatever hunters were still there, with their guns, and to see if there were any DOW folks there or at Spud's.

With Trbovich dead, that left Honeycutt.

He considered calling in Jones and Ortega. He'd feel better about sending her home with two officers, instead of just one.

But they were performing a useful function, and Honeycutt, as far as he knew, was sitting alone in the squad room drinking stale coffee.

He turned to the mayor. "Alden," he said. "I'm going downstairs for a minute. I'm gonna send Christy home. Don't go anywhere. When I come back, we'll hash out a plan."

Alden might have nodded. Deeds was a little surprised that he remembered to swallow.

When Howie Honeycutt opened the back door of Town Hall for Christy, the wind snatched it from his hand and blew it wide, straining the hinges. Snow blew against her face, stinging, as if tiny ice crystals had been hurled at her. She had lived in the mountains a good long time, and she didn't mind a winter storm, but this was something different, almost sinister. It was ferocious and it didn't let up.

She caught the door and shoved it back toward Howie, who took the handle in his free hand. His right gripped an ungainly looking shotgun that she'd heard Morris call a "street sweeper" when he suggested that Howie take it along. It had a round drum at the bottom, just in front of the trigger. She didn't know much about guns, though Morris had insisted she own a .38 snubnose and take a refresher course at the range down in Fort Collins every couple of years. She supposed she should be carrying it now, what with all the disappearances and the wolf attacks. But she was used to keeping it locked in a gun safe in the bedroom closet, and really, the thing was brutish and unpleasant.

She started down the steps toward the Tahoe they had arrived in, but Howie touched her lightly on the shoulder. "Let me go first, ma'am," he said. "If you don't mind." He raised the shotgun barrel, as if she might have forgotten he carried it. "Want to keep an eye out for them wolves."

"Be my guest," Christy said. She had scanned for anything as soon as she stepped into that biting wind, but she could barely see beyond the edge of the parking lot. An army could be positioned in the trees there, and she wouldn't know it.

Howie descended ahead of her and walked to the vehicle, swinging the gun barrel from side to side as he went. She followed in his path, wishing he would move a little faster. Caution was fine, but if there were any wolves around, getting inside the SUV and locking the doors seemed like as good an idea as trying to gun them down.

He went to the passenger side and opened her door, then stood there like an attendant at a valet stand while she got in. She half-expected him to show his palm for a tip. But when she was inside and buckling her seatbelt, he just released the door, which the wind slammed for him. He hurried around to his side and slid in behind the wheel, positioning the shotgun barrel-down in the footwell.

They saw a wolf in the first block, trotting along beside the road with a human arm, torn off just below the elbow, in its mouth. Howie touched the shotgun's stock, but the wolf paid them no mind and he drove on.

"These are strange times," he said. "Almost biblical, you might say."

"I guess you might."

"You really learn what a person's made of, times like this. Times of crisis."

"I suppose."

"It's true."

"I don't doubt it."

They reached the end of downtown. The road made a wide curve toward the northwest, and halfway through it three wolves stood on the pavement, in the other lane. Christy thought he would drive past them, maybe even speed up, but instead he stopped the Tahoe right in the lane and opened his door, the engine still running.

The wolves' ears perked up as he stepped out, and she saw their muzzles twitch, smelling him. The one in front peeled back its lips in a snarl, and its golden eyes narrowed.

Howie scooped up the shotgun and stepped away from the door. With it open, the cold clutched at her like a fist.

The front wolf's muscles tensed as it prepared to charge. Howie sighted on that one and pulled the trigger, twice in rapid succession. The blasts seemed incredibly loud, the flash from the barrel blindingly bright against the gray day. The rounds tore huge chunks from the animal's right side and back, staggering but not dropping it. Christy's grip tightened on the sides of her seat as the thing took another unsteady step toward Howie, and the two behind it readied for their own attacks.

Howie wasted no time firing again and again, unleashing two more shots at the lead wolf and two each at the others. The top of first wolf's head sheared off and it finally fell. The second one jumped over the first and Howie's volley caught it in mid-air, knocking it back and down. The third animal took Howie's first shot square in the face, turning it to red pulp, and the second shot savaged it still more.

When all three wolves were still, Howie returned to the SUV. Christy noticed that his left hand dropped to his crotch on the way, like a baseball player adjusting himself.

"We should get to my place," Christy suggested. "You can hunt more after you've dropped me off, if you want."

"I didn't like the way those ones were looking at us," Howie said, as if that explained anything. He shifted gears and pressed on the accelerator, and the vehicle moved forward, passing over the parts of the road that were slushy and red from fresh wolf blood.

"Well, Morris wanted me to call him when I'm there. Don't want to keep him waiting." That was a lie; Morris had told her the phones would be off. When Honeycutt returned he would know she'd made it up.

Howie didn't respond at first. He drove slowly, carefully, keeping the SUV in its lane and trying to see through the snow. After a few minutes, he said, "No, you wouldn't want to keep him waiting. Especially considering the way you whore around on him."

She couldn't have heard that right. "Excuse me?"

"I've seen you at Reverend Fuckbuggy's, going over there to spread your ladybits for his fucking fuckstick."

"Howie, I think you had better not say another word and just get me home. If you do that, I won't tell Morris what you said."

"You think he doesn't know?"

"I'm sure I don't know what—"

"Don't bother to deny it, Mrs. Deeds. Mrs. *Whoredeeds*. I'm not blind, you know. People think I'm not paying attention, that's all. But I am. I do."

"Maybe you had better just let me out here," she said. Middle of nowhere, woods on both sides of the road. She regretted the suggestion as soon as she'd made it. Their street was coming up in less than half a mile, she would be able to see it if not for the snow. But between here and there was open forest.

"My first time, I was scared," Howie said. "So scared, you wouldn't believe."

"First time what?" Christy said. She wanted him to remember that she was there, and who she was. Howie respected Morris, she was sure. He was having some kind of breakdown, but that respect wouldn't wane.

"She wasn't the first I'd seen. But after I saw that one, Karen, I couldn't stop thinking about her. And I knew one day I would have to try it. I just had to."

"Howie, I really think you should shut up and drive."

He didn't seem to notice that she had spoken. He still had control of the vehicle, but his eyes looked glazed. She wondered exactly how much trouble she was in. She wished she'd put that .38 in her purse, like Morris wanted her to.

"So I found this one who reminded me of Karen. I wasn't in high school anymore, but she was, and she had that same way about her, that sluttish way like Karen had, jubblies hanging out all over the place, you know. I saw her and I followed her home and there wasn't anybody else there. I knocked on her door and she opened it and acted like I was some kind of idiot for standing there, so I just up and did it. First with my hands and then when they got sore with this metal vase they had there. It got pretty messed up, that vase, dented and all and of course blood all over."

Christy watched the street for a chance. He was going too fast, and if she jumped out on that snow-slick road she would fall and likely split her head open. But he would have to slow to make the turn. She would go then. She'd run to the first house, the Nelson place, and she'd call Morris and tell him that one of his officers had gone completely insane.

Except the phones were off at Town Hall. So she couldn't.

"But anyhow, it worked, and of course there were knives in the kitchen, and what I really wanted, what I couldn't do with Karen, was to find out what the taste was like."

Her stomach gave a flip and her bowels turned to water. She clenched to keep everything inside. The turn was coming up, but he wasn't slowing, and then he drove right past it, still heading away from town.

"Howie, that's my street!"

He ignored her, and pressed harder on the gas. His left hand dropped, seemingly unconsciously, to his lap, and he rubbed himself as he talked. She wondered if she could get the shotgun, or unsnap his handgun from its holster. Probably not without killing both of them, at the speed he was reaching.

"It was raw, of course, and it made me sick after. It was kind of chewy and a little bit salty and sour. Of course, organ meat's better."

Christy bit her lower lip, fighting a sudden need to vomit. She tasted bile and her body hitched and spasmed.

"Nobody ever caught me, but like I say, I was so scared. Scared of being caught and scared of myself. I never laid a hand on anybody after that, not for years. I moved away so I wouldn't see the street where Karen was or the house where this other girl was whose name I never knew. I came here and your husband, Mrs. Whoredeeds, he saw what I had in me, saw the greatness that's in me if only I had a chance to show it, and he gave me a job and I put that all behind me, for so long. I thought I was over it. Up until Mike Hackett, anyhow. And then when I saw him all opened up, well, I remembered those others, Karen and that other girl that I did myself, and then it was back. Those old feelings were back."

He braked suddenly, causing the Tahoe to fishtail. He maintained control, though, and he pointed it up a narrow dirt road. Christy had never been here, had no idea where Howie was taking her, but he had to move more slowly on this road, where the snow was thick and the surface uneven. The act of making the turn seemed to have restored some of Howie's focus, but she expected that it would lapse again, and as soon as it did she would jump out.

The road led up over a low rise and down into a dip, with a bigger hill on the other side. By the time they hit the downslope, he was talking again. "Your husband, Chief Deeds, he can see what others can't. He saw the makings of something special in me, that's for sure. Lot of people can't but he did. He could do more about it, too, except that he's blocked by his few blind spots. You're one of them, too, Mrs. Whoredeeds. He doesn't know about you spreading yourself for the fucking right fucking reverend. Not yet, anyhow. If he did then he would be free to—"

The urge to vomit was growing in her again and she knew she had to get out. The Tahoe reached the bottom of the slope, and the road was flat for about a dozen feet before it started to rise again. There might have been a stream bed in the low part; she couldn't see it through the snow but it seemed to meander through the trees, offering an open path back toward town.

She wouldn't get a better chance.

Just before he started up the far side, Christy undid her seatbelt and threw her door open and jumped. She landed on her feet but off-balance, and she fell forward in the snow, trying to catch herself on hands that sank down. When she got her feet under her again her front was covered in snow, and the cold—which had been bracing for an instant when she opened the door—was once again stultifying. It would slow her down soon, which meant that she needed to make progress in a hurry.

The Tahoe stopped, its engine shutting off. Christy didn't look back, but ran as fast as she could through the snow. She heard the sound of Howie's door opening and then closing. She had reached the nearest trees before she heard the first blast from his shotgun, and although she thought the stream's course would be more direct, it wouldn't offer much in the way of protection, and if she fell through into water that would slow her down, possibly finish her.

Shot ripped through the trees all around her and a couple of pellets punched at her clothing but didn't penetrate. She kept going, weaving from tree to tree.

He fired again, twice, then he swore and started running after her. Christy knew he had a handgun on his belt, and wondered if he remembered it was there. She had put enough distance between them that the shotgun's blasts were scattering, but if he was any good with a pistol, he could still bring her down.

She had to get away, before he thought of it. She was no athlete, but she was in decent shape. And she was desperate.

She ran.

CHAPTER THIRTY-SIX

Alex couldn't stop thinking about Conklin, out there in the store. He was sure the same was true of Robbie. They collapsed together in her big old chair with the busted springs, just long enough to catch their breath. To shift his attention, and hers, he ran his fingers down the scar on her cheek. "What was he like?" he asked. "Your dad."

Robbie sucked in a breath, then let it out. "He was a simple man, I guess. A country man through and through. He could fix any kind of engine you can name, car, truck, lawnmower, whatever, and that was mostly how he earned his way. We never had much money or nice things, but he didn't care, and if my mother did I never knew it. She died when I was three, so I never really knew her. But Dad, he could fix things, and he raised a few chickens and kept a milk cow. He could take a knife and peel a whole apple in a single piece. He had a limp from a bullet he took in the hip, in Vietnam, but he never complained about it and if you didn't know that you wouldn't think he had ever been more than ten miles from home." She let out a laugh, so sudden it was startling. "And he could hunt. I tell you, people think I'm good? They should have seen him. Everything I know about tracking and shooting, about how animals behave, it all came from him."

"Sounds like a great guy." He tried to stifle a yawn, then gave in.

She matched it with her own. He was so tired, and it sounded like she was too. He had to get up, check the peepholes, see if it was safe to go out. But first he had to close his eyes. Just for a minute.

The tunnel was black and he couldn't breathe. When the coal dust got this way it went everywhere, and for days after your spit would be black, and you would cough up great blobs of stringy mucus. Every miner got a handkerchief for Christmas if his family could afford it, and they'd all be trash by spring because the black wouldn't wash out anymore.

This way, boss, Flannery said. His eyes glowed like the headlights on a truck. *Follow me.*

Alex followed, unable to see Flannery's face most of the time, but watching the way those headlight eyes burned through the black fog. Up one sloping, curving tunnel and then down a straight one and then through an opening into another one leading away at an angle, and he wondered if Flannery was just taking him deeper and deeper under the ground. But then they were in a shaft that had no opening, except, no, that was a door, not a solid wall. Alex cringed from it, afraid he would hear the growling and snapping behind it, but he didn't. Flannery seemed confident. He pressed his ear to it only for a second. *This is the way, boss,* he said. *Trust me here. This is the place you want.*

Trust didn't come easily, but Alex didn't see much choice. Flannery worked the latch and the door swung slowly open, squealing on seldom-used hinges. Light splashed in and Alex had to close his eyes, had to throw up a hand to shield them. When he lowered it, squinting, he looked for Flannery but the man was gone, so he stepped through the doorway not into the soft hills of Kentucky but into a winter snowscape, jagged and thick with pine trees and standing among them, a little cabin, worn and aged but sturdy enough, he guessed. And it looked familiar, and he wondered where he had seen it before, and why it mattered.

A thumping noise outside prompted Alden Stewart to get up from his desk and walk to the window. He walked slowly, heavily, afraid that what he would see outside would be bad. He knew Morris had lost all respect for him. He had lost it for himself. He had considered government, public service, a useful profession. But he had harbored certain beliefs about it, about the challenges he would face, the demands that office might make on him.

Wolves had not been one of those. Wolves had not factored into his expectations at all. And yet here he was, facing the worst crisis of his life, and it was wolves after all.

When he got to the window, at first all he could see was fog on the glass and ice around the edges and snow blowing against it from outside. He got closer and looked through the snow and after a few seconds he located the source of the thumping noise, which was—not surprisingly, he thought—wolves.

They were jumping against the big plate glass windows of the Cup & Cow. Over and over. Even from here, he could see the glass shake with every impact.

He returned to his desk, more quickly this time, and snatched up his phone. Eight missed messages. Because Morris had convinced him to silence the thing, and he thought he had it on vibrate but maybe not.

Belinda was inside the restaurant. Probably calling for help.

He wasn't sure what he could do, but something had to be done. He went to the door. The hallway was quiet. Most of the staffers had already been sent home, if they could be spared. And since no town business was being done today except that dealing with wolves, most of them were expendable.

He rushed down the stairs, urgency lending him speed. Maybe courage, as well—he wasn't sure about that, but he felt that he could charge across the street and battle the wolves with his bare hands, if they threatened Belinda. Maybe at the last moment he would lose his nerve, but he hoped not. "Morris!" he called as he descended. Downstairs, he pushed through the door to police headquarters. "Morris, where are you?"

Morris was in his department's conference room. Officers Ortega and Jones were in there, as were seven men Alden didn't know. They were wearing hunting clothes, though, and there were guns all over the place. "Morris, the wolves are trying to get into the Cup & Cow. Belinda's in there, and some others. You've got to do something."

"We were just hashing out a plan," the police chief said.

"There's no more time for a plan. Either you get out there and kill them, or let me have a gun and I'll do it myself."

"That'd be suicide, Mayor Stewart," Jones said. "Pure and simple."

"I don't care. I won't stand here and watch them break the glass and eat up my wife."

"Fine," Morris said. "Let's get this done, men. When we finish these ones off, we can start working our way through town."

The men grunted or mumbled their assent. The language of the overtly masculine, the testosterone-fueled, had always been as unfamiliar to him as Greek or Norwegian. But he got the gist when they gathered up their weapons and headed for the door.

"Morris, I need a gun," Alden said.

"You wouldn't know what to do with it. Just let us handle it."

"I'm not staying in here while you go out there," Alden said. "And I can't go out without a gun."

The chief stopped and eyed Alden for a long, uncomfortable moment. Then he went to a gun rack on one wall, unlocked it with a key from his ring, and removed a rifle. Or was it a shotgun? Something long, anyway.

"Is it loaded?"

"It's loaded."

"How do I work it?"

Morris turned away and followed the other men out. "Figure it out," he said as he left.

Alden rushed to catch up, turning the thing over in his hands as he did. The trigger he understood, that was obvious. And it wasn't like he had never fired a gun. He had, mostly as a boy, plinking at cans. What he didn't know was whether this gun had a safety, or whether he needed to cock it, or what.

At the Town Hall's big double front doors, Morris shouldered the right one open and looked out. "Six of them," he said. "Everybody watch both ways. Keep an eye on each other's backs."

He gave a soft three count and shoved the door wide. He went first with the others right behind, shouting as they went. The wolves across the street spun around to meet the new threat. As the men raced down the stairs, they opened fire. Their guns roared again and again. The wolves were beaten back by the assault. One of them, with two bullet holes in it already, tried to slink away, but somebody saw it and unloaded a couple more rounds in its head and it fell, twitching, on the snowy street. Another lunged at the men but at least three of them shot it at the same time. Blood and tissue blew out its other side, spraying across the sidewalk.

When the wolves were all down, Morris crossed to the restaurant's door. The men were loosely grouped behind him. Alden hurried to be there when Belinda opened up. As he passed, one of the wolves—still twitching, its blood pumping from several wounds, scarlet trails on dark fur—snapped at his leg. The thing's teeth caught his pants and tore them, and Alden cried out and yanked his leg away. The nearest hunter put another bullet into the beast and it dropped back to the road, quiet at last.

By the time he reached the doorway, Belinda was unlocking it. Morris opened it. She gave him a grateful look and then ran into Alden's arms. He tried to hold the unused rifle away so it didn't hit her, but it was awkward and heavy.

"Are you okay?" he asked.

"I'm fine, fine. We were scared, but that's all."

"I'm so glad you're safe," he said. He looked past her at the people gathered inside. Maybe ten or eleven of them, most looking glad to see the men with all the guns.

"Everybody, go home if you can," Morris Deeds declared in his loudest police chief voice. "Not alone—you're not safe out here alone. But if you've got a gun and someone who lives close by, and ideally a vehicle, then you're probably better off locked inside your own house than here. Stay upstairs if you've got an upstairs, and keep away from the windows. If you want to stay here and join us, we're going to sweep the town and kill as many of these damned things as we can."

A woman who had been inside the restaurant started to ask a question, but she never got to finish it. A racket erupted from the kitchen— what sounded like the rear door banging open, the clatter of cookware, the unmistakable growling of wolves, and the click and scrabble of paws on the slick floor.

The people inside the restaurant screamed first, and some of them bolted from chairs and rushed toward the door. But the doorway was blocked by Morris and Belinda and Alden and behind them, the armed men who had shot the wolves. They raised their weapons again, but this time the wolves were behind glass and behind innocent, terrified people trying to get out.

Alden couldn't keep track of everything that happened next. Somebody opened fire. The big window shattered and glass crashed down like another, noisier snowfall. More guns went off, and inside a couple of people cried out and fell. Alden saw one whose skull erupted in what looked like a pink cloud, and he didn't think the wolves could have done that. But he didn't get a chance to try to figure out who did, because the people inside were coming out no matter what, knocking aside Morris and tearing Belinda from Alden's grip. She fell and he tried to catch her but a shoulder or an elbow or both bowled him over onto his back, the wind knocked from him. He lost his grip on the gun and when he tried to get up, someone else slammed into him and he couldn't see for a few seconds, could only hear gunfire and terrible, plaintive screams and the sounds of the wolves. When he got his bearings and could make out his surroundings again, he saw Belinda, her face a mask of terror and pain, being whisked back through her doorway by something that had her legs and had incredible strength. Her eyes met his for an instant and then her head was whipped out of sight, and he saw her flopping briefly, like a dog's tug rope being shaken, and then he couldn't see her at all. He got unsteadily to his feet. Inside the restaurant was blood, blood everywhere, and Morris was dragging him away, saying, "No, Alden, you can't do anything now."

They fell back to the Town Hall, taking occasional shots through the restaurant's windows, one man even taking the time to gather up the guns that had been dropped. But there were only six people now, two who had come from inside, the rest the hunters that Morris had led and officer Ortega. Jones was dead on the street, as were others, and inside the restaurant it was impossible to tell who was alive and who was dead, because the screams could have been anybody's.

CHAPTER THIRTY-SEVEN

R obbie handed Alex a shotgun and a semiautomatic pistol and gave him the quickest of reminders on how to use them. He would if he had to, though he held onto hope that it wouldn't come to that. He looked through the peephole into the store, where there were still several wolves gathered around what was left of Conklin's body. At the same time, Robbie checked the alley behind the shop. "Looks clear this way," she said.

"Good, because it isn't here."

"We should head for Town Hall," she said. "See if the police need any help." She had tried calling police headquarters a couple of times, even tried the reception desk at Town Hall, and the mayor's direct number. No answers at any of them, which Alex didn't interpret as anything good.

"Okay," Alex said. He didn't have any better ideas, since he couldn't figure out how to put *never having come to Silver Gap in the first place* into action.

"So, when we go out the door, we go right. At the end of the block we'll cut over to Main. Unless we see wolves there."

"Got it."

"I just don't want to get separated."

"Believe me, neither do I."

She smiled and quickly kissed him, and then she opened the door.

Nothing jumped in at them. She looked right, then left, then right again. She had a rifle in her hands and two pistols, one in a coat pocket and the other jammed into her pants. Alex only had the one, in his pocket, since he was certain if he tried the pants trick he would end up shooting his own dick off.

"Clear," Robbie said.

He followed her example, checking both ways before he joined her in the alley. They moved at a quick, steady trot, fast enough to cover ground but not likely to leave them winded, should they need to fight. At the alley's end, Robbie peeked around the corner, again looking in both directions, and scanned the alley they had just covered. "Looks good," she whispered. She gave a little nod in the direction of Main Street, and started that way.

Robbie reached that corner about six paces ahead of Alex. He saw her tense up and drop into a crouch and snap the rifle into place. She squeezed off three quick shots, then raised her left arm and waved Alex back. "Wolves," she said. "They've got some people surrounded. Stay put a minute."

Alex wanted to move up, to play his part. But would he be a help or a bother? If the people were surrounded by wolves, he wouldn't dare shoot because he'd be as likely to hit them as the animals.

She disappeared around the corner and he heard gunfire. He risked going that far, to make sure she was okay and to see if there was anything he could do. The situation was worse than she had implied. There were three people on the sidewalk, two women and a man. One of the women was sitting down, bleeding heavily from a gash that ran from her right elbow most of the way to her shoulder. Robbie had dropped one of the wolves that ringed them, and wounded another, but there were still four, huge and menacing.

Alex tried to gauge the distance to the wolves versus his nonexistent skill with a gun, wondering if he should try to shoot one. As if it sensed his gaze, the one closest to him—and therefore to Robbie, who was moving forward, trying to keep the people calm with a steady, soothing patter—whirled around and saw him at the corner. It charged suddenly, racing right past Robbie and coming toward him. At the same moment, the other wolves lunged at the woman on the ground.

"Alex, run!" Robbie shouted. "Meet me at Town Hall when you can!"

Alex fired his shotgun at the oncoming wolf, but largely missed. Then he saw a second one emerge from the nearest doorway. Robbie was shooting at the wolves surrounding the people, and couldn't help.

Instead, he took her suggestion.

He was both tired of running from wolves, and getting better at it, however mutually exclusive the two might have been. He figured the best place to go was back to Robbie's shop, where he could lock and bar the door, and where he would have as much ammo as he could ever need.

But when he reached the alley, there were two wolves coming toward him from that direction. That changed the plan. Instead of turning, he ran straight across the alley. Robbie's house was in that block, so maybe he could go there.

Before he had covered half the block, he knew he'd never make it.

The shotgun was slowing him down, for one thing. He hurled it over his head, hoping that if nothing else it would hit one of his pursuers. No luck; he heard it clatter to the ground.

Even without it, he just wasn't fast enough to outdistance them for long. He could hear the huff of the nearest wolf's breath. He still had the pistol in his pocket, but feared that trying to retrieve and use it would slow him down just enough.

He made it to the corner, saw Robbie's house. It seemed so far away.

Then he saw a truck, idling at the curb, almost right in front of him. Nobody behind the wheel, the door open. It was almost too good to be true, as if the wolves had laid a trap for him. He shifted course and circled around it, heading for that wide-open door.

It was only when he got to the other side that he saw the driver, half-dragged from the seat, dangling onto the road. Most of his face was gone, his throat torn open, blood everywhere.

Alex glanced up at the wolves. They had hesitated when they reached the corner, as if concerned there might be danger behind the truck.

He couldn't count on that hesitation lasting. He tugged the body from the door, silently apologizing, and dumped it in the road. Then he got in and slammed the door. The wolves sprang at him, one of them smashing against the door and bouncing off, another hanging on for long, terrifying moments, by claws and teeth, before releasing and dropping back to the street.

He could shoot through the windows, but that would weaken the glass and increase his own vulnerability. Instead, he shoved the gearshift into drive and pulled away. The wolves gave chase, like dogs after a car. But the streets were empty, so he floored it and left them behind.

Robbie had told him to go to Town Hall, and he knew that's what made sense. That's where the cops would be, and being around trained people with guns seemed like a good idea.

But ever since that dream, that flash of one that he'd had in Robbie's office, he hadn't been able to shake the feeling that the cabin Flannery showed him meant something. And driving that truck away from the wolves, he realized where he had seen it before.

That first day out with Robbie. That was the cabin they had found when they'd heard the elk in the woods, and weren't sure at first what was making the noise. It had been padlocked from the outside, he recalled, and the lock had been considerably newer than the cabin around it.

It hadn't been too far from town, but it was isolated, and far enough away that people weren't likely to casually happen across it. He and Robbie had, but their intent had been to get away from civilization.

He thought he remembered how to get to it. They had found it on foot, but there had been a dirt road leading almost straight to it, and on the way home Robbie had pointed out where that road met the highway.

The snow made driving in anything but a straight line on a clear path difficult. But the truck had good clearance and its tires seemed to grip the roadway. He couldn't do anything about the lack of visibility, but if he didn't try to drive too fast, he thought he could manage.

And he thought it was important enough to try.

He still couldn't begin to understand what the whole dream business meant, or how Jared Flannery—years after dying in a mining disaster—had directed him to Silver Gap, where his sister was in trouble. But he believed that Clara was the key. She was the reason Jared had come to him. And if that was true, then the cabin had something to do with Clara's disappearance.

At any rate, he had to check it out. He had already failed Jared once, in a big way. He couldn't do it again.

On the way out of town, he saw a few wolves. They looked up at the truck but none bothered to chase him. One group, chowing down on somebody just off the edge of the road, didn't even bother to glance his way.

Whatever Conklin had believed about the number of these hybrid beasts had to have been way off. There must have been hundreds of them. That was unheard of for a wolf pack, according to what Robbie and Conklin had told him.

What if it wasn't one pack, though? Conklin had suggested that there might be many such packs, spread out along the highest spine of North

America. That was sheer speculation, based on having seen wolves here in Colorado and evidence that might have pointed to others in northern Canada. Could the truth be that there had been multiple populations, but some force, climactic or otherwise, had brought them together? Maybe they were all right here, gathered in the mountains around Silver Gap— and moving lower in elevation all the time.

He was lost in contemplation and trying to peer through the snow and he almost missed the turn. But he saw the dirt road as he was passing it, and managed to brake without losing control of the truck. He backed past it and took the sharp right slowly. The road was thick with snow, but there had been traffic on it recently; the tracks of passing wheels were still visible, the snow not as deep in those depressions.

He took the road as fast as he dared, feeling the truck's tires slip on the snowpack. He hadn't seen any wolves for a while, which he knew didn't mean they weren't around. Most people never saw wolves, but that didn't mean wolves didn't see them.

He came over a rise and saw the cabin on the far side of another hill. But between here and there was a police department SUV, stopped and seemingly abandoned at the road's low point. The passenger door hung open.

What that was doing here, he couldn't tell, nor could he interpret how it might affect his mission.

He pulled up behind the Tahoe, hoping there was a way around it. When he reached it, though, he could see that it blocked so much of the road that he couldn't pass, and with the snow he was unable to tell if the surrounding ground was safe to drive on. Instead he turned off the truck, which he had come to think of as a gift, a deliverance of some kind, and pocketed the key. Before he got out, he tried his phone, to call Robbie and let her know he was okay, but he had no signal at all.

He put the phone away and took out the gun. It was a Colt, she had told him. Semiautomatic. Nine millimeter. A little bit of a kick, but not too bad. Fifteen-round magazine. He knew what the words meant, but that was about it.

It didn't feel good in his hand. He put it back in his coat and got out of the truck, and as soon as he did he heard a loud crack, not far away, that over the past few days he had come to recognize conclusively as a gunshot.

It was off to his right. A snow-covered path snaked through pines, some of them the very same ones he and Robbie had been looking at, their branches orange and sparse. Now that he was standing here, he saw two sets of footprints cutting through the snow in that direction.

So a cop was shooting at wolves. That wasn't a bad thing. He looked back at the cabin up on the hill, surrounded by pines.

He heard another shot and then he heard a woman scream, and then he decided he needed to check it out after all.

It was cold and the snow was blowing and the sun, which he hadn't seen all day, was heading for the horizon. If he was going to find out what was going on, he had to do it fast, and then get back to the cabin. But if the woman who had screamed was Clara, he had to do something. Even if it wasn't, it sounded like somebody in trouble.

Alex Converse was nobody's idea of a hero, he knew.

But it looked like he was the closest thing around.

He pulled the gun from his pocket again and followed the path of the footprints.

CHAPTER THIRTY-EIGHT

Alex huffed his way up a steep hill. At the top, he started to think this whole escapade was hopeless—by the time he caught up to whoever was out here, he would be out of breath, ready to collapse.

But then he heard the woman's voice again, and a man's. It was familiar, and it was nearby. He looked down the other side of the hill and there, in a clearing, stood Howie Honeycutt. He held a shotgun and he was pointing it not at a wolf but at a woman, and it took Alex a minute because he had only met her once, hours that seemed like days ago. The police chief's wife.

Christy Deeds.

She was on her knees in the snow, twenty or thirty feet from Honeycutt. Honeycutt was maybe forty yards from Alex, down a hill that was covered in snow, but not enough snow to hide the big rocks studding it.

No way could he get down the hill in time. And at his range, no way would Honeycutt miss the woman who was kneeling—or praying —before him.

But Alex had a gun, and his gun had fifteen bullets in it. He didn't know what was going on here, but he could tell who the bad guy was.

He started down the hill, trying not to slip. He took a couple of steps and then he stopped and aimed at Honeycutt and squeezed the trigger. Three shots rang out in quick succession, and the gun's kick was much stronger than he had anticipated. The first shot hit the ground a dozen feet ahead of Honeycutt, and the second sailed well over his head and the third would have been dangerous only to passing avian life.

He took a few more steps and stopped again. Aimed. Fired.

Just two shots this time. Closer, but no cigar. By now Honeycutt was staring at him and the woman was halfway to her feet, also staring.

He took a couple of steps. Stopped. Honeycutt dared to look away from him, back at Christy. She must have looked like she was thinking about running, because he leveled the shotgun at her and Alex could see him pull the trigger, and he pulled it again and again, but nothing happened.

Alex fired three shots. He was getting closer still, but he had not yet come near enough to his target to seriously threaten Honeycutt's health.

Honeycutt had his duty belt on and what looked like a holster with a gun in it, but maybe he had forgotten about it, because he glared at the shotgun as if it had betrayed him.

Alex fired, missed.

Honeycutt threw the shotgun at him. It twirled end over end but fell well short.

Alex fired three shots. One came uncomfortably close to Mrs. Deeds. One could have hit Honeycutt if he had weighed about two hundred more pounds. Alex was getting better all the time.

As if he had finally remembered it, Honeycutt reached for the holster on his hip. If he drew that gun, Alex was dead and so was Christy Deeds. Alex raised the Colt and aimed it and blew out his breath, steadied his right hand with his left, and squeezed the trigger.

The gun barked and shot flame and danced in his hand, one shot, two, three, four, and click, and click.

Honeycutt laughed and drew his gun.

Alex tried Honeycutt's stunt, throwing the pistol. It soared through the air, coming closer to the cop than any of the bullets had, but in the end falling into the snow eight feet away from him.

Honeycutt examined the weapon in his hand as if he had never seen it before. He glanced over his shoulder and saw that Christy was still where she had been, and then looked at Alex, and he smiled and raised the gun. He said something, but the wind snatched the words away and Alex couldn't tell what they were. He raised the weapon and sighted in on Alex and—

The wolf was only a blur against the snow, a dark streak hurtling through dusk-shrouded air.

When it stopped, Honeycutt was on the ground and the wolf was standing on his chest. Honeycutt wore a look of utter terror, and blood was spreading into the snow around him, and the wolf's muzzle was poised above his throat.

Alex darted forward, and as he did he saw that the wolf's right ear had a wedge-shaped piece missing from it, and he knew that this was the wolf they had called Notch.

The wolf—Notch—paused, as if waiting to see what Alex had in mind. Alex wondered that himself.

He had no weapon. He wasn't sure what had happened to Honeycutt's gun when the wolf jumped on him, but it wasn't in sight. And less than a minute ago, he had been trying to kill Honeycutt, and Honeycutt had doubtless intended to kill him.

But Honeycutt was a human being and, for the moment, he was alive. The wolf was a savage animal, leader of a pack that had been slaughtering humans.

Really, there was no contest.

He reached a high spot above the clearing and he jumped.

For an instant—less than—he was sailing, soaring, airborne, one with the blowing snow.

Then he made impact. Fur and fangs and smell, grunting and clawing, the taste of dirt in his mouth and he couldn't see, it was all too fast. He got an arm looped around the beast's thick neck and the wolf snapped at him and it was so, so strong. Alex tried to press a knee against its spine, thinking if he could do that and pull on its neck maybe he could break it.

The wolf writhed and twisted from his grip and batted at him with a paw, cutting his forehead, and almost instantly his eyes filled with blood. He blinked and punched the beast in the nose, hard, and Notch blew out a breath and drew his lips back in a vicious wolfen grin and he was about to bite, about to finish Alex.

One bite.

One bite would do it, now.

But the wolf didn't bite.

Instead, it backed off.

Alex was on hands and knees, bleeding, panting, gasping for breath. Eye level with Notch. And Notch was gazing at him with those big, golden eyes, and there was intelligence in that gaze, there was understanding. Notch was no dumb animal, acting on pure instinct. He knew what was going on. He knew what Honeycutt had done and what Alex had done and he knew everything else, about Silver Gap and the people there and he probably knew that Alex was the one who had blown up the rendezvous site.

He could easily kill Alex. That much was certain; Alex knew it and so did Notch. For a long moment Alex was convinced he was seeing the last thing he would ever see, the wolf, muscular and beautiful and deadly, and Christy Deeds behind it and Honeycutt bleeding in the snow, staring at them.

But without breaking eye contact, Notch took a step backward, then another and another. Somewhere there was a gun, and if Alex could find it he could kill the wolf.

But Notch seemed to know that he would not. He broke the mutual gaze at last, and glanced once, dismissively, at Honeycutt, for a longer time at Christy, and walked out of the clearing.

Within moments, he was gone.

Invisible.

Christy got to the gun first, and she picked it up and held it on Honeycutt, who was weak, losing blood fast, and didn't struggle when Alex took the handcuffs from his belt and clamped them over Honeycutt's wrists. Christy told him which pocket of his belt her husband kept his key in, and sure enough, Honeycutt's was there. Alex pocketed it and they walked at a quick but manageable pace back toward the vehicles. On the way, Alex scooped up snow and held it to his bloodied forehead.

When they came to the police SUV and the truck, Alex pointed toward the cabin. "Do you know what that is, Mrs. Deeds?"

She shrugged. "Looks like somebody's hunting cabin, I guess."

"What about you, Officer Honeycutt? If I went in there, what do you think I'd find?"

Honeycutt hadn't said a word. He still didn't. He tried to look casual, but Alex wasn't buying it.

"Keep that gun on him, and keep your distance," he said. "I've got to check it out."

"I don't know if Howie is aware of my husband's demands or not," Christy said. "He's a good husband, and he doesn't demand a lot. But he does insist that I own a gun, and that I know how to use it. I do." She smiled. "A whole lot better than you, I guess."

"I never claimed to be a marksman," Alex said. He felt confident that she would keep Honeycutt in line, and he climbed the hill. The snow was maybe slacking off a little, but the sun was nearly gone.

The cabin door was still padlocked. He pounded on the door, and in response he heard a thumping from inside, and what sounded like a muffled but feminine voice. He dug in the snow until he found a good-sized rock, one he had to hold with two hands, and he smashed it against the lock, again and again.

He could barely scratch the lock, but the hasp was old and the wood around it older still. Instead of breaking the padlock he tore away at the wood until the hasp fell free and the brand-new lock was lost in the snow at his feet.

He opened the door.

Inside, Clara Durbin, bound and gagged, was on her feet, trying to get to the doorway. Beyond her were two women, for whom his arrival was far too late. He guessed they were the other two missing women, Marie Hackett and Barb Johnston.

He stepped forward and took hold of the duct tape over Clara's mouth and tore it free, and then realized that the other two also had their mouths duct-taped shut.

And he remembered his dream of the silver-mouthed women, who had looked just like Clara and the other two, none of whom he had known at the time, and he wondered—not for the first time in the past few days—how much he would never know about the world he lived in, how much of what passed for daily life was really magic, thinly disguised, barely sensed.

And then he laughed, and Clara Durbin looked at him as if he were a crazy man. "Maybe I am crazy," he said, putting an arm around her back to help her from the cabin. "Maybe I am at that."

CHAPTER THIRTY-NINE

On the way back through town in the police department's Tahoe, Alex driving while Christy held the gun on the handcuffed Honeycutt, Clara clearly uncomfortable to be riding in the same vehicle with him, much less in the same seat, they saw plenty of evidence of wolves. House doors hung open and people were in their yards or sprawled in the streets, draped over vehicles, bloody and torn.

And they saw wolves.

They weren't attacking, not anymore. They were standing in clutches of three or four or six, looking for all the world like they were conferring, discussing what steps to take next.

Nobody in the vehicle was speaking, not even Honeycutt, who in Alex's admittedly limited experience rarely shut up. The sights were too awful, too numbing. Alex couldn't count the dead. He didn't want to try.

They were almost to Town Hall when they saw two more department SUVs heading their way. Christy showed him how to flash his rooftop lights and he got a flash in return, and he stopped in his lane and the front vehicle pulled up alongside. Ortega was at the wheel, with Deeds in the seat beside him and Robbie in back with the mayor. Alex killed the engine and got out at the same time that Robbie did, and she stepped into his arms and he breathed in the scent of her and tangled his fingers in her hair and lost himself in her eyes until she closed them because their lips were together.

After they broke, she held onto his arm and said, softly, "We've been talking."

Chief Deeds got out, and the mayor, and they told Alex what they had in mind. There were problems, they said, issues. They told him what those issues were and he understood why they were talking to him about it. Well, that and Robbie would have made them. She would have insisted, but it wouldn't have taken much arguing. Because he had what they needed.

It took most of the night, but the wolves didn't interfere. The snow continued to fall, but the wind dissipated, and the snow was soft now, caressing instead of stinging.

They stopped at every house, even the ones where it was clear that no one still lived. Those, they entered, looked around, checked in closets and under beds in case there were survivors. In the end, they found two hundred and eleven, out of what Mayor Stewart said was an official population of five hundred and ninety-two.

Alex made to each one the offer he had discussed with the others, and when the mayor and the police chief and Robbie weighed in, everybody eventually agreed to it.

The first blush of pink in the morning sky found Frank Trippi driving his precious snowplow down the mountain, carving a path through snow that was three and four feet deep in places. Behind the plow came a convoy of other vehicles, trucks for the most part, with a few SUVs and passenger cars and a school bus mixed in. Few carried just one person; most, like the snowplow, were packed to capacity with people and pets and things, possessions too precious to leave behind. No one had time to pack completely, but everyone was given a few minutes to grab whatever was most likely to be missed.

Alex rode in the open back of the snowplow with Robbie, and Morris and Christy Deeds. Robbie and the chief both held rifles and scanned opposite sides of the roadway. Alex's Lexus followed behind, driven by a waitress who had worked for Belinda Stewart. Her three golden retrievers were her passengers, along with the mayor. Officer Ortega drove a department Tahoe with Howie Honeycutt in the back, handcuffed to a D-ring mounted between the seats.

"This was awfully generous of you," Robbie said quietly. "You didn't have to."

"I know," Alex replied. "But I figure it'll cost about the same as the movie would have. Since I'm not ever gonna finish the movie, why not?"

"Don't get me wrong. It's appreciated, even by those who are too proud to want to accept it. Nobody likes the idea of leaving, and nobody likes the fact that some rich guy can make it so the hit is more emotional than financial. So yeah, they resent it, but they're grateful at the same time."

"Wolf," Morris Deeds said. This had been an ongoing thing—wolves standing by the side of the road, watching them pass. None had attacked, though, not since around dusk, according to Robbie.

Not since around the time that Alex had encountered Notch, the time that some unspoken understanding had passed between them.

Deeds didn't raise his gun, and neither did Robbie. The peace was uneasy, but it looked as if it might hold.

Something else nobody liked—which no one had phrased in quite this way, at least not in Alex's earshot—was admitting defeat.

But that's what they were doing. They were abandoning Silver Gap, leaving it to the wolves, in hopes that it would be enough. In hopes, Alex thought, that whatever force had drawn the wolves together, brought them to this place, made them strike out against humanity, could be halted or reversed.

Alex would cover resettlement costs for the survivors, because what he could offer was money. He wasn't good with guns or tracking game or building houses, but he had plenty of money and sometimes that had to be good enough.

He stood next to Robbie, the motion of the snowplow jostling them so that they were always in contact, shoulders or hips or thighs or hands, and he looked at her profile in the morning's half-light, at the way her straw-colored hair fell across the scar on her cheek, and he thought that something good had come from this ill-fated journey, because if a woman like her could come to love a man like him, then miracles were possible after all. He thought about Christy Deeds and her husband, on the other side of the truck bed, and he thought about the widowed Clara Durbin and Titus Johnston and Alden Stewart and those who hadn't made it, whose loved ones were trekking down the mountain without them, and that filled him with sorrow, but then he thought about those who had survived and he knew, he *knew*, that magic infused the world and touched everyone in it.

Not all the time, perhaps, but often.

Enough.

He took Robbie's hand in his and he felt her warmth against him and she graced him with a smile. "It's been snowing pretty much since you came to town," she said. "Global warming, my ass."

And she laughed, and he joined her, and that simple universal thing, laughter shared between lovers: that was magic, too.

ACKNOWLEDGMENTS

This book has been a long time coming, and it wouldn't exist at all but for the assistance of the many people who helped it along. That list includes Ted Adams; Carlo Soriano; Greg F. Gifune; the Colorado Division of Wildlife; Dianne Larson; Rebecca Moesta, Kevin J. Anderson, and the great team at WordFire; and my family.

Only a mountain has lived long enough to listen objectively to the howl of a wolf.

—Aldo Leopold

ABOUT THE AUTHOR

Jeffrey J. Mariotte has written more than seventy books, including original supernatural thrillers *River Runs Red* and *Missing White Girl*, horror epic *The Slab*, and the Stoker Award-nominated teen horror quartet *Year of the Wicked*. Other works include the acclaimed thrillers *Empty Rooms* and *The Devil's Bait*, and—with his wife and writing partner Marsheila (Marcy) Rockwell, the science fiction thriller *7 SYKOS* and *Mafia III: Plain of Jars*, the authorized prequel to the hit video game, as well as numerous shorter works. He has also written novels set in the worlds of *Star Trek, CSI:, NCIS, Narcos, Deadlands, 30 Days of Night, Spider-Man, Conan, Buffy the Vampire Slayer* and *Angel*, and more. Two of his novels have won Scribe Awards for Best Original Novel, presented by the International Association of Media Tie-In Writers. He is a multiple Stoker Award nominee, and has been a finalist for the International Horror Guild Award, the Spur Award, the Peacemaker Award, and the Glyph Award.

He is also the author of many comic books and graphic novels, including the original Western series *Desperadoes*. Other comics work includes the horror series *Fade to Black*, action-adventure series *Garrison*, and the original graphic novel *Zombie Cop*.

He is a member of the International Thriller Writers, Sisters in Crime, Western Writers of America, Western Fictioneers, and the International Association of Media Tie-In Writers. He has worked in virtually every aspect of the publishing businesses, as a bookseller, VP of Marketing for Image Comics/WildStorm, Senior Editor for DC Comics/WildStorm, and the first Editor-in-Chief for IDW Publishing. When he's not writing, reading, or editing something, he's probably out enjoying the desert landscape around the Arizona home he shares with his wife and family and dog and cat. Find him online at www.jeffmariotte.com www.facebook.com/JeffreyJMariotte, and @JeffMariotte.

IF YOU LIKED ...

If you liked Season of the Wolf, you might also enjoy:

River Runs Red
by Jeffrey J. Mariotte

Zomnibus
by Kevin J. Anderson

Selected Stories Horror
by Kevin J. Anderson

OTHER WORDFIRE PRESS TITLES BY JEFFREY J. MARIOTTE

Empty Rooms

The Slab

Missing White Girl

River Runs Red

Cold Black Hearts

Our list of other WordFire Press authors and titles is always growing. To find out more and to see our selection of titles, visit us at:

wordfirepress.com